THE SWEETBRIAR BRIDE

BRENDA WILBEE

Guideposts.

CARMEL • NEW YORK 10512

Scripture quotations are from the King James Version of the Bible.

This Guideposts edition is published by special
arrangement with Harvest House Publishers.

THE SWEETBRIAR BRIDE

Copyright © 1986 by Harvest House Publishers
Eugene, Oregon 97402

Library of Congress Catalog Card Number 85-081933
ISBN 0-89081-482-1

Printed in the United States of America.

FOREWORD

The Dennys founded the city of Seattle. They were a large family, the combination of two: the Borens and the Dennys.

The Borens were Ma (Sarah Latimer Boren) and her three grown children: Mary Ann; Carson Dobbins and his wife, Mary Kays (called Anna); and Louisa.

The Dennys were Pa (John Denny) and five of his eight sons: Arthur, James, Samuel, David, and Wiley.

Mary Ann Boren and Arthur Denny first brought the families together. They married in 1843. The subsequent marriage of Ma Boren and Pa Denny five years later united them as a family, and the birth of little Loretta on Valentine's Day 1851 cemented them firmly, their bloodlines mixing and crossing in the child and sister they all shared.

Other children were born. Arthur and Mary Ann had three: Kate, 9, Nora, 4, and Rollie, 2. Dobbins and Anna had one: Gertrude, born December 12, 1850, on Dobbins' 26th birthday.

Together they took four wagons west. Ma and Pa stayed in the Willamette Valley in Southern Oregon with baby Loretta and three of the Denny brothers—James, Samuel, and Wiley. The other two brothers (Arthur and David) and Dobbins Boren moved on. They wanted to build a city. They moved north, over the mighty Columbia River and up to Puget Sound of Northern Oregon.

Then, on January 23, 1853, Louisa Boren married David Denny, intermixing the families once again.

"...and the old settlers called Louisa Denny the 'sweetbriar bride.' "

—Brenda Wilbee

For
DAVID LAMBERT

ACKNOWLEDGMENTS

I thank first and foremost Sally Rosamond, my friend and neighbor downstairs, for making me quit when I was too tired to see straight, for making me laugh when I cried, and for sliding peanuts, coffee, fresh fruit, and sometimes even dinner under my nose as I struggled eternally to crank out this manuscript.

I thank David Lambert, my friend, for providing me with the inspiration to make David Denny into a man of heroic proportions, and feet of clay. And for spending hour upon hour providing editorial criticism, too much money on long-distance phone calls so that I might not lose heart and quit, and for promising me over and over that I could do it again.

I thank Tresa Wiggins, my sister, who has remained with me forever as a constant supporter and source of encouragement. And for taking my children when they needed the attention, giving of herself above and beyond the call of duty.

I thank Greg Lange, friend and fellow researcher, for unearthing the impossible, and for negotiating a contract with JK Gill bookstores.

I thank John Watt, great grandson of Arthur Denny, for his interest and help in my project, and for insisiting I push on and write this sequel.

Most of all I thank my three children: Heather, Phillip, and Blake Kent. Heather for putting up with too many hours at the computer late into the evening. Phillip for missing his school conference, and Blake for catching the screws I threw all over the room in a fit of despair when my computer broke down yet once again.

THE BORENS AND DENNYS

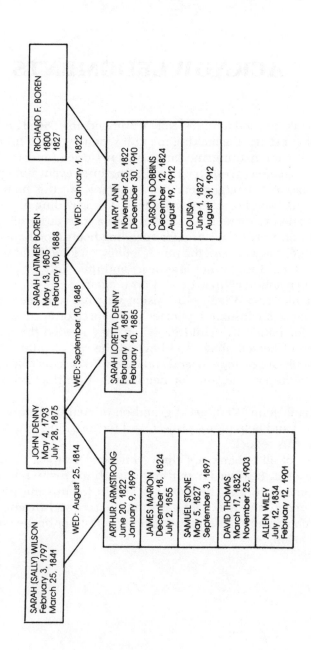

RICHARD F. BOREN
1800
1827

SARAH LATIMER BOREN
May 13, 1805
February 10, 1888

JOHN DENNY
May 4, 1793
July 28, 1875

SARAH (SALLY) WILSON
February 3, 1797
March 25, 1841

WED: January 1, 1822

WED: August 25, 1814

WED: September 10, 1848

MARY ANN
November 25, 1822
December 30, 1910

CARSON DOBBINS
December 12, 1824
August 19, 1912

LOUISA
June 1, 1827
August 31, 1912

SARAH LORETTA DENNY
February 14, 1851
February 10, 1885

ARTHUR ARMSTRONG
June 20, 1822
January 9, 1899

JAMES MARION
December 18, 1824
July 2, 1855

SAMUEL STONE
May 5, 1827
September 3, 1897

DAVID THOMAS
March 17, 1832
November 25, 1903

ALLEN WILEY
July 12, 1834
February 12, 1901

Family Group 1

ARTHUR A. DENNY
June 20, 1822
January 9, 1899

MARY ANN BOREN
November 25, 1822
December 30, 1910

WED: November 23, 1843

Children:

LOUISA CATHERINE
October 20, 1844
March 22, 1924

ORION ORVIL
July 17, 1853
February 26, 1916

MARGARET LENORA
August 14, 1847
March 30, 1915

ARTHUR WILSON
August 18, 1859
November 14, 1919

ROLAND HERSCHEL
September 2, 1851
June 13, 1939

CHARLES LATIMER
May 21, 1861
May 13, 1919

Family Group 2

CARSON DOBBINS BOREN
December 12, 1824
August 19, 1912

MARY ANN KAYS (ANNA)
November 6, 1831
June 21, 1906

WED: February 18, 1849

Children:

LEVINIA GERTRUDE
December 12, 1850
June 3, 1912

WILLIAM RICHARD
October 4, 1856
January 19, 1899

MARY LOUISA
1858
1926

Family Group 3

DAVID THOMAS DENNY
March 17, 1832
November 25, 1903

LOUISA BOREN
June 1, 1827
August 31, 1912

WED: January 23, 1853

Children:

EMILY INEZ
December 23, 1853
Unknown

ANNA L.
November 26, 1864
May 5, 1888

MADGE DECATEUR
March 16, 1856
January 17, 1889

DAVID THOMAS, JR.
May 6, 1867
October 4, 1939

ABBIE LUCINDA
August 25, 1858
June 25, 1913

JONATHON
May 6, 1867
May 6, 1867

JOHN BUNYON
January 30, 1862
Unknown

VICTOR W.S.
August 9, 1869
August 15, 1921

SEATTLE 1853

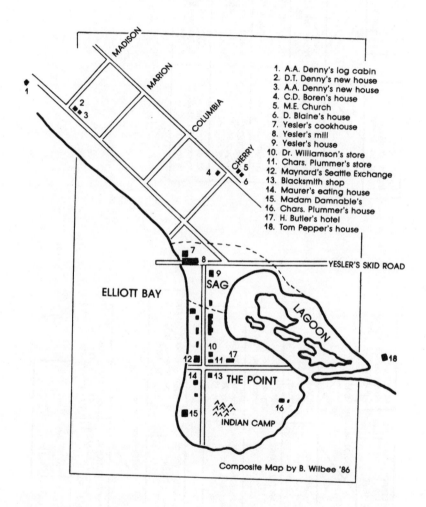

1. A.A. Denny's log cabin
2. D.T. Denny's new house
3. A.A. Denny's new house
4. C.D. Boren's house
5. M.E. Church
6. D. Blaine's house
7. Yesler's cookhouse
8. Yesler's mill
9. Yesler's house
10. Dr. Williamson's store
11. Chars. Plummer's store
12. Maynard's Seattle Exchange
13. Blacksmith shop
14. Maurer's eating house
15. Madam Damnable's
16. Chars. Plummer's house
17. H. Butler's hotel
18. Tom Pepper's house

MADISON

MARION

COLUMBIA

CHERRY

YESLER'S SKID ROAD

ELLIOTT BAY

SAG

LAGOON

THE POINT

INDIAN CAMP

Composite Map by B. Wilbee '86

Prologue
January 24, 1853

"On January 23rd, 1853, in the cabin of A.A. Denny, on the east side of Elliott Bay, Louisa Boren was married to David T. Denny.... The young couple moved their worldly possessions in an Indian canoe to their own cabin on the bay, about a mile-and-a-half away, in a little clearing at the edge of the vast forest."
—Emily Inez Denny in *Blazing the Way*

For a moment Louisa Boren thought she was back in Cherry Grove, Illinois, in Pa's big farmhouse. But then she saw the fir poles of the double bed, covered still with bark and twigs, and beyond the posts—her mirror. Her wedding present to David.

I'm not Louisa Boren anymore, came the delightful, shy thought, seeping in like a secret. She felt a smile come to her face, and her heart skipped. *I'm Louisa Boren Denny.*

Suddenly she was aware of him beside her, the warmth of his thigh touching her own, the even rise and fall of his chest disturbing the blankets. She was aware of him, and strangely frightened. She had waited so long. How could this be, that she finally lay beside him, waiting in the cold dawn of morning for him to wake?

Their cabin hung in shadow, both the window and door bolted tight against the bitter January cold. Sunlight crept through the chinks in the logs. The light fell in slivers of yellow-gray through the shadows—over their hats, a sunbonnet and cap on the back of the door—and over her mirror. There the yellow-gray turned to gold, and dust motes danced in the golden beams. Yellow-gray and golden slivers stretched across the room to the bedcovers. When she dared to look, they lay softly over David's face.

He slept like Pa—cheek turned to the pillow, left arm flung over his head. She watched his face, the way his eyes moved under their lids, the stillness of his cheek, the cold air passing in and out of his nose in foggy swirls. He was hers. She had done it. Despite all the odds, despite the age difference, despite Ma and Pa, despite James, despite everybody, she was David's wife at last, and if she didn't move, if she didn't disturb the quiet, the dream could last forever. She glanced to the mirror.

• • •

Ahead and down the hill were the wagons, four humps of white in the moonlight. She looked into the back of each, trying to find Ma and Pa's. When she found it, she struggled to mount the feed-box nailed to the backboard.

"Can I help?"

Louisa gasped and lost her balance; the ground spun and drew close. But the man who had spoken was quick, and he caught her as she fell.

"David!"

His arms were tight. Dizziness descended, and she fought it. Her heart hammered against the mirror, wedged tight between them. Time stood still as David's eyes bore into hers. She wondered if she might faint.

Still he stared into her face, and unconsciously she swallowed to rid her mouth of the dryness that had come. But David blinked, and the tiny movement broke the spell and he let her go. Then she saw the corners of his mouth turn up, slowly at first, the way she loved and had admired from afar. "I might have known you'd be up to something," he said.

She said nothing.

"You've got your mirror."

It was her father's, her real father's, wall mirror, and she loved it. She couldn't leave it behind. She clutched the mirror in her arms and spun so that her back was to him. "You know nothing of the kind," she said sternly, in a tone not unlike Ma's. Her voice caught with the sudden fear of being stopped, but then she felt his hands on her shoulders, the way Pa would do to Ma when she was upset. Louisa took a breath to calm the inner storm and pain that his touch created.

"It's all right. I won't tell." He propped himself against the back-board. She clambered into the wagon, too clumsily, and felt the rise of color in her cheek.

"Are you sure you don't want any help?" he yelled up after a bit. She said no and hurried to finish. Her dresses, schoolbooks, and sunbonnets, already squashed flat, lay in a disheveled heap

on the floor of the wagon. Moonlight spilled into her empty trunk. Breathing a prayer of forgiveness for her disobedience, she wrapped the mirror between layers of an old comforter she had made as a child and set it carefully along the back wall of her trunk. She folded the rest of her clothes in and around it.

She could see the back of David's head as she worked, as well as his shoulders, broad and muscular, and his cap—the one she had given him for Christmas. His hair was long, and it curled a bit under the edges of the hat. Finally she was done, and the rounded lid of her trunk banged shut. Ma and Arthur would never know. Her secret was sealed.

● ● ●

Louisa sighed and slid deeper into the covers, crossing her arms over the comforter, the same one she had wrapped her mirror in nearly two years ago. She smiled triumphantly. The trip across the prairie hadn't hurt her mirror at all! And just last night she had given it to David for a wedding present. So there it was—she had her mirror, and she had David.

"What do you see?"

He was awake, watching her, both arms clasped behind his neck. Self-consciously she drew the quilt up and averted her gaze to the ceiling. The cedar shakes ran evenly across the fir beams.

"You were looking at your mirror. What did you see?"

She felt the bed move, then he was over her, looking down, catching his hand behind her neck and lifting her mouth to his. She murmured, feeling like a kitten in the sun's warm path. "I saw the night I snuck my mirror out to the wagons in Illinois—and you caught me."

He chuckled; she could feel it deep in his chest. "Oh, Louisa," he whispered tenderly. "How I love you."

She reached for him, and hung to him, her face pressed tight to his shoulder, smelling the sweet scent of his skin. With half a groan and sigh he took her face in his hands. He ran his fingers over her eyes and her cheeks, as he caught her hair behind her neck and lifted it clear so he could kiss behind her ears. "I wanted to do this way back then," he whispered. "You looked like a scared little jackrabbit."

"You *should* have kissed me then, David Denny."

He answered quietly and quickly. "You were too old for me."

She laughed. "Go on with you! I'm *still* too old for you! And it's not stopping you, I see!"

He pulled back so she could see his smile.

"Kiss me," she scolded, taking his hand to put over her heart. The room spun round, tipping, sliding away from her. He whispered things in her ear, but she felt only his warm breath. "We have all day," she told him. "Mary Ann promised to keep Arthur away."

He touched the tip of his nose against hers and she laughed out loud as he planted flowers of kisses over her face. It was just them, fighting Arthur and the world together. "Wouldn't surprise me a bit," he whispered between kisses, "if that brother of mine came barging in anyway. Those cows are getting pretty hungry, and he's anxious—"

"I don't want to hear it! Not today. And I told Mary Ann to tell Arthur that if he got any foolish notions, he was to take *my* brother—not you! You are mine all day!" She threw her arms around him.

"Liza," he teased, "what are we going to do with ourselves? We can't stay in bed all day!"

She pulled back to see his eyes. "David." His face was so intense, so full of love for her. A shadow crossed his eyes, a flicker, then it was gone. "I changed my mind," he said, reaching for her, but she rolled away, and he caught her wrist just as she was about to toss the embroidered pillow Ma had made. The sheets tangled and twisted as they wrestled in the cold, laughing and giggling and fighting for the covers. But then she was pinned to the feather mattress, her arms held flat against the sheet. "You're beautiful!" he exclaimed, ducking his head to hers, and it took her breath away.

"Oh, David!" she cried, so powerful was his love for her. She clasped her hands behind his neck and he sank into her arms. "Oh, Liza, I love you," he whispered. "My heart is so full of you."

She liked the way he said things. "And mine is full—"

"*Hey! Dave!*"

David jerked up just as the door flew open. Louisa screamed and dove for the tangled bedsheets, clutching frantically, missing, hearing a tear somewhere down by her feet. David threw her a blanket and she pulled it quickly over her face. She wanted to die. Arthur stood in the doorway, and behind him stood Mr. Bell.

Part One
Winter 1853

"The pioneers struggled for existence, for winds and storms on the high seas prevented the sailing vessels from coming in with supplies. The settlers were entirely cut off from any source of provisions outside Puget Sound. That winter Arthur Denny described later as 'a time of great scarcity amounting almost to distress.'"

—Roberta Frye Watt in *Four Wagons West*

1

January 24

"When we selected our claims we had fears that the range for our stock would not afford them sufficient feed in the winter, and it was not possible to provide feed for them, which caused us a great deal of anxiety. From statements made by the Indians, which we could then but imperfectly understand, we were led to believe that there was prairie or grass lands to the northwest, where we might find feed. . . . It was slow and laborious traveling through the unbroken forest, and before we had gone far Bell gave out."

—Arthur Denny in *Pioneer Days on Puget Sound*

"Think maybe I'll go back now."

Arthur Denny pulled off a mitt and stuck his fingers down his neck, scratching carefully. David Denny asked, "You sure you don't want to go on a bit more, Bell? Daylight awhile yet."

"Worried about my wife. This snow."

All day there had been snow, a wet, sleeting fall. The Denny brothers exchanged hesitant glances. Maybe they ought to go back. But no. Somewhere out here, if they just kept on, they would find the grass that Salmon Bay Curley had told them of. They *had* to keep on. They had to find that grass or the cattle would die.

"Sally, she'll be needing help with the little ones," said William Bell, peering at the sky, powder gray in the thick dark of the woods.

"All right, you go on back. We'll keep at it."

David tensed at the sharpness in his brother's voice. Sally Bell wasn't well. She had weak lungs and the cold was taking its toll. Why couldn't Arthur understand that?

"Hey!" Arthur hollered at the retreating figure, cupping his mouth to propel his voice. "HEY!"

William Bell turned, a slumped man almost lost in the swirling snow. "Come after us if we're gone too long!"

Bell waved, arm pumping like a broken windmill.

"Well, that's that," sighed Arthur. "Come on. We'll freeze standing around like this."

David trudged after his older brother, older by ten years, stamping his feet with each step to bring the circulation back. Numb. Always numb these days. "Got any idea where we are?" he called, trying not to think of Louisa. She was upset with him, he knew, for letting Arthur ruin their plans. "Hey, Arthur!" he shouted. "Where are we?"

" 'Bout five miles north of your place, I'd guess!"

They took turns hacking away at the forest undergrowth. It was monotonous work as they dropped their hatchets against low tree limbs, slicing back large ferns and bushes. They checked the compass frequently, pushing north-northwest. Would they find Curley's Bay? Would they find the grass?

They spoke little, saving their energy. When Arthur stopped it was simply his signal for David to move ahead, to take over the blazing. He thought of Louisa, alone in the cabin, and fretted. Their first day and he was gone. What was she doing? Was she lonely without her sister, or Anna? The other women from the settlement? Two miles out of Seattle was a long way. Longer if you were by yourself. The more he thought about it, the worse he felt. He shouldn't have come. He should have told Arthur to go on without him. No, he couldn't have done that. They had to find that prairie grass, and with this snow it was even more important now than before.

"You're slowing down! Let me go first!"

David let Arthur pass. Snow lay thick along the forest floor—unlike last year, when the temperature hadn't dropped below freezing the whole winter long. But this winter was something altogether different. Might as well be back in Illinois, he thought glumly. Weeks of driving winds, sleeting rain, and snow. Ships unable to get in. Food running low. Flour gone a long time ago. He couldn't even remember the last time he'd had bread. Mary Ann had cooked a fancy spread for the wedding last night, but now there wasn't a whole lot left. They'd been making do with potatoes, and now even the potatoes were just about gone. Game wasn't plentiful either, not like last year, when all they'd had to do was go out in shirt-sleeves and drop ducks out of a pale blue sky. Shortage of grass, freezing temperatures, timber wolves coming out of the mountains—it was all taking its toll. And if they didn't find something for those cows to eat they would lose any chance at milk come spring, or fresh beef.

The woods broke suddenly. Snow fell white instead of gray, and ahead lay a body of water—with the foggy outline of more woods along the far side. "What the..." Arthur stood perplexed.

A lake? David's mind raced back over the conversation he had had with Curley. He was *sure* Curley hadn't said anything about a lake—just the bay. Had they gone too far east and run into the little lake that nudged the back of his claim? He suggested it to Arthur.

"We're too far north." Dismay and numb shock rooted Arthur to his spot. "It just can't be," he mumbled, standing stiff in the open wind. "Unless there's another lake up here. Curley say anything about a lake?" He took long strides down to the shoreline, breaking snow as he went. He squatted and peered into the icy surface. Suddenly he raised back his arm and dropped the blunt end of his axe over the ice. The shatter echoed across the stillness. Water gurgled. "Saltwater!" He jumped to his feet and shoved his hand under his armpit to warm it. "Can you beat that, Dave? Saltwater!"

"This is Curley's Bay, then?"

"You're darn right it's Curley's Bay! We did it, Dave! We did it! We found it!"

David laughed, relief flooding through his gut like warm fluid. But then the laughter stopped fast. "Where's the *grass?*"

Arthur started at a quick pace west along the edge of the water. David half-jogged to keep up with him, lumbering painfully through the snow and salt marsh. "Where are you going?" he demanded, worry gnawing.

"We've got to find the outlet! Maybe the grass'll be out there!"

"But Curley says it grows along the bay!"

"Then it must be between here and the Sound!" snapped Arthur. David knew better than to say anything more, and they raced along for close to 15 minutes until Arthur's sense returned. He slowed and drew in long, shuddering breaths. David caught up, panting, axe and rifle slung over his shoulder. Both of them looked wildly around. The afternoon had lengthened, and again he thought of Louisa. She would be checking the front door every 15 minutes, expecting to see him at the step any moment. He chuckled suddenly and Arthur looked up. "Just wondering if

Liza'll let those fool chickens in—the ones Maynard gave us for a wedding present yesterday."

"Probably." Arthur pocketed the compass. "Come on. Maybe this marsh grass will turn into something decent. Maybe. You got any of that hardtack left?"

"No."

"Well, if we don't freeze, we'll starve."

Nothing to say to that. They walked silently. Snowflakes fell steadily, dropping all around them. But it was easy going compared to the forest, and before they knew it they had reached the beach.

But there was no prairie grass. It was a bitter disappointment.

• • •

Louisa put David's supper away, then went to look out the door again. *Where was he?* Fresh snow covered the tracks he had made earlier, erasing any sign of him. It was as if he had never been there. Dusk had deepened, and an eerie feeling caused her to shut the door quickly.

"No, I am not going to worry," she said out loud, looking anxiously about for something new to do. All day she had kept busy, forcing time forward. But now it just sat, thick and heavy, like a woman waiting her time.

"*I-am-not-worried.*" But faces didn't lie—she *was* worried. She could see it in her face in the mirror—eyes dark and darting, mouth pulling at the corner, quick, shallow breaths fogging the glass. Impatiently, almost angrily, she rubbed the glass clean with her palm. *Now stop it!* she told herself sternly, watching the movement of her lips, the tension in her cheeks. *Stop it! Calm down! He'll be home any minute!*

But it was no use. She flung herself into the rocking chair, eyes still focused on the mirror. She rocked madly, trying to drive the worry from her head. She could feel it throb through her body with each beat of her heart: *Boom. Boom. Boom.*

Another time she had been afraid like this—coming across the prairies and that awful buffalo stampede. Opening her hands and forcing her fingers flat, she held them up to see, peering closely at the smooth, even skin. No sign of the lacerations now. Her wrists, too, were smooth. But the memory was still there, pounding, pounding, pounding, not knowing where David was. Her heart had pounded like this then.

"They probably will be home any minute now." The words bounced around the empty room, hanging off the walls. "Any minute I will hear him singing 'Watchman, Tell Us of the Night.' " But there was just silence, unbearable silence.

She sang David's favorite song softly, rocking in her chair, fingers curled tightly around the smooth, cold armrests.

> Watchman, tell us of the night,
> What its signs of promise are;
> Traveler, o'er yon mountain's height,
> See that glory beaming star?

In the growing darkness it seemed as if by singing she might bring him home.

> Watchman, doth its beauteous ray
> Aught of joy or hope foretell?
> Traveler, yes; it brings the day,
> Promised day of Israel.

When it was dark she lit the lamp and set it on the table in front of the window.

● ● ●

"Now what are we going to do, Dave?" Arthur smashed his boot into a log, knocking snow loose. The log rolled and he kicked again. It cracked.

David took his eyes off the bare patch of sand and focused on the gray, choppy water. He shivered in the beach wind. "Guess I didn't understand Curley. Thought he knew we were looking for grass for the cattle." His stomach felt a little sick. "That," David waved his arm backward without bothering to turn, "that's worthless. Totally unfit." He spat the "t" into the biting cold.

"Sorry, old man."

David started. "For what?"

"Fine time to be out, just married and all."

"Yeah, well. . ." Arthur's understanding was unexpected, and it left David feeling self-conscious. He started south along the beach, kicking icy stones and seaweed as he went. They were miles away from home, and it was getting late. Maybe another hour of sunlight left—if you could call it sunlight. They weren't going to make it.

"Hey, Dave! Let's head north! Curley's place should be up there somewhere!"

North? The thought hurt. He couldn't go north when Louisa was south. He couldn't go north and leave her alone, worried sick about him. No, he would keep south. "Bell might be out with a search party!" David yelled. A wave washed too close and he danced free, shaking the foam from his foot. "Bell won't think to look for us at Curley's. But if we hurry," he added, seeing Arthur's expression, "maybe we could make it to Smith's Cove before nightfall."

"What good is that going to do us?" Arthur asked.

"It's on the way home."

"But it's empty!"

"I *know* it's empty," David shouted, irritated now, and that made him angry. He didn't like raw expression of emotion. It was fine for other people, but not for himself. He prided himself for the quiet, thoughtful image he portrayed. "You're the one who asked Bell to come look for us," he said on a more even note. "And he's going to look there before he ever knocks on Curley's front door."

Arthur marched past, hands shoved into his pockets, gun and axe wedged between his arm and side. "Just don't be letting Henry know we're using his place as a hotel."

For another half-hour they tromped side by side, snow flurries wetting their faces as the afternoon ripened and turned. David peered ahead, expecting to see the log cabin any minute. Good old Henry. He had come up the spring before, staked his claim and built his cabin, then hustled back to the Willamette for his mother and sister. Being unmarried, he had only been able to claim 180 acres, but it was a valuable 180 acres according to the way Henry figured it—and there was no reason not to figure it that way. Henry was convinced that the Northern Pacific Railroad would find its terminus on his land—the northern edge of Elliott Bay. And if he was right, he would be a wealthy man someday. But in the meantime, like the rest of them, he was going to have to make a living selling timber to Henry Yesler, once Yesler got his sawmill in operation—come spring, when the ships could get through again. A lot of things would happen come spring—if they made it that long. Returning settlers, the new sawmill, big contracts, more ships, better supplies. Food.

"We should have gone up to Curley's."

David ignored him.

"I said we should have gone up to Curley's."

David felt the bite of the remark. The worst of it was that Arthur was right. Arthur was always right. They were not going to make it, not even to Smith's Cove. Arthur veered to the left, off the beach to the tree line. "Better make camp!" he hollered, "before it's too dark to see. Try and get a fire going. You got the matches?"

David fumbled in his pockets and held them out. Arthur snatched them. "Soaked!" he cried. "Every last one of them *soaked!*" He flung them into the trees.

"I'll go see if I can't get us some supper," David offered, shivering. His teeth had begun to chatter.

2

"In the afternoon we unexpectedly came to a body of water and at first sight thought we had inclined too far eastward and struck the lake (Union), but on examination found it to be tidewater.

"From our point of observation we could not see the outlet to the Sound. Our anxiety to learn more about it caused us to spend so much time that when we turned homeward it soon became so dark that we were compelled to camp for the night without dinner, supper or blankets."

—Arthur Denny in *Pioneer Days on Puget Sound*

Louisa shivered, knocking something from her lap, and with a start realized that she had fallen asleep in the rocking chair. Disoriented, she stared into the dull gloom, the darkness of the cabin rubbing her face like a thick, frosty blanket. An ember from the hearth exploded. It was then that she became aware of the intense cold, and that David was not back.

The realization came slowly in her groggy, numbed state. Heavy, thick cold pressed in on all sides. She sat stiffly in the inky blackness, too groggy and too cold to think further.

What was that? A sound. A far-off cry. She strained to hear, the grogginess leaping back. Again the cry. She stumbled to her feet. A sharp, mournful bleating. A *cow*! It was one of Mr. Bell's cows! Over a mile away! Why did it cry so? The sound seemed to bleed into the quiet. Then sudden snarls bit the silence, furious staccatos in the black night. *Wolves!*

The hair crawled up her neck as the howls rose. The howls blended and competed. She stood paralyzed, fixed on the violence. The very woods resounded with vicious snaps. When it was at last quiet her heart lurched with fright for her own safety, and she threw herself at the door to check the latch. It was bolted tight, and she breathed a quick prayer. Then she remembered David. He was out there. He was out with the wolves...

Other noises came—a sharp crack, then the slow wheeze of a tree. "David?" Frightened by her own weak voice, she moved too quickly and tripped. "David? David!" The edge of the table caught her along the hip. She winced and rubbed the spot, then fluttered her hands over the tabletop, searching for the lamp. Her empty supper plate. Crumbs from the last of the potato bread. A book. The shatter of glass told her she had knocked the lamp somehow. Stifling back a cry, she forced her fingers over the jagged, thin pieces.

The bowl was intact—but empty. Bone dry. And the rag wick was dry. She was lucky there hadn't been a fire. How could she have been so foolish? She started for the mantel, but the sound of wolves came again. They were close, and her breath escaped in long, loose shudders. The candle she had found fell with a thud, and she heard the soft rolling sound as it turned slowly over the floor. Just as it collided against the wall and stilled, she remembered Doc Maynard's chickens.

She waited, breathless, half-expecting to see the door break apart in the battle. But all was quiet. The wolves passed on and the sick, aching knowledge that David was out there somewhere snuffed any relief she felt. She sank back into the rocker. A beam of light leaked through the far window.

David had put a wooden shutter with an inside clasp over the opening. Louisa rose and slipped the bar loose and cautiously peered out. The moon was full, a silver dollar to pluck and put in your pocket. It had quit snowing. The sky was clear. The moonlight cast soft rays into the small clearing, but beyond the clearing, cedar trees and Douglas fir and giant hemlocks stood secretly. All around were the strange forest sounds.

Is this what it's like to be married? she thought dismally, staring out to the wild gloom. Alone, afraid, so far from everyone? In Seattle she at least had her sister and Anna.

What was Mary Ann doing right now? Was she afraid? And Sally Bell? If only they could wait together, it wouldn't be so bad. A flicker of resentment ignited. Arthur had demanded that David go. It was all his fault. No, that wasn't fair. David had gone out that door with no one pushing him, and if she was going to be angry, she had better be angry at the right person.

Her bottom lip trembled. Didn't he care that this was their first day together? Didn't he . . . No, this was not Illinois. They *had* to find grass for those cows. And when they did, they would have to find food for themselves. It would be like this so long as the dreadful winter kept on. She wanted to scream. This was why they had left Illinois—to get away from the snow, the biting cold! What were they doing here?

David! Where are you? Tears leaked out despite her resolution not to cry, freezing on her cheeks. She didn't know how long she stood there, shivering in the biting cold, growing more frightened with each breath. She tried to imagine how cold David might be. Was he this cold? So that his teeth chattered and cut his tongue?

Don't be foolish. Both of us catching lung fever won't do anybody any good. She forced the window shut. A flash of an old memory verse came to mind, and she yanked the shutter back open. She searched the dark forest for any sign of movement. "I will lift up mine eyes unto the hills, from whence cometh my help." Beyond the quiet, dark glen were the hills, the Olympic Mountains. What was the rest of that verse?

Tucking the blanket more snugly about her shoulders, Louisa felt along the floor for the candle. Her fingers closed around the cold wax. The matches were in a dish on the stove. Scratch. Scratch. *Come on, light!* A puff of smoke and the flame leaped high, putting shadows over the walls. Trembling, she pushed the candle into the brass candlestick, took her Bible from the mantel, and set it on the table. It fell open to the place where she had kept her sweetbriar seeds.

She stared numbly at the page. Her sweetbriar seeds. All the way across the prairie she had kept them hidden between these pages. Her sweetbriar—her tryst with Pamelia. Pamelia. She could almost see her dearest friend on earth, the laughing blue eyes, the long, spun-gold hair catching sunlight on an Illinois spring breeze.

• • •

Arm in arm they walked through the carefully cultivated flower beds. Tulips nosed green spikes up out of the cold, hard earth and daffodil stems crowded the fence. Louisa reached out to the sweetbriar and rubbed a tiny bud between her fingers. "If only there were just one bloom." She wanted to see the pink rose, the five petals, the threaded veins of darker pink. "I just wanted one, Pamelia, just one. I need something to take with me, to hold onto."

They both cried then, overcome with sorrow. "I can't say good-bye," Pamelia cried. A robin hopped close and cocked his head, then hopped away unnoticed.

"The seeds!" Louisa shrieked suddenly. "Pamelia, the sweetbriar seeds we gathered last year! You have them in your bureau! Go get me half! As soon as I get my own home in the Promised Land I'll plant them and send word to you, and you can plant yours! It'll be a tryst between us!"

In a moment Pamelia was back. "It's a promise," she said breathlessly. "Blossoms cover thorns! Just remember that, Louisa! Look for the beauty, the spring! Always!"

"It's a lovely thought . . . straight from God, I think!"

• • •

Louisa pushed aside the seeds and memories and began to read. "I will lift up mine eyes unto the hills, from whence cometh my help." With a start she realized it was the very verses she had been thinking of! Psalm 121. Feeling a sense of wonder, she read on.

> My help cometh from the Lord, which made heaven and earth. He will not suffer thy foot to be moved; he that keepeth thee will not slumber. Behold, he that keepeth Israel shall neither slumber nor sleep. The Lord is thy keeper; the Lord is thy shade upon thy right hand. The sun shall not smite thee by day, nor the moon by night. The Lord shall preserve thee from all evil: he shall preserve thy soul. The Lord shall preserve thy going out and thy coming in from this time forth and even for evermore.

Goosebumps crawled upon her shoulders and neck, and then down her arms. She looked out the window, to the moon and dark treetops. She snuffed the candle flame. The goosebumps spread across her back. Drawn to the window, she looked out to the silver-dark world. The promise of sweetbriar, that's what she would call this promise. It *was* a promise—straight from God. The tryst between herself and Pamelia had taken on new meaning. Not only would spring come, but God was there.

Everything would be all right. God would bring David safely home.

Whoo-oo! Whoo!

She jumped. There was a rush of wings, and an owl, large and white, descended out of the forest, taking something away in his talons. She shuddered. Just owls.

3

January 25

"Of course, our failing to return at night caused great anxiety at home."

—Arthur Denny in *Pioneer Days on Puget Sound*

In the morning Louisa cracked the door, just enough to see out. It was charcoal gray and dismal. The chickens were clucking and making a fuss, protesting the foot of snow banked over the stoop.

The chickens. After the wolves had gone on she had forgotten them again. It was a wonder they hadn't frozen, but she pushed aside any sense of guilt. *David wasn't back.* "Scoot!" she hollered, stepping out.

They would not let her go. Rooster and hen, they trailed after her down to the beach, and no amount of scolding would turn them back. Hot tears stung. David was out there, and here she was screaming at some stupid chickens. "Scoot! Scram!" she hollered again, smacking her mitted hands, flapping her arms. But they persisted.

Clouds spread over the water, and although it wasn't snowing, an impending snowfall was in the air. She could feel it. And it was so cold. The warm assurance from last night was gone. "Scram!" The chickens were so stupid, stabbing at her boots with their beaks, lifting their skinny, scaly feet up and down. It dawned on her that they might be hungry, and she hastily retraced her steps, plowing back through the snow to the cabin.

"Lots of chicken feed, but no flour. Chickens get plenty to eat, but we go hungry." She scooped a cup of feed out of a fat sack behind the stove. One quick flick of her wrist and the millet fell in a golden arch, splattering over the front stoop. The chickens pecked and clucked joyously, heads jabbing the snow. She headed south.

Icy froth clung to frozen seaweed and broken shells all along the shore. An ice shelf extended a foot over the water and choppy gray waves sloshed over the shelf like dirty clothes on an old washboard. She pushed through the snow without seeing. She had to get to Seattle. She had to get help. How silly she had been to think that God would just take care of things. Terrible things always happened. People froze to death. Wolves came out of the hills. There had been plenty of graves along the Oregon Trail— even baby graves. God had let babies die. But the verses of last night kept coming back. What had God meant? Did He mean to protect her? Her family? In this bitter winter? *Where was David?*

The Bell's cabin poked out of the snow-blanketed trees and she took the path up the short cliff at a run, slipping on the ice. She wasn't quite sure what Sally Bell could do for her, but it was William who answered her frantic pounding.

"Where's David?" she stammered, shocked and surprised to see him. "*Is he here?*" She stumbled in, looking around, confused, half-expecting to see him sitting somewhere.

"I came back yesterday. They wanted to go on and... *They didn't get back last night?*" he demanded, sudden worry lining his face.

"No. They're still out there."

He helped her to a chair and she sat gratefully. Sally poured a cup of coffee but Louisa waved it away.

"I'll go out and see what I can find," said William, pulling on his boots as he spoke. "Was sort of expecting Arthur to hail as he went past. Should have figured they were still out."

"I waited and waited and... David never came home," Louisa whispered, growing more frightened by his expression. "You don't suppose—"

"They'll have holed up somewhere, Louisa. They're smart men." He shrugged into his coat and pecked his wife on the cheek. "You sure you'll be all right?" he asked her. "Here, do you have anything they could eat?" Sally handed him some hard-tack and he stuffed it into his pockets. The door clicked shut and Louisa stared at the split-cedar plankings.

"Don't worry so," suggested Sally, sitting in a chair beside her. "They'll be all right."

"But it was so cold last night. And this morning... I think we're going to get another storm. This is worse than Illinois." She felt a twitch in her right cheek. The four little Bell girls looked at her solemnly from the table. They sat in absolute quiet, eating their porridge. "The wolves," Louisa said, twisting to see Sally. "Did you hear the wolves?"

Sally got up to do something with the fire. Her frail voice was full of defeat. "William checked this morning. Bossy got stuck in some tree roots—out scrounging for something to eat, I guess. They polished her off. They're so hungry they're coming out of the hills."

Louisa jumped to her feet. "I must be going."

The wind lifted her hair off her shoulders when she stepped outside. It whipped the loose ends of her scarf and she grabbed them quickly, bringing them over her mouth and nose. "Thank you!" she called, but Sally had already shut the door.

Head down, she began again to push through the snow-covered beach toward Seattle, grateful at least for the low tide. If the tide had been in there would have been no way she could have gone for help. She would have been stuck at home, the water cutting her off. She walked quickly, blocking out the creeping panic, determined to keep her sense.

BOOM!

A second crack split the air and she looked up, startled. A third boom ripped loose and she plunged forward, leaping logs and at times slipping on the slick, icy sand. What had happened? Had they found David?

"Hey, there!"

"Dobbins! Oh, Dobbins!" she burst out, seeing her brother coming toward her. He closed the gap and took her firmly by the elbows. "What's happened in the village?" she demanded.

"Nothing. It's just gunpowder bombs. Mary Ann sent the little girls over with the news that Arthur hadn't come back—thought maybe it'd point 'em in. Doc Maynard's going to keep it up every 15 minutes."

So he hadn't been found. She rubbed her face with both hands. "Well, I'm off to find them."

"Let me come with you."

"No, I can make better time without you. And besides, you're not dressed for it. No telling how long I'll be gone."

"But, Dobbins!"

"Are we going to stand out here arguing all morning? *Arthur! David!*" he hollered, making his way back over where she had come. He pointed his rifle every once in a while to the gray sky and fired. "*Ar-thur! Da-vid!*"

What if Dobbins and Mr. Bell got lost? Four men swallowed up by the fog and snow. She stood alone in the wind and shivered.

Dobbins fired again, and she heard the faint call of his voice. "Arthur... David..."

Sudden gunfire came from the distance, catching her off guard. It wasn't the gunpowder from Seattle, either. It was from the north. She heard the crack of Dobbins' gun. Her heart stopped, then pounded hot when the distant gunfire answered.

"DAVID!"

It had to be! Relief shot through her fright, driving her forward. She rounded the corner and swept past Dobbins. He was safe! He was alive! Back over the old logs and bits of driftwood. Past the madrona tree hanging too low. Then around another bend. "David!"

He was running, stumbling toward her. Frantic with relief she flung herself headlong down the beach, remembering last winter when she had first come to Puget Sound...November rain driving out of the sky, running over sandbars, David standing ankle-deep in water, waiting for her, clutching his walking stick, head bandaged, sick with fever and too weak to do more than hold onto her when she at last was in his arms. "Oh, David!" she cried, and she was in his arms again. His nose was cold in her neck, his words kind and soothing in her ear.

"Well, well, well. What a sight," said Mr. Bell, drawing close. Suddenly everything was all right again. How could she have been so angry? So frightened? She laughed, clutching David to herself, unable to let him go. He swung her into the sky and she laughed giddily, catching his shoulders as he twirled her around. The first snowflakes touched her face, icy and wet and melting. Then she was falling, falling back into his arms, caught by his merry eyes, crinkled at the corners and holding her in his gaze. She didn't care. She kissed him, right there in front of them all.

• • •

"How come David is always the one that has to go?" Louisa asked. They were seated around the table at Arthur and Mary Ann's house, eating breakfast, celebrating David and Arthur's safe return. Her sister had fried up the last of the potatoes, and it was comfortable in the warm, cozy cabin. Dobbins and Anna were there too. It was a regular family party.

The little girls, Katy, Nora, and Gertrude, sat quietly. Rollie, the baby, slept on Arthur's lap, his red curls tight and sweaty from the fire. Katy, nine years old and the oldest of Arthur and Mary Ann's children, sat on David's lap. She nestled her head against his shoulder. She held his cheek in her hand, and whenever he finished telling how they had built the cedar-bough shelter just the way the Indians did, she would look up and smile. "And now tell us about the part where Pa had to rip the stuffing out of his coat," she would say, "to start the fire," and David would tell all over again how they had set the cotton into a hole of a fir tree and fired their muskets into the dry cache. He had caught a pheasant and they had broken it in half to roast close to the little tree fire.

"And then Mr. Bell came and found you on the beach!" said Gertrude (Anna and Dobbins' daughter), taking out her thumb long enough to be a part. She was three years old. "And he had hard bread."

Louisa glanced nervously out the window. It was deep charcoal now, with a splintered and broken sky. Tiny flakes fell, but the wind had weakened. "David always has to go out," she tried again. "If it isn't hunting, it's scouting. If it isn't scouting, it's fishing. If it isn't fishing . . ." She stopped abruptly. She was sounding just like Anna, complaining about what had to be. "If it isn't fishing, it's something else," she finished lamely, embarrassed, yet feeling stuck. The plain fact of the matter was that she hadn't even been married 24 hours and now they were talking about sending him across the bay to New York! To see if anybody over there had any potatoes or flour! It just wasn't fair.

She wanted to make them see, to understand. But they didn't. They just sat there, staring at her, waiting for her to go on, making her feel silly and demanding and very childish. For the first time she understood a little of how Anna must feel, and she looked sympathetically across the table to her brother's wife.

"I'm not always the one," David said patiently, breaking the awkward silence. "And besides, Liza, it's got to be done. You know that."

"Why can't Dobbins go over?" She turned to her brother. "Dobbins? Why can't you—"

"Don't you be telling Dobbins to go now," Anna interrupted. "If we're going to keep score on whose husband is out all the time, it won't be David who wins. He's *not* the only one who has to go out, and you know that. Dobbins is gone *all* the time—hunting or whatever he does out there."

"Would anybody like anything more to eat?" Mary Ann asked. She pushed back her chair and stood at the end of the table, looking weary, her face too flushed. She was pregnant again, and Louisa worried for her. Mary Ann couldn't keep the wild game in her stomach, and with the flour gone and now the potatoes, what would she eat? The realization sent a chill into Louisa, and she felt sudden shame for her selfishness. Of course someone had to go over to New York. But today?

"Where do you think that duck came from, Louisa?" Anna went on, not leaving well enough alone. "Do you think it just flew in to land on your plate?"

"I'm sorry, Anna. I didn't mean—"

"Dobbins got that duck yesterday while David and Arthur were out. No one's sitting around by the fire, Liza."

"I realize that, Anna," she whispered, looking helplessly at David. He was watching her, his eyes unsure.

"And now because David didn't understand Curley properly, a whole day's been wasted and Dobbins has to go out and see if *he* can't find something for the cows."

"Anna, I'm sorry!"

"Anna," said Mary Ann with a stern kindness, "it's just that Louisa has only been married one day, and . . ."

She was going to cry. Right here in front of everybody she was going to cry. Mary Ann poured coffee into enamel mugs and concentrated on the steaming fluid going from kettle to cup.

"There's a little bit of the potatoes left," said Mary Ann, sounding like Ma trying to be chipper. "David?"

"No thanks, Mary. A cup of your coffee is fine."

"David, it doesn't look good out there," Mary Ann said. "Do you and Louisa want to stay the day, and go over tomorrow? I'm afraid—"

That was the last thing she wanted to do—spend the day with Arthur, waiting out a storm that might or might not come. "No, Mary, that's all right," she interrupted. "We have the chickens at home. David, if we left now . . ."

Arthur stirred. He had been sitting a little apart from them, lost in his own thoughts. He put Rollie over his shoulder and the baby opened an eye, then fell back to sleep. "I thought it was settled. I thought you were going over to New York today, Dave."

"For heaven's sakes, Arthur! What's wrong with him going tomorrow?"

"Something's got to be done!"

How *dare* he yell at her! She threw on her coat. Especially after he had barged in on them yesterday morning—and with no apology. Why, it made her cheeks burn even now thinking of it.

"A civilized man has *got* to have bread, Louisa," Arthur said. "We can't go on like this. We've got to have flour, or potatoes. The children—"

"Don't shout at me, Arthur Denny," she declared, marching across the room. "Mary Ann? Can I borrow a dry pair of mitts?"

David bundled into his own coat. "Arthur, I'll go over as soon as I see what this new storm is going to do."

"Da-*vid!*" She yanked on the door. Wind hurtled in, throwing papers off Arthur's desk. She didn't care. She stormed out, slamming the door behind her. Anger, pity, guilt, regret—they all bounced around inside her head. Why was she acting so foolish? This was not Illinois, where all you had to do was go into town and get what you needed. Arthur was right. Something had to be done. *But why did it always have to be David?*

David didn't say anything when he passed her on the beach trail, and she followed him home in silence, chin tucked behind her collar, listening to the wind howl past her ears.

4

"Not all the cabins were 'papered,' but this one was."
—Emily Inez Denny in *Blazing the Way*

The storm struck just as David and Louisa got home, blasting against the log walls and whistling around the corners. David kicked in the door. He didn't even wait to take off his coat. "Do you mind telling me what that was all about?" He threw his hat against the door. It missed the hook and slid to the dirt floor. "Well?" He snatched it up and slapped it against his thigh, then jammed it onto the spike. He held out his hand for her own hat. She handed him the bonnet without a word and turned her back.

"Might as well clean my gun," he said when she didn't answer. He set to work, propping his stocking feet up on the puncheon tabletop. "This isn't Illinois, Liza." He blew into the muzzle with short, quick bursts of air. "We can't take the day off just because we got married, you know."

If she heard anymore about Illinois she would scream. She pulled a bolt of cloth, pink cattice, from her trunk, and began to measure curtains for the corner dish crate. The blue-down dishes David had gotten for her from Captain Plummer sat in the crates. How carefully she had washed them and set them out, putting the teapot in front so anyone who came to visit might see what a fine set it was. So why was she making curtains and covering them all up?

She could feel his eyes upon her. He was waiting for her to apologize. Well, she wasn't going to; she wasn't sorry. Arthur had no business ordering everyone around, telling them where to go and what to do. He was getting absolutely awful with this dreadful weather, and David, if *he* had any backbone at all, would stand up to it and say no. He certainly could have told Anna to shut up. The shears made sharp snips. She listened to the sound and watched the scissors open and close. Snip-snip, snip-snip.

The morning advanced. They left the disagreement alone, but it was there nonetheless, like a heap of laundry in the middle of the floor. In their minds they stepped around it, and sometimes over it. Their minds had to gauge the distance, and steer clear in words. But neither of them could put it away. They both wanted to talk about it, but couldn't.

By dinnertime the wind was delivering a storm gone wild. It sliced through the unchinked logs of the cabin, teasing the candles and blowing sleeting, wet snow. "I think we better mix some glue," said David at last. Evening had set. "Then we can paste up some of these newspapers." A pile of back issues of the *Columbian*, the newspaper out of Olympia, sat in a heap by the dish crate. "It'll keep out the worst of the wind."

"Stick it up with what?"

"I guess there's no flour, is there?"

"No."

"We could grind some of that chicken feed. See how it works."

The chickens were nesting behind the stove. It had been David who had taken pity on them, not her. Now he took a pot out and scraped the built-up snow from off the log rounds. He swept the snow into the pot with swift strokes. He helped himself to a scoop of feed and used the end of an axe to mash it into a powder. She watched him work, his body rigid, bottom lip caught between his teeth. Shirt-sleeves rolled back, he worked patiently, grinding the grain, stirring it into the boiling water. He didn't speak to her, but kept his eyes on his work. It was a sorry, miserable day.

He was still standing over the stove when she put her arms around him, laying her cheek against his back. She felt his surprise. "I'm sorry," she whispered, all the sorry coming out in a rush of two whispered words.

He stiffened, and when he turned at last she slid into his arms, toasty warm from the heat of the stove. He tilted her head back by pulling gently on her hair. "Oh, it's all right," he said. Suddenly he caught her in a fierce grip, pressing her to his chest, almost hurting her. "Oh, Liza, I love you. Don't be mad at me. I don't know what to do with you when you act like that."

She didn't know what to say. She had been beastly. Well, she would make up for it—somehow. "You want to know something?" she whispered into the blue flannel that was his shirt. "I don't know what to do with me either when I act like that."

He laughed softly, and the world was good again on the wave of that sound. "Ah, Liza," he said, sighing deeply, laughing still, "you're so funny." Suddenly he swiveled. "Whoa!" he shouted. "Where's the mitt! Quick! It's boiling!" Paste bubbled and spit over the stove. *Plop, plop.* "Where'd it go?" His face was red, his eyes frantic.

"I don't know!" she cried. "Didn't you have it?" Spitting blobs threw themselves onto the floor.

"No! I mean I don't know!" *Plop, plop.*

"Here! Use this!" She grabbed her coat off a spike and he slid the pail off the stove plate. "Whew," he said, laughing hard as he surveyed the mess. He blew air and shook a finger. "Next time it's your turn."

• • •

"What's so funny?" David eased the newspaper out of her hands. All evening they had worked, pasting old sheets of the *Columbian* to the logs like wallpaper while outside the wind howled, whistling around the corners of the log cabin and screaming down the chimney. "Oh, David! Let's get into bed and I'll read it to you! It's the funniest story!"

He fixed a cup of tea for them both. She snuggled against his warm, strong arm, thinking that this was as it should be—just the two of them, safe in their cabin, the world angry and cruel but barricaded beyond the sturdy log walls.

"Well?" he said, taking a sip of his tea, waiting for her to begin.

Nearly a dozen years ago, I was on my return to the old homestead in the good State of Connecticut, having just completed my studies as a student of medicine. In company with a goodly number of people, I stopped for the night at a country inn, not being able to resume my journey till a later hour on the following day. I was not at all dissatisfied with the arrangements, and my pleasure was further enhanced by finding at the well-laid supper table two ladies of surpassing loveliness, the younger of whom I thought the most bewitching creature in existence.

She delighted in David's smile, and the way it grew as the story progressed. Quickly she found her place, hiding her own smile.

The ladies were accompanied by a young gentleman about my own age, with whom I could not but feel exceedingly annoyed. He not only engrossed all their attention, but lucky dog as he was, seemed determined that no other person should participate in the amusement. An offer of some little delicacy by myself to the younger of the two ladies was met with such antagonism on his part that it effectively chilled any further attempts at intimacy.

I retired, but for a long time I rolled and tossed about in my bed sadly; now one plan by which I might make acquaintance with the young lady would suggest itself, and then another, until at last I found myself in a state of dreamy languor.

I fancied I had heard a sort of little bustle going on near my bed, but it gave me no uneasiness until someone sprang into the bed, and clasping her around about me, whispered, "Ugh, how dreadful cold it is to be sure, Julie. We shall have to lay spoon fashion or else we shall freeze."

"Now here was an incident."

David laughed, unable to hold it in anymore. Louisa grinned and went on, snapping the newspaper and finding her place.

What to say or how to act was a question not easily solved. At last I mustered courage enough to ejaculate, "Dear Madam, here is some mistake, I'll—"

The lady did not wait for me to say more. With a sharp, quick scream, she sprang from the bed and bolted from the apartment. I was wondering what the deuce it could all mean, and you can well believe, gentlemen, that my slumbers were far from quiet.

In the morning, I know not how it was, but I was vividly impressed with the idea that my nocturnal visitor was one of the two ladies who had supped with me the evening previous, but which, I could not conjecture. On taking my seat at the breakfast table I placed myself opposite the ladies. The younger of the two passed her plate, and begged me to favor her with the preserves.

"Certainly, ma'am," said I, and as the thought sprang into my mind that she might be the lady in question, I added, "Will you take them spoon fashion?"

David dropped his head against the freshly papered logs, laughing hard.

Eureka! What an explosion! The lady's face instantly assumed the hue of a crimson dahlia—

"Why, Louisa Boren Denny, you're turning the hue of a crimson dahlia!"

"I am not!"

"You are too!"

—while her companion seemed so cold and passionless as I could desire. I was satisfied she had kept her own counsel—scrapped an acquaintance—fell deeply in love, and when I reached home I had the pleasure of presenting to the old folks my esteemable lady, the present Mrs. Maddox.

She dropped the paper over the edge of the bed and slid beneath the covers, embarrassed beyond belief, feeling the red-hot sting on her cheeks. David tugged against the sheets, but she hung on hard, holding them over her face. "Liza," he said.

"What?"

"Look at me." he insisted.

"No!"

He laughed softly. "Want to go with me to New York tomorrow?" he asked. "Soon as this blasted storm lets up?"

She inched the sheets off her face. She could only stare at him as he smiled down at her, his eyes crinkled, hair messy. "Now why didn't I think of that? I would get to see the baby, too, wouldn't I?" mused Louisa.

"Does that mean you'll go with me?"

She laughed and dove for the covers again. "Of course I'll go with you! I had fully intended to all the time, David Denny!"

5

January 26

"On Mr. and Mrs. Denny's first visit after their marriage to the home of John N. Low and family, who had remained at Alki Point, they were treated to a nearly tragic scene."
—Emily Inez Denny in memoirs

Arthur's red flannel longjohns hung on a peg. He grabbed them and stuck his left foot through. Today he was off to find some *wapatoes* for Mary, and to look for pasture grass for the cows. At the same time he stuck his right foot into the longjohns, David, two miles north, was pulling his own longjohns off the wall.

David had two pairs. They both hung on pegs the same way Arthur's did—along the logs, beside the bed. "Here, put these on," he told Louisa, throwing her the second pair. "It'll be bitter on the water today."

She pushed them beneath the covers, and David laughed while she drew them on in the dark warmth. "It's not funny!" she yelled.

But he just laughed harder. "You stay put until I get a fire going! And you get your clothes on!"

"I'm not *shy*, David! I'm just worried that Arthur might come busting in!"

He lit the lamp, striking a match to a rag wick that sat in a small bowl of dogfish oil. A rancid odor rode the flame. Splintered sunlight poked through the shutters. Shadows drew back. He had to nurse the fire, blowing steadily so that the flame could catch. At last there were crackles and hisses, and he called, "Louisa! You can get up now!"

She put on a brown wool dress and buttoned it over the red flannel. She wore two pairs of socks and the moccasins that Jim Seattle, one of Chief Seattle's sons, had made for her when the weather had turned bad. They were plain moccasins, the fur laid to the inside—not like the fancy beaded kind the Plains Indians made. "I feel like a Mountain Man," she said, laughing at herself. She stood before him, tossing her still-tangled hair. It fell about her shoulders like black silk that needed ironing.

"You don't look like a Mountain Man."

He had seen her do it a hundred times, brushing her hair like that when they had lived with Arthur and Mary Ann. But this morning it was different; he couldn't get used to the idea that they were married, that she was his. He watched the quick strokes, the flash of her hands. Midnight hair, flashing brown eyes, creamy skin. The Oregon climate had put a rose flush to her face, and it made her prettier than ever. "Coffee, or tea?" he asked, resisting his impulses.

"If we're going all the way to New York, we better have coffee."

"Coffee it is."

The sky was a brittle blue. Sunlight spilled out of the heavens. Everywhere snow glistened and reflected, and when the dry, cold wind lifted it off the rooftop the powder cut the air with sharp rainbows of color. "Louisa! Come here!"

He had built their cabin overlooking Elliott Bay, and this morning the water rippled like a great pearl before him, catching and throwing back light. The Olympic Mountains across the Sound to the west cut the brittle sky with jagged white edges, and David took great breaths of the cold, fragile world. He was struck dumb with the glory.

Everything was a dazzling white—even the trees. Two feet of the dazzling snow lay like a thick blanket over the earth, and he had to shovel a path to clear the door swing, then tromp a path down to the beach where the canoe was tied. When at last they pushed off into the glimmering, quiet water, neither of them spoke, both caught in the spellbinding beauty.

In the distance was the western promontory of land that the Indians called Sqwudux. It framed Elliott Bay, and around its point was New York, six miles distant. New York was the original settlement. It was where they had first come a year-and-a-half ago, John Low and David Denny, scouting the land. Everyone else had been too sick with the ague to come north. So they had stayed behind in the Willamette Valley of southern Oregon, and when John had gone back to get them, it had been just him—alone with the Indians.

When John had returned with the others three weeks later, there were 24 of them: 12 adults and 12 children. Now only John and his family, plus Charles Terry, the proprietor of the New

York Markook Trading Post, lived there, as well as a few bachelors headed for gold and the Queen Charlottes come spring. The rest of them had abandoned New York the year before to move inside the bay, where the harbor was deeper and the winds less fierce. There was more timber, too. But John and Charles had stubbornly held on, refusing to admit the inadequacy of the location. They insisted they were in the best spot to pick up the Puget Sound trade. "It's the best spot to go slowly mad," Arthur had said. A sense of anticipation marched through David's veins as he set his paddle into the clear water with deep, even strokes. The canoe glided easily along.

"There it is! There's New York!" he hollered when they rounded the promontory. He felt an emotion of pride nearly lift him from the canoe. It was beautiful to him, those first four sturdy cabins and this lonely, rocky beach.

New York. A pretentious name for this lonely, rocky beach. Columns of smoke rose from two stone chimneys. Smaller clouds of smoke from numerous Indian fires scattered along the shore came into view as they drew near, and when they landed, pebbles and small rocks chewing under the canoe, the odor of rancid dogfish oil assaulted her nose.

The Indians smeared themselves with the oil to keep warm and to repel the snow and rain. Salmon cooking over alderwood fires and clams boiling in large tin buckets mixed with the stink, and decaying seaweed and ocean salt added pungent odors. The air was heavy and difficult to breathe, and Louisa gagged and coughed. She had forgotten how bad it could be when the Indians congregated in large numbers.

New York was a common camping ground for Chief Seattle's Indians. Sometimes as many as a thousand pitched their cedar-bough tents, although today there appeared to be only about a hundred. They gathered quickly, whispering curiously, admiring the canoe. "*Kloshe!*" said Suwalth, one of the tribal elders. He spoke Chinook, the simple Hudson Bay Company trade language, and when it was understood that the canoe was a gift from their chief to David, he resorted to Duwamish, the native tongue.

"What's he saying, David?" Louisa asked, unable to decipher the difficult sounds.

"He says that the sea gull is Seattle's spirit power."

She shivered. She didn't want to hear about spirit powers—

they scared her. It was as if ghosts came out when the Indians danced and chanted on dark nights.

"Oh, come on," he laughed. "Don't look so frightened. It's an honor to have a dugout with the chief's spirit powers carved on it."

She rolled her eyes and let him guide her through the thick throng. Before they got to the cabin she spotted Jim and George Seattle, and waved. "Hello!" she greeted. "Where's Kickisomlo?"

They shrugged, unconcerned with their sister's whereabouts, and David stopped a moment to chat. She felt cold and went up to the cabin alone.

Lydia Low cried when she saw her. David caught up and Lydia cried again, welcoming them both in with a lot of fussing. The four oldest Low children added to the fuss, pulling them through the open door at the same time, hugging and asking questions and showing David their new toys, hand-carved soldiers from Charles Terry.

It surprised Louisa to see how Lydia had aged. But it was no wonder, the life she led—alone for months at a time while John went clear across the Sound searching for timber on the Olympic Peninsula. There was no white person to talk to except Charles— when he wasn't running his store or chewing tobacco or getting drunk with the bachelors in the cabin next door. But John was home today, Lydia said. He had pilings just sitting in Port Madison, waiting to be loaded—whenever Captain Howard made it up with the *Leonesa*. "Until then there ain't much he can do." She stuck her hands on her hips and gave David and Louisa a strong smile, unwilling to let the hard times spoil the visit.

"We came to see if you folks had any flour," said David. He and Louisa stomped the snow from their boots. "We haven't had any in Seattle for six weeks. And the potatoes are gone."

"There's flour . . ." Lydia shuffled to the stove, the fun gone out of her voice and face. "Not much of it, though. John paid 40 dollars for that barrel last fall. We haven't been using any of it for ourselves. Don't think we've had bread for two whole months. Been using the flour to trade the Indians bit by bit for fish and venison, sometimes even just *wapatoes*."

"You don't have any potatoes?"

"No, not since before Thanksgiving."

David groaned and dropped into a chair. He took off his hat

and laid it on the table. Louisa caught his eye and he managed a weary smile. "Where's John? With Charles in the store?"

"They're going over the books. But you just sit and rest yourself. I'll fix you a cup of tea. One of them Indians is bound to let them know you're here."

"May I hold the baby?" Louisa asked.

"Help yourself." Lydia wiped her hands on her apron and waved the last lingering Indian from the door. John had designed it in two pieces to keep the Indians out. The top half was able to swing open to satisfy their incurable curiosity, but the bottom half could be secured to a floorboard and bolted shut. "Takes 'em longer and longer to get their eyeful," she muttered.

"What did you call her?" Louisa asked, picking up the 3½-month-old infant.

"We gave Charles the honor of picking the name. Amelia Antoinette."

"It's a beautiful name," said Louisa.

"How's that sister of yours?" She was looking a bit peaked last October—when Nettie was born. Nettie, that's what we call her. Don't know if I said my proper thanks—her coming over and helping me out like she did." The water began to boil, and Lydia rushed about. "Well? How is she? I keep telling John it's a cryin' shame she ain't built any bigger. You, too, I might add."

"She's doing better. Having no bread has been hard, though. She can't eat the wild game—and that's all there's been. She'll be glad when the baby is born."

"She ain't pregnant again, is she?" asked Lydia.

"Maybe I'll go ahead to the store," said David, pulling his hat back on. But a commotion outside interrupted and John appeared, elbowing the Indians from his front step. Charles Terry followed on his heels.

"Well, well," John drawled, offering his hand and stomping more snow into the growing puddle in front of the door. "Suwalth told us you were calling."

"It's good to see you!" said Charles, reaching around with his hand and grinning widely. "Ah, it *is* good to see you."

Charles was 23, with black eyes, bushy black hair that couldn't settle, and a black beard. Full and running over with humor, he was the direct counterpart to John Low, a slow-moving, stubborn man with thin cheeks and sharp eyes. Charles had a smile lingering about his face. His eyes were not black like empty dark nights; instead, they held the sparkle of stars. His step was quick. He laughed easily, and told tall stories that made Lydia laugh.

Lydia laughed now. "It's like old times," she declared. "Children, shoo!" They scrambled up the ladder to the loft overhead, petticoats swishing and giggles falling behind as they disappeared over the loft-edge. "Here now, Louisa, you just have a sit in the rocking chair. And let me get you a cloth so the baby won't burp on your pretty dress. John? Ain't that a pretty dress?"

But the men were engrossed in talk of the weather. They sat around three sides of the table, elbows on the puncheons. "Big clouds forming in the south," said Charles. "And they look mean."

Louisa rocked Amelia Antoinette, patting the baby's small, warm back, listening to them, watching Lydia's face and the lights in her eyes. The men switched to politics, and Louisa listened with one ear, curious to know whether Congress had granted Puget Sound a separate territorial government. Besides the weather that's all anybody talked about these days. Just before Christmas, Arthur and George McConaha and some others had gone to Monticello to draft the petition.

"How's Doc Maynard, Louisa?" asked Lydia. "Miss him like an ache in a back tooth. Him and Arthur still have their rows?"

Louisa smiled. "Yes, they do."

"And what's this about a sawmill? John's pea green, though you could skin him before he'd admit it."

"Soon as the ships can get in they'll be bringing the engines for the mill. Mr. Yesler's got the ground marked. And the cookhouse is already built."

"How are the McConahas? They had a little girl, didn't they?"

"Eugenia. Born right before Amelia Antoinette."

"It's Nettie," said Charles.

"What?" Louisa looked up, surprised to see that Charles had been listening.

"It's Nettie, Miss Boren. You called her Amelia Antoinette just now." He laughed.

She laughed. "And you called me Miss Boren just now."

Charles broke into a grin. "No! Good Lord, when did you do that?"

"Two days ago," she said, smiling triumphantly. Charles

whistled and rubbed back his hair, looking at David so that they all laughed. The door banged.

"Now who can that be?" Lydia mumbled, pulling herself out of the chair. "And I was just going to have you tell me about that brother of yours, and Anna." The top of the door flew open before she could manage it, and an Indian whom Louisa recognized as Old Alki John stuck his head through.

"Flour!" he bellowed.

"What you got to trade for it?" John asked, not getting up at all.

"Salmon. Three." He held up three fingers.

"Very good, Old Alki. But that's what you traded for last time. We're sick of salmon. How about a great big buck?" asked John.

"You *wa-wa*," said Charles, jumping to his feet. "I'll go get it." He winked at Louisa on his way out, still shaking his head.

"It'll be ten dollars," said John. "Ten dollars or one buck with great antlers. That's the trade."

"I not pay that much."

"Then get the buck."

"No!"

"Ten *dolla*, Old Alki John," said John impatiently. "Take it or leave it."

The Indian's skin glistened with the dogfish oil. In the small room the stench was almost overpowering. "No," he wheezed, anger seeping into his face. "Bostons always want more and more. Bostons always take! They take our land! *Cultas!* No more!" he shouted, and surprised them all by spitting against the leg of the table.

John sighed and tipped back his chair. Louisa set her teacup into the saucer. The baby stirred. Lydia, she saw, bit her lips and waited. The wrinkles cut deep across her brow, like cracks.

"How do I explain to these savages that the price of flour *has* to go up?" demanded John. "When there ain't none!" He swore and looked at no one in particular. "What I wouldn't give for a piece of bread myself! But I been saving what's left for them! If Howard or Plummer or *anybody* for that matter don't get up here... Ah, David. You tell him! Tell him in his own language what the problem is. I'm sick of it."

"No!" Alki snarled. "Too much!" He waved David back, letting the knife he kept tied to his wrist swing free. John scrambled up behind his chair, fastening his hands to the back posts so tight his knuckles turned white. Lydia reached for the baby. Overhead one of the children whimpered.

"Alki," said David firmly, in English, rising and putting out a restraining hand. "Put away your knife." But the old Indian slid the blade through the air. He flung David aside, and when Charles came through the door John leaped for the far wall and snatched a hatchet off a spike. His face grew pale, the Indian's dark. They stood unmoving, judging each other's strength and hostility.

Old Alki darted forward.

6

"The women, seated chatting at one end of the cabin, were chilled with horror to see the white man, his face pale with anger and excitement, raise an ax as if to strike the Indian."
—Emily Inez Denny in *Blazing the Way*

"Drop the hatchet, Low," said David, breaking the unbearable silence. "Now."

It fell with a thump, and Louisa stared hard at the dark, shiny blade against the beaten earth. John wiped his forearm across his brow and collapsed into his chair with a long, drawn-out breath. He didn't even look up.

Old Alki spoke. "Before many moons have passed," he said with little ceremony, "there will be no Bostons on our waters. Chief Seattle, he is a coward. But Nelson and Leschi—there is much *wawa*. You will see. *Chuck chako*, the tide is rising." He stood on the threshold. "David Denny," he said in a kinder tone. "*Tillicum. Skookum tillicum.*" He smiled, then plucked the sack of flour from Charles' hands and let the heavy door slam. The bolt fell into place with a thud.

It was a different world when David and Louisa stepped out—a day turned inside out. Louisa skirted an Indian fire, cold and already laced with blowing, fresh snow. It fell lightly, from a sky that was no longer blue, but dull white. Heavy, dark clouds rolled out of the south. "David, what is to become of us...if what Old Alki John said was true?" A few of the Indians leaned out of their cedar-bough shelters long enough to call and wave goodbye. It was hard to believe there could be any truth to what Alki had said. She shivered and looked out over the water, gray and choppy now. "David?"

"It's all right. John came to his senses."

"But what if he hadn't? What if you hadn't been there?"

"There's no sense in asking those questions, Louisa. You want to take the stern this time?" She nodded and climbed in. He climbed in after her and pushed off. She felt the bob as the boat cleared. They moved out into the wind.

What if, what if, what if. The questions came with each paddle stroke. What if they hadn't been there? What if David hadn't been able to stop John? What if... The Indian law was simple enough—an eye for an eye. Only the Indians didn't care *whose* eye. Any Boston would do. She concentrated on David's back and the distant shore that was home. Surely the Indians wouldn't try to take revenge on them. But then there was nothing to take revenge on, was there? Nothing had happened. "David? What do you suppose Alki meant by Chief Nelson and Leschi?"

"Making threats, that's all. He was angry."

"But—"

"Stop it, Louisa!" He turned, and the canoe bobbed without the even, steady strokes. "He was just being belligerent. You can't go around acting like you believe him. You saw him. He walked in there, looking for a fight."

"But what about the Muckleshoots?"

"Nelson's not stupid. He knows there's nothing he can do to stop the whites from coming in. Seattle knows that. Leschi knows that. Patkanem, Johnkanem—all the chiefs know that. *None* of them are stupid. We're just all going to have to do our best not to step on each other's toes."

"David?" asked Louisa.

"What?"

"I forgot to ask Charles if he had a catalogue from San Francisco I could borrow."

He laughed, and it was good to hear. "Maybe Catherine Maynard has one!" he said.

"Maybe."

"Don't worry, Liza. Chief Seattle will keep things in line."

David was right. The Indians got out of hand only once in awhile, and Seattle always straightened them out. There was no point in worrying. And she could hardly blame Alki for getting so nasty. John should have known better.

Suddenly she was tired. It would be good to get home and put on a fire. Just she and David. No Indians. No snow. No frights.

The wind picked up as they entered the bay. Soon it was blowing hard, throwing spray and waves alike into the canoe. In no time the freezing water collected and soaked through her longjohns and skirts, and she began to shiver from the terrible cold. David paddled quickly, sloppily, racing the wind.

"Synchronize your strokes with mine!" he hollered. "That way we'll have a paddle in the water all the time and the wind can't blow us as much." But when he paused to check the sky, and to turn and look at her, she knew they were in trouble.

"We've got two choices!" he yelled. "Keep trying, or let the wind set us back where we can hopefully pick up the point and go along the south beach!"

"But what if we miss it? What if we get blown out into the open sound?"

There was a moan in the wind now, blowing steadily out of the south, pushing the clouds low, as if to set a dark cap over the world. She pushed aside thoughts of yesterday's storm and the fury of that wind. "You rudder us into the wind!" he hollered. "I'll paddle straight!"

Dip, pull, lift. Dip, pull, lift. One more stroke. One more stroke. She prayed while she worked. It blotted out the creeping panic and eased the pain in her feet and hands and the cold in her lungs. She worked mechanically, blindly, the ache across her shoulders tight and cruel, a stinging burn in her fingers. Dip, pull, lift. Dip, pull, lift. One more stroke. One more stroke. The wind grew icy, drawing tears. The boat rode high and dropped, slamming her knees into the icy base of the canoe. But she kept on until she could hardly grip the paddle for the cold. One more stroke. One more stroke. One . . more . . . stroke. *What was the Psalm she had found?* I will lift up mine eyes . . . Her promise of sweetbriar.

Pamelia.

Spring.

"Louisa!"

She jumped, guilty.

"Can you bail some of that water out?" he hollered, worry distorting his face. The water lay nearly an inch thick in the bottom. She lay the paddle crosswise, across the rim of the canoe, and leaned over it. Cupping both wet, mitted hands, she managed to toss out only a little. "How far?"

"I don't know! I can't see!"

Sleet lashed her face, and frantically she tried again, over and over and over until she was dizzy. Prayer did nothing now to keep at bay the frightening realization that they were caught in the teeth of yet another storm. The moan had gone deep, a wounded sound.

"Forget it!" yelled David. "Paddle!"

They weren't going to make it. She fought the sob that wanted to escape. They were going to freeze to death out here on the water, maybe even capsize and drown. Then she heard the muted sound of the Duwamish war cry. "David!" she screamed.

He whirled. Red blazed in his cheeks. Ice caked his beard. He squinted, body rigid. Suddenly he broke into a wide smile. "It's Jim and George!" he yelled, and she half-twisted, then fell sideways as a wave slammed crosswise into the canoe. Painfully she righted herself.

"My father say to come for you! It is Southwind!" Jim shouted, pulling alongside. Too weary to even nod, Louisa watched weakly, as if in a dream, while the braves lashed the two canoes together and began to pull them through the water to home.

"It is Southwind!" explained George when they pulled up at last onto the beach just below the cabin. "The old woman, she need to catch waves in net. Then wind will stop. When she catch waves, maybe Chinook come then!"

"Will you stay with us?" Louisa asked at the door of the cabin. She wondered where they would go now.

"No. We take you home."

"You stay with us," said David.

"No-no. We go now."

• • •

A crack broke the raging wind, and Louisa, buried beneath the heavy covers of the bed, trying to get warm, heard the ominous sound. There was a slow wheeze, then a sudden, rushing roar and terrific jolt. Flinging back the covers, she stared wide-eyed from the bed to where David stood across the room, trying in vain to corner the chickens behind the stove. "What was that?" she whispered.

"A tree."

"A tree?" She sprang from the bed, tripping over a bucket of water in the middle of the floor. He caught her as another broke caught the wind. The jolt was worse, shaking the cabin.

"Louisa, get back into bed," he said, trying to disentangle her arms.

She dove under the covers and pillows in one leap.

"Good thing Jim and George got us when they did," he said. "That's a devil wind for sure." He moved to the window and tugged on the latch. Sleeting rain-snow whipped past, driving against his face. He threw his weight to the shutter. "Whoa! How'd it get so bad so fast? Boy, it's a good thing we're not out there."

They had been back nearly three hours now, but still she couldn't get warm or shake her fright. "A tree is going to fall on us." She could feel herself losing control. A sudden thud hit the roof and she ducked. When nothing happened she hesitantly peered up at the even rows of cedar shakes, expecting them to splinter and rain down at any moment. When she looked at David his face was white, and it terrified her.

"Must have been a tree limb," he said.

"*A tree limb?*" she shrieked. "*On our roof?*"

"Don't worry. Chodups and I built this pretty sound. It's taken more than a . . ." The chickens flew out of the corner and over the table, landing on the dish crate, squawking, screeching, stirring up the panic. The panic squeezed about her throat. The teapot went over. She couldn't even hear the crash in the noise. All reason fled as the china scattered silently. Again she was out of bed. She slipped in the puddle, but caught herself on the edge of the table. Painfully she slid to the ground. "My teapot," she whispered hopelessly as she knelt and swept up the broken, scattered shards of her beautiful china teapot, gathering them into her lap. She started to cry, unable to find the blue slivers in the dirt and pick them free. The whole miserable day came crashing in on her, and she sat back on her heels. "*We should never have gotten married!*"

"That's silly."

A rock hit the front wall, a small thud just over her shoulder, and she jumped. The broken pieces of china fell from her nightgown over her bare feet.

"Don't move," David said quietly. "Let me get this stuff off your feet. No! Don't move!"

She stood shivering, crying, holding her fist to her mouth to stop the hysteria. She could feel his fingers move gently over her feet, then the sharp pain as a shard bit.

"Hold still!"

"I can't!"

He grabbed a tea towel off the chair and started to rub away the mud and loose pieces of glass. She winced. "First you get lost, David!" she cried behind her fist. "And then the wolves get Mr. Bell's cow. It was Bossy, David! Our best milk cow! And then Anna is so mean! And our food is running out! And then we had that terrible fight! And today Mr. Low . . ." She hiccuped. "Mr. Low pulls that stupid hatchet off the wall, and makes Alki threaten us. And then another terrible storm and we nearly die out on the bay. And a tree is going to fall on us!"

"A tree is not going to fall on us!"

"The cows, David! The cows are going to die, David! The children will get sick! Little Rollie! Katy—"

"Stop it!"

"We're all going to die in this place! The snow! It'll never go away! We'll starve! Captain Plummer won't make it in time!"

"Stop! Liza! Stop it! I said STOP IT, Liza!"

"And tomorrow you're going to go out again—to find food—and leave me here all by myself! *And my brand new teapot is all smashed!*"

He slapped her. She blinked, stunned, but when he pulled her close she could feel the quiet vibrations of his voice deep in his chest, and the quiet, sure beat of his heart. Another thud hit the roof, and she threw her arms around his neck. All around the wind howled. The candle had gone out. "David? Aren't you scared?"

His answer was quiet in the raging storm. "No."

7
January 27

"About one o'clock the storm abated...."
—Emily Inez Denny in *Blazing the Way*

It was dark. Absolutely black. David rocked Louisa in his lap in the inky blackness. He rocked slowly, listening to the wind weaken, feeling Louisa relax. He could hear the soft creak-creak of the chair runners whisper against the abating storm. He wanted to cry with relief. Never did he want to live through another day like this. Now that it was over, it did seem that Louisa was right: Ever since they had gotten married, terrible things were happening.

"David?"

"Mm?"

"Will you sing?"

"What do you want me to sing?"

"Watchman, Tell Us of the Night."

He began to hum, holding her close. He rocked evenly, listening to the wind, her soft breath against his neck. She grew heavy in his arms. Oh, Liza, he sighed, laying his cheek against her silky hair. How I love you. How long he rocked he didn't know. In time a new noise came to his ears. *Rain?* Louisa sighed and he began again to rock. He ached to get up and see. Was it the Chinook, the gentle wind that Curley and Chodups had told him of, that Jim and George had spoken of—the good, gentle wind that followed snow and drove it from the ground?

His thoughts wandered. What were they doing here? Building civilization out of this God-forsaken place—without sawmill, without a smithy, without even a church—of this place they called Seattle in the wilds of Puget Sound. It was just a few cabins, really, tucked beneath the dark shadow of thousands upon thousands of cedar trees, and pine and hemlock and Douglas fir along a lonely shore. They were an isolated place, a small island surrounded by dangers. What a flimsy thing this was, this civilization they sought to build! It was nothing more than a flimsy coat, shielding them from hunger and wind and thirst and cold. It was a thin coat drawing the line between them and death. And if a man grew careless, the enemy was there to win. Sometimes it won anyway. It nearly had this afternoon.

David shivered. He should never have taken Louisa over to New York. For the first time the icy blade of fear lay against his skin where his heart beat in the hollow of his neck, and it was a new feeling for him. Oh, he had been frightened before, but those had been momentary times—fleeing usually from some sort of danger. But this, this was different, sucking the air from his lungs, suffocating him. *What were they doing here? What had he done?*

He understood Louisa a little more. It was this fear that had taken her by the throat, he realized. Ah, poor, dear Liza. He rubbed his cheek in the coolness of her hair. His heart hammered with the tension of their fear, hers expressed, his hidden in secret doubt. But then he yawned, and the yawn ridded him strangely of the fear. The fear drained from him as he expelled the air from his lungs and breathed back into his lungs the cold, sweet scent of rain. It *was* raining! He could hear it now pummeling the roof and beating the sides of the cabin. Rain! The Chinook. God had sent the Chinook!

The old sense of manifest destiny came surging upon him once again—that same sense that kept thousands of other men tramping the prairie grass to Oregon, planting wheat and alfalfa and new towns. Yes, it was a good thing they were doing. Civilization was a mighty thin coat against the enemy right now, but they would make it strong. This was no time for slack. It would take each of them—Maynard, Yesler, Collins, Bell, Boren—everybody. It would take discipline and hardship. No one could lose his head. As for John—well, he knew better now, and would be more careful.

It was a good thing they were doing, bringing civilization to these shores. And it was an inevitable thing, too, he reasoned. Give a man a pile of sticks or a wagon of bricks and he would build. Man built bridges and barns and towns just as beavers built dams. For no other reason than it's just what men did.

No, there *were* reasons. Civilization wasn't just the coat that kept off the wind and held the hunger and thirst at bay; it brought music and art and study. Without civilization a man had to grub in the dark for fuel and food and look over his shoulder. But with civilization a man could sing and paint and learn. And come spring, when the sawmill arrived and the settlers came, when the ships and trade plied the sound, when that new preacher that Arthur kept talking about got here, then... then... "Liza?" he called softly.

She stirred.

"Liza? Do you hear?"

"What?" she asked sleepily, opening her eyes to his.

"The wind, Liza. It's gone."

• • •

Louisa knelt in front of the cabin, turning the soil with a large wooden spoon. It was the best she could do for a shovel, and she paused to take a deep breath, the spoon resting easily in her hand. When she sat back on her heels and turned, the beauty of the day caught in her lungs, and she made an involuntary cry. The Olympic Mountains stood jagged and white against the blue of the sky, like torn pages of a book. Elliott Bay glistened in the sun's soft song, a friend and no longer an enemy. She bent to her task again, tongue caught lightly between her teeth.

"Liza?"

She looked up, and David was there. Her heart gave a thump, so quietly had he sneaked up, so good was his smile. "I'm planting my sweetbriar, David."

"May I help?"

She nodded and he picked up her Bible. "What's this?"

"It's where I kept the seeds." He handed it to her and she tipped the Bible to the earth. The tiny seeds fell into a line all along the row she had made. "It's my tryst with Pamelia," she said when it was done.

"And what does it mean?"

"It means that she and I shall never really part. And that spring will always come." She paused, and looked into his eyes.

"It means something else, too, David," she said.

He waited.

"It means that God is with us. I know that now."

He picked a few of the crowded seeds out of the line to lay in a space where they had not fallen. Then quietly he folded the earth over and patted it flat with his palm. Somewhere a bird called. Together they went down to the beach and sat on a log, watching the sun slip low into the dawn of spring.

Part Two
Spring 1853

"Since the advent of the white man, no springtime in Seattle has ever come as joyously and with such a sense of resurrection and hope as the spring of 1853, because none has ever followed such a lean and hungry winter."

—Roberta Frye Watt in *Four Wagons West*

8

March

"The Seattle settlement that a few months before had been isolated and hungry now hummed to the tune of the sawmill. The
new arrivals added their vitality and energy to the village group.
All worked from sunup to sundown to supply trade, and, though
they worked for revenue, they were at the same time clearing
the town site of its heavy forest—accomplishing two tasks with
one axe."

—Roberta Frye Watt in *Four Wagons West*

Spring came in a fury.

It melted worry like it melted snow, and the sunshine sang
softly in colors of lime-green and earth-black. It swept over Elliott
Bay like a magic wand.

Elliott Bay was shaped like a broken "O," and the tide swept
in and out of the cut to the northwest. The very western edge
of the "O" was the promontory of land the Indians called
Sqwudux. On the far side was New York, and on the inside, trees
like giant sleepy sentinels grew thick and unrelenting all the way
to the base. There, at the mouth of the Duwamish River, sandflats
spread like an apron off the shore.

Luther Collins had a farm along the mouth of the Duwamish
River; his newly planted peach orchard grew out of the apron
band. The Maples (Sr. and Jr.) and Henry VanAsselt each had their
own farms further down the snaking river, and together they
were called the Collins Settlement.

The shore curved north. The beach narrowed and the trees
picked up the guard again. The Hanfords and Holgates had claims
along this space, the dividing line between the claims splitting
the number "5" if the "O" was a clock. Their cabins sat along
the beach but their claims extended deep into the woods, ending
parallel to the twist in the Duwamish River. New settlers took
homesteads along the twist, even as far as Mox La Push, where
the White River met the Black to form the slow-moving
Duwamish.

The very north end of the Bay was Dr. Henry Smith's place.

Before he returned from the Willamette, Thomas Mercer arrived and took the claim just south of his, toward the one o'clock hour. David and Louisa's log cabin sat back under the trees on the two. William and Sarah (Sally) Bell's cabin sat at two-thirty, Arthur Denny's at three.

And the village of Seattle lay right between three and five o'clock.

Dobbins Boren, Henry Yesler, and Doc Maynard held the three claims that made up Seattle, and as spring came the settlement grew out of the three claims like embroidery being stitched to a patchwork quilt. Wildflowers burst from the muddy ground. Pussy willows plumped and glistened. Spiders hatched and crept free. Then Henry Yesler's sawmill arrived in the middle of March, and the soft, magic days of spring turned. Now Seattle, once isolated and hungry, hummed to the tune of the sawmill.

The mill easily dominated the village. It sat near the beach in the very center of the settlement on a small stretch of muddy flatland. With its shrill whistle and whine of saws, it ran two 12-hour shifts, from midnight to noon and back again, and the blue smoke never let up. Every man from around the bay was needed to run it—or supply it. The Maples brought timber from their farm, rafting it down the Duwamish River. The Holgates and Hanfords together carried their timber to the shore over shoulders, and Timothy Hinkley drove an oxen team up and down the beaches, dragging the timber into town. Arthur Denny tended the screw that gauged the sawing of the boards. David drew in the logs.

And so spring plunged forward, days spilling over each other in a rush. Seattle came to smell of burning wood and smoke and fresh-cut lumber and upturned earth, and the evenings were filled with the scent of sweet pine. Popping sparks like a thousand fireflies lit the smoky shadows. Hectically, almost frantically, the men of the village threw themselves into the work from sunup to sundown, and from sundown to sunup, clearing the land and filling the contracts, building their city and building their homes, accomplishing the two tasks with one axe.

For Louisa these were happy days. She listened eagerly to the news when David came home each day at noon from the mill, but her happiness came not so much from the excitement that seemed to catch everyone else—that of building a new city—as

in the tumbling, reckless return of spring. She welcomed it as
no other, for no other had come after such a hard and uncertain
winter. Sunlight filtering green through trees to warm the earth,
Indian women clamming on the tideflats, seagulls dropping clams
from the sky—this was music, and she left the cabin open each
day so that she might hear the song. Spring had exploded out
of winter like a ball from a cannon, and never had she known
such a rapid and heady rush of new life.

Leaves unfurled. Black currants ripened. Berry bushes drooped
sweetly to mossy banks. Wild roses grew thick and brambly,
sprawling along picket fences and log walls. It was a spring that
forgave, and Louisa, as the others, forgot the brutal winter.

There were times, though, when she remembered spring in
Illinois. *What would she and Pamelia be doing today?* was a question she often asked herself. Sometimes the loneliness went deep,
and often she would cry in secret. But always she found her
comfort by looking to the spring outside her door. She only had
to sit on the front stoop to know God's healing. Across the bay
and climbing the sky were the faraway hills of the Olympic
Mountains, their snowcapped peaks all that remained of winter.
*I will life up mine eyes unto the hills, from whence cometh my help.
My help cometh from the Lord, who made heaven and earth.* She
could repeat the whole psalm. It was memorized and sealed in
her heart.

There was something, too, about the sheer height of the tower-
ing trees all around that put into her heart a sense of eternity,
of serenity, of offered hope. The winter's dreadful storms had
not gone unchecked. God in His mercy had sent the Chinook. God
in His mercy had given her this place, this patch of ground that
was her new home. And God had given her David. Her tryst with
Pamelia had come true, and by thinking of all these things she
found that her loneliness for Illinois softened. God's guiding hand
was upon this place. The soft, easy days slipped into joyful
routine.

Mondays were for washing. All day buckets of water boiled
on the stovetop. As soon as one bucket bubbled and then cooled
enough to put her hands into it without scalding, she took David's
mud-soaked pants and soiled shirts to the washboard. Bucket after
bucket was needed, and when his clothes were all finished and
hung over the berry bushes, she washed her own.

Tuesdays were for ironing. David made an ironing board out of a cedar slab, nailed over two high stumps just outside the cabin door, and she covered the slab with newspapers and heavy white cotton, stretched and stitched tight. She heated two five-pound sadirons over the stove and traded them off, singing while she worked and watching the Indian women clam.

Wednesdays were for cleaning the hearth and making strong lye soap made out of the ashes. Every day of the week had a special chore: baking bread, digging her own clams, sewing, or mending. And then there were the things that had to be done each day: The stove, a regulation ship's cookstove, had to be blackened and polished. She had to sweep and shake mats and plump the pillows. There was always knitting and cleaning and cooking. Sometimes David brought fresh game, and it had to be dressed. And there was her garden.

It was her garden that held the days together. Hours were spent transplanting wildflowers, the sun upon her back, baking through her bonnet and coaxing the flowers to plump and grow bright. Dobbins, her brother, brought pink Mission roses from Fort Steilacoom after taking a turn on the road that Arthur was trying to put through. David found wild trilliums. Catherine Maynard's dandelions (a wedding gift) came up in full force. Soon bees found the place, and birdsong and bees laced the soft breath of spring.

But Louisa's happiest times were when David came home from the mill. The sun was at its warmest during those early, balmy afternoons, and she liked to lean alongside a mossy log in the woods, reading or mending while he chopped and grubbed the stumps. Their cows, brought up from Dobbins' claim, bawled with content now, dripping saliva and mucus over the succulent new growth; the chickens, two broods of Rhode Island Reds, ran and pecked and got underfoot. They strutted about like tiny feathered kings, and the gentle cows allowed them their vanity. In the distance she and David could often hear the echo of their new neighbor's axe, Thomas Mercer adding to the sharp sounds of progress through the trees.

"Liza?" David asked one afternoon. He stood winded, bare back against the bark of a Douglas fir. His axe was propped against his thigh and weathered pants. Yellow chips splattered the earth by his boots. "You hear anything?" His chest rose and sank with each heavy breath. She sat still, listening, sorting his sounds from the wind-whispers of the cedar boughs.

"No."

"It's the cows. They're awfully close to the house."

She turned, aware now of the quiet tearing of grass, the mush-mush of slobbery teeth grinding, the soft, hollow clang of cowbells. Whiteface and her calf nosed the ground 20 feet away.

"Maybe they feel safer."

"*Why?*"

The book closed on her thumbs and the tree welcomed her head as she leaned back. The sky, bright blue, swayed overhead. "Wolves?" she asked, hesitating, glancing at him, trying to read his expression.

"Not now."

He slung the axe again. His muscles tightened and loosened. She sat content, watching the play of his muscles, the sweat leak over his brow and wet his cheeks. She liked the way he took quick swipes at his brow and cheeks with the back of his hand. She liked to watch his hands grip, then slip, as the axe slid. She thought of his hands, how gentle they were, how warm and safe and good. And swiftly came the realization how deeply she loved him, probably more now than ever.

" 'Bout to go over," he said, smiling when he saw her watching him. "Want to help?"

She jumped to her feet. Her favorite job. Together they braced their feet in the thick mossy floor of the woods and secured their hands side by side on the tree trunk. David counted. They both pushed. She screamed, "*Timber!*" The exhilaration, the energy, the roar of the air, the sudden, terrific jolt of the earth. She never tired of it.

• • •

If Seattle hummed to the tune of the sawmill, it was the politics that added the harmony and discord. Men and women talked of building roads and Luther Collins' new ferry across the Duwamish River. They dispelled or cemented rumors regarding the coming of the transcontinental railroad, depending on their confidence or lack of it. And of course they talked of Separation.

Arthur was the ringleader, never quiet when he could speak.

"We are like two sisters," he would say. "Oregon is the big sister, and of course she must be served first. But I will do her justice. She is always willing that we should have what's left over, and will even try to help us get it. *But we are still clad in her cast-off clothes!*"

Tempers and debates flared, and with each passing day of spring the need to know the outcome grew sharper. Had their petition been presented to the Session yet? Would the newly elected President Pierce sign it? Or were they already the Territory of Columbia and just didn't know it? Weekly issues of the *Columbian*, the newspaper out of Olympia, kept them hanging.

Saturday, March 26, the paper reported: "*The question of a division of the Territory is THE question of the day. Let there be a suitable expression of the voice of the people, and the thing will be done—the 'Territory of Columbia' will be organized!*"

Two weeks later word came that "*we have received by the last mail a 'Bill to establish the Territorial Government of Columbia' sent to us by our Representative in Congress, Hon. Jos. Lane.*"

So it had been presented. Had it passed?

9
April 10

"On March 5th, the King County commissioners, appointed the preceding winter by the Oregon legislature, held their first meeting. Mr. Low did not qualify since he was preparing to leave 'New York'; but Collins and Denny met with Boren, sheriff, and Yesler, county clerk. All during that year these four men met and slowly, painstakingly, conscientiously laid the foundations of King County."

—Roberta Frye Watt in *Four Wagons West*

Soon the rooster would crow and it would be time to get up, to tumble out of bed. David stirred and shyly Louisa reached for his arms. She wasn't used to waking with him, not since the mill had gone in last month. But it was Sunday, and he wouldn't be working today.

"Liza?" he whispered, welcoming her. She waited in the dark for him to call again, just for the pleasure of hearing his voice. "Liza?"

"Yes, David." She kissed his eyes and he reached up, catching her face.

"Do you know what day it is?" he asked.

"It's Sunday."

"No. I mean the date."

She thought a moment, then remembered. "April the 10th. Two years ago today we left Illinois." She slid back beneath the covers, her head resting in the hollow of his shoulder. *The wheels turned and the wagons moved. Pa led the horses into town, turning them to Main Street, where he stopped to let the other three wagons lead out. All along the white picketed fences their friends stood, and Louisa gasped at the roar of shouted goodbyes. Arthur and Mary Ann pulled out first. Dobbins and Anna, with little Gertrude on a lap, went next, and James third. Pa cut in, and slowly they made their way through Cherry Grove. All the friends held handkerchiefs high overhead, and the white fluttered against the blueness of the sky, like little clouds skittering in the wind beyond. Louisa looked back, out to the mass of friends, blurred now by* her tears. Someone ran to the middle of the road. It was Pamelia, her arms raised high, waving, disappearing, swallowed up in the distance. A wave of overwhelming sadness burst from the pit of Louisa's stomach, and she rose up on her knees as if to see better was to ease the pain. She waved until her shoulders ached, until her arms dropped without feeling. Too soon the friends were gone, and only the ruts of the wagons marking the mud trailed out behind, stretching like spoiled ribbons back to world gone forever.

"Two years ago today . . ." David whispered, kissing her.

"A long time ago," she whispered back, taking his hand beneath the blankets.

"It was forever ago. I was just a child then."

"You were not."

"I was."

"Let's not argue about it."

• • •

The sky stirred. A pink ribbon unraveled over the trees to the east, and Arthur Denny moved quietly out into the early Sunday morning. He stopped for a moment on his front step, shivering, his jaw set, his cap set. Then suddenly, pushing his hands into his pants' pockets, he set out along the trail. Dew twinkled as he passed, but he didn't notice.

He was headed for the Point, passing the mill, the swampy neck of Maynard's spit of land, and finally, on past a cluttered Indian camp. He came to a stop on the south bank and stood motionless, staring. April the 10th. Two years ago today.

The pink ribbon opened and bled into the brightening blue of sky, the blue in turn stretching and expanding. He watched the sun rise to top the trees, throwing dark shadows across the lagoon. He turned, his own shadow falling long and dark, a mark against the wet earth. When he looked north he saw it all, the sun rising upon his town, waking it.

April the 10th. Two years ago on this date there had been no name—just the embryo of his dream. But here it was, Seattle, wrought from swamp and eternal trees.

It was what he had worked for. It's why he had left Illinois. It's why he had endangered his family and left his father's home. It's why he had turned his back on the Willamette Valley, and even New York, or Alki, as Charles Terry was calling the place now that John Low was gone. It was here, right here, right beneath these very patched and resoled boots that had brought him across the country, that he would see his dream come true. He would build the greatest city of the world. He would name the streets, build the political foundations, fight for what was right in legislature. He would bring in a minister, too—if he could talk the Methodist Episcopalian Church into sending one. He would be like Pa.

A sudden wave of nostalgia for the old days blew like a breeze, ruffling his memory and making him smile. Pa was a Whig. Once, in Illinois, he and his friend, Abraham Lincoln, had jumped from a two-story window to prevent a quorum, and so stopped the passage of an "obnoxious" bill. Abe went home limping, but Pa had had to have a splint for weeks. Even yet it bothered him when it was cold. But that was Pa, tough and determined. Yes, he was like Pa.

Like Pa, he had called the meetings of the King County Court commissioners. Appointed the winter before by the Oregon Legislature, they were supposed to lay the political and economic foundations of the county, and if granted separation, help establish the territorial seat and legislature. It had been he and John Low and Luther Collins, with Yesler as court clerk and Dobbins as sheriff.

They had worked hard since March 5th, their first meeting. They had appointed grand jurors and petit jurors. They had hired Bob Moxlie to make weekly mail runs between Seattle and Olympia, with a stopover at New York—Alki. They had instituted taxes. And they had finally gotten the fares set for Luther Collins' ferry across the Duwamish River: 12½ cents for a man on foot, 50 cents for his horse. Wagon and team were a dollar-and-a-half, sheep and hogs a nickel each. It seemed ridiculous to Arthur, since there wasn't a sheep, pig, or horse in the whole county!

But now John was disqualifying himself.

Arthur fingered John's letter of disqualification in his pocket. He never thought John would actually do it—give up. The business with Old Alki must have really bothered him, not that he could blame John. It must do something to a man to threaten another's life. But it was probably just as well. There had been whispers of repercussions. David brought word from time to time, and Maynard had heard things. Granted, they were just whispers, but they were enough to make a man careful.

It was too bad John had to go. It was going to be harder to get that Fort Steilacoom Road put through—and that was top priority. It was imperative to their survival as a city to open the way up so settlers from the Willamette could come up in a wagon schooner rather than having to book passage around the Peninsula.

Olympia was building north, and they were to build south and meet at the government post midway. They had ordered volunteer labor to insure its completion. Had they assigned anyone yet for the job of collecting fines from those that didn't volunteer?

He returned home thinking hard.

• • •

David lathered his face and stood shivering in the chill, razor in hand. He stared at himself in Louisa's wall mirror, towel around his neck, remembering suddenly that last night in Illinois when she had sneaked out to the wagons, and how afterward when she had gone up to bed he had felt along the empty wall to pull the nail. Well, he had saved the nail, and now it was imbedded into the logs, holding the mirror again.

He squinted. His face had changed a lot since leaving home. He *had* been just a child then. Now . . . well, now he felt like a grown man. He grinned and drew the blade over his upper cheek, being careful not to touch the growth along his jaw. Louisa said she liked his beard, and he wasn't about to shave it off!

"Liza, let's go visit Salmon Bay Curley today," he said. "And celebrate April the 10th."

10

"There is a legend about Bear and Ant."
—Hagen Sam in *Huboo*

Salmon Bay Curley lived in a shack along the beach north of Elliott Bay, not far from Salmon Bay. He had a head of tight, coarse curls, a rare thing for an Indian. His old name, Hu-hu-bate-sute, had disappeared when the Bostons came, but he didn't mind. He liked his new name because David Denny had given it to him.

Curley's shack was right on the beach, huddled against the wind on a four-foot bluff. Cedar slabs propped against each other and held together by Boston nails kept out most of the wind. The roof, cedar shingles slapped across cedar poles, kept out most of the snow and rain. The sunlight, though, found its way through the cracks.

The beach was a good one, with sand and driftwood. Further out were rocks of oyster shells, and even further out were the sandbars with clams. Way out, in the water, were salmon.

Long cedar plankings joined the shack to the beach. Along the bluff and directly in front of Curley's door were berry bushes. Behind were birch and alder trees, and beyond them were the hemlocks and cedar and fir. Hunting trails led through those trees, so it didn't matter whether Curley went out the door and down the plank or out the door and around back—there was food in either direction.

Salmon Bay Curley sat on a log to think. Spring had come too early this year. Bear must be awake, he thought. Whether to go out and get clams, or to take his Hudson Bay musket and see if he could find a rabbit, he didn't know. His *klootchman* didn't care. She never cared. He didn't either.

"Yahoo!"

"Ah! *Kla-how-yah*! David Denny!" Pleased, he watched his friend paddle toward shore, although he didn't bother to stand. It was too much trouble.

"How are you?" David called to him in Duwamish.

"Mmnph." He watched David climb from his canoe and shake

the stiffness out of his legs. "Where is your *klootchman?*" Salmon Bay Curley hollered, combining his own tongue, Duwamish, with the easier Chinook.

"Louisa? She's tired. I left her at home—sleeping."

"Ach!" Curley laughed, seeing his friend make such a thin excuse for his woman. He laughed because he liked Louisa, and it didn't matter to him if she was lazy.

"She must be pretty lazy these days. She's been taking a nap every afternoon," said David. The dampness of the log soaked through his pants while they sat in quiet companionship. He was disappointed that Louisa had decided not to come. It wasn't like her, and he couldn't help feeling a bit resentful. But it was a beautiful day and he wasn't going to let her absence ruin it. The sky was a deep blue, the treetops so green that they looked black. It had been a day just like this when he and Low had come up, looking for a place to build Arthur's city. It was too bad John had pulled out.

• • •

David and John leaned over the splintery rail of a small boat, watching the western shore of what was called Puget Sound. The tang of early fall was in the air, and David breathed in the rich scent of earth and sea. A seagull cawed. David tilted his head to the gray-white arch of spread wings and smiled. He flung a bit of hardtack; the bird swooped low to catch the bread in its open beak.

A serenity enveloped the sound. It could be felt easily in the peaceful sound of wind in sails and of fish breaking water, and in restful colors of green forests, blue skies, and ocean. "The Promised Land," David said. He watched the seagull fly back to the sky. "That's what Louisa calls it."

"Who is this Louisa Boren you keep talking about?" the captain of the boat hollered.

"My stepsister."

"Sounds like this could be interesting!" the man hollered again.

"There's not much to tell you, sir."

"I got all day!"

He shouldn't have said anything. Now he was going to go through the whole story. "My brother married her sister eight years ago," he said. "And my pa married her ma three years ago."

The captain raised a brow—a bushy, heavy covering atop his pale blue eyes. "Now that IS interesting, lad!"

"No law against it," said David defensively.

"I suppose you aim to marry her, this Louisa Boren?"

"I do."

"And just how old of an upstart are you, anyway?"

"Nineteen, sir." He braced himself for what would come next.

"Nineteen, eh? And how old is she?"

"Twenty-four."

"Twenty-four! Holy cats a-matin', boy! So the young lad is going to marry himself a lady five years older than himself, and his sister to boot?"

It was always like this. Ma, Pa, James. David tried to ignore it, but found that his teeth were clenched, that his jaw ached. He concentrated on the shoreline, the trees that grew thick and green, so green that they almost looked black.

• • •

"What do you think?"

Salmon Bay Curley interrupted his thoughts, and with a start David turned to look at his friend, chin still caught in his hands, elbows on his knees. "Oh, nothing much," he said slowly, unwilling to dilute the strong memory with talk. It had seemed so hopeless back then, he and Louisa. But now . . . now he was married, and he loved her more than his life. And she loved him too. It really was the Promised Land. No, it was better than the Promised Land. Here they didn't have to fight the giants like the children of Israel had had to. This land of milk and honey was simply theirs for the taking.

And enduring.

He thought back to the hard, cold winter, and how the Chinook wind had come just in time. There *were* battles to be fought, and he couldn't forget that. But God had led them here, and He watched over them. He couldn't forget that either.

"Curley, have you heard anything?" he asked.

"No."

"What do the Indians say about John Low leaving?"

"Nothing."

Again they sat in quiet companionship. David couldn't help but contrast it to the hustle-bustle that was always about whenever white men got together. "Curly, isn't this spring a bit strange? There's been no tease to it."

"Bear woke up early this year."

"What?"

"Bear woke up early this year. That is all." Curley stood. He walked along the beach, batting at the black currant bushes. He stopped to eat a currant and whistled on the tartness, then wandered to the water. He squatted, letting his seat hang low over the beach. "There is a story of my people about Bear and Ant," he said in Duwamish. He picked up a stick and began to make marks in the sand. "Want me to tell you?"

"I like to hear your stories."

"This Bear, he just walks around," said Curley. "That is all he does is walk around."

For some reason David was reminded of Jesus—the way He answered questions with stories and drew circles in the sand. He didn't know if he liked the comparison or not. He began to feel uncomfortable.

"This Bear," continued Curley, cutting the circles deep with this stick. "He just walks around and around. But Ant, Ant hurries everywhere." The stick lashed back and forth and made a mess. "I will tell you about Bear. He goes inside his house and comes out. He wants something to eat.

"But Ant, she is working. Working, working, working. She is always working, gathering food to put away. But Bear. Look at Bear—he just walks around. He eats the berries until he is full. He fills himself full. Then he goes and lies down with his bottom in the air." Curley bounced on his seat.

"And then what happens?"

"The Bear and Ant. They start to fight. They fight so loud all the people come to hear. Ant says, 'I want it to be night for awhile, then day.' She say that six times, then three times more. But Bear, he just lies there with his bottom in the air. He just says, 'No, next year it will be day again.' Bear, he just wants a nice long sleep between each day.

"They dance. Ant tightens her belt and dances. But Bear just puts up his head and says, 'Next year it will be day.' That is all he says.

"Ant tightens her belt some more and dances some more. She sings. She sings, 'Night, and again day.' She sings five times, then five more.

"Bear, he is asleep. There he is, all full, with his bottom in the air. The Great Spirit sees Ant and Bear and says, 'Ant is the winner. It will be day and then it will be night.'

"Ant is happy because she wins. But her middle is squeezed in two from tightening her belt. And Bear, he still sleeps, even when it is day, then night. He only wakes up when the berries are ripe. That is the story. The end."

"So we have night and day," said David, although he knew Curley hadn't told him the sacred legend to explain night and day and the end of winter. Why *had* Curley told it to him?

"Only Bostons wear belts."

David shivered even though the air was warm. Goosebumps crawled over his shoulders.

"And the Great Spirit picked Ant to win," said Curley.

"No." But even as he protested he knew he had assumed God's blessing upon his own race. It's what he had just been thinking, wasn't it—that this land was theirs simply for the taking and enduring? His own assumption disgusted him.

"It is just a story, David Denny."

"Will there be a fight between Bear and Ant?" he asked.

"If you have ears, hear."

The goosebumps spread, like great spiders walking across his skin, and he paddled home with Curley's paraphrase of Jesus' words ringing in his ears. "He who has ears, listen." It wasn't until he was climbing the trail to the cabin that he realized he had forgotten to ask Curley to come for supper. Louisa would be disappointed.

"Louisa?"

The cabin was empty. Outside the cows milled close. Whiteface and her calf mooed dismally. "Louisa?"

"*Louisa!*"

She was nowhere to be found.

11

"The old hen that Dr. Maynard gave the 'newlyweds' made a nest under the doorstep, and went to sitting as soon as the nest was full of eggs."

—Roberta Frye Watt in *Four Wagons West*

As soon as David was out the door, Louisa wrote a quick note: HAVE GONE TO TOWN. She set it on the table, right by the lamp where he could see it when he came in, then picked up her basket and was out the door herself. He had gone north, but she turned south, a slight smile upon her lips. Two years ago today she loved David secretly. Today she had a different secret.

The shift of sand under her feet as she walked along the beach was a sound she had come to love, and she listened to it with both ears...the soft grinding, the gentle push. She held the basket tightly, one that Betsy Foster, Chief Seattle's granddaughter, had made for her, and kept her eyes focused on the dark hull of a ship anchored close to Seattle.

She hadn't realized it was there until she had gone nearly a quarter of a mile. The sight of its black profile interrupting the waterline stirred quick in her chest. The ships tied them closer somehow to the States, to home. They reminded her that they were still a part of the world, not just an isolated shore. Would there be a letter for her? Without knowing it, her step quickened.

She could smell Seattle long before she came to it. The scent of sawdust and pine and fir and cedar, mixing and galloping in the breeze, came sweet and stinging to her nose. Rounding the last break in the trees, it took her breath to see the busy triangle of cleared land where the mill and cookhouse stood.

The mill was an open structure with a corrugated tin roof at the foot of Skid Road, a narrow strip of Henry Yesler's land that ran straight uphill into the forest. Stripped of trees, the steep, narrow road was used to skid the logs from Henry Yesler's back claim down to the saws. A tall, blackening smokestack stuck through the mill's tin roof, the whistle fastened right beside it. Trash was burned in a silo with a screened oval top, and it was out the silo that sparks like fireflies flew.

The sawmill split the village exactly in half. To the north and above the bank where she stood, small frame and log houses popped up, tucked beneath thick trees. Front and Second Streets were still paths, cluttered with stumps and brush and chattering squirrels. Meadowlarks and steller jays scolded. Lady's slippers and skunk cabbages grew over the forest floor where hitching posts might have stood back East.

To the south of the mill was the Point, Doc Maynard's claim, a spit of land that rose out of the muddy tideflats, gawky and ugly—but the very core of the business district. David had told her that Hillory Butler and William Gilliam were clearing the thick firs for Doc Maynard, and that Maynard was selling the city lots as fast as the trees could come down. Board cabins with false storefronts sat in hurried construction, sleepy-looking or slapped, with wooden signs banging over doors.

Commercial Street was the "road" that joined the Point to the mainland and mill, but to Louisa's way of thinking it could hardly be called a road—not by any stretch of the imagination. It was just a series of wide cedar plankings strung end to end over the muck. It ran from the sawmill all the way south, past Maynard's Seattle Exchange and Real Estate office, and ended abruptly at the Indian camp, a sporadic collection of cedar-bough shelters and open fires along a 16-foot south bluff.

At times the tide washed over Commercial Street between the mill and the Point, creating an island of the business district. The "Sag" was swampy and offensive, but it didn't stop anyone from building. Doc Maynard and Henry Yesler simply hired Old Dutch Ned to haul sawdust between mill and swamp, and every day the simple Dutchman could be seen wheeling his barrow back and forth, snuffing the stench and filling in the "Sag."

Pride burst from Louisa's heart as she saw it all—this town born of trees and brush, growing with sawdust and sweat. In that instant she knew the feeling that lived in Arthur, the feeling that drove him forward so hard, and that sometimes took hold of David. And she forgave them a little. They had seen this from the beginning.

She picked up her basket resting at her feet and stepped over seaweed, twisted coils of battered bark pieces, foam, and kelp, and stepped off the beach onto the sawdust of Arthur's city.

She wondered how many settlers had come this spring. A hundred? There were few families—she knew that. Most were bachelors. And there were the Indians. They milled about, braves dressed in buckskin breeches or just loincloths and blankets. A few ran naked. Squaws wore cedar-bark dresses or else Boston clothes. About 20 of their dugouts sat along the beach, cluttering the shore at odd angles. Some had pulled up alongside the mill onto the sawdust.

The sawdust filled much of the clearing. Everywhere it was sawdust and mud. And men. And noise—dogs barking, saws whining, hammer blows, men hollering. It was all so wonderful, and she was glad she had come. She would see Catherine Maynard first and ask about the catalogue. If there was time, she would stop in to see Mary. Maybe Arthur would have the mail delivery sorted, and maybe there would be word about the minister.

One of the millhands whistled, and Louisa bent her head to hurry past. Even though it was Sunday, the saws still ran; Henry Yesler didn't hold much to the notion of taking the Lord's Day off. Why was the mission board taking so long in sending Arthur word? Didn't they understand that Seattle was in need of the gospel?

The first plank on Commercial gave way when she stepped onto it. Mud oozed over her polished boots and she fished in her pocket for her handkerchief. But it was no use. Another step and more mud. Sighing impatiently, she gave up and went on her way, up the slight incline to Doc Maynard's Seattle Exchange. There was one consolation: Everyone else had muddy boots and skirts too.

When she got to the corner of Commercial and Main (the only intersection on the Point), she took a deep breath and mounted two splintered stairs. She didn't know Catherine Maynard, and she was nervous, more nervous than she would have thought. They had met only once—when she and David were married 2½ months ago. Doc Maynard had given them the chickens and Catherine the dandelion seeds, but somehow since then, what with the awful winter and then the hectically busy spring, they had never really had a chance to get acquainted. I should never have come, she thought.

"Ma'am." A man passed, carrying a crate over his shoulder.

He smiled, his face grizzly and rough.

"Sir."

She looked at the door again. On April the 10th last year Doc Maynard had opened this door for business, and had just about lost everything on his salmon-packing business. She wondered how he was doing now, especially with the new stores in town. Well, you're here now, she told herself. You might as well go in. She can always say no.

It was chilly inside, with merchandise that smelled of leather and wool and scented soaps. She stood blinking, and in a moment glass jars of penny candy and lemon drops took on color and shape in the gloomy light. Where was Catherine? Indians talked somewhere behind a shelf. They spoke their own tongue, the guttural, harsh Duwamish. Hesitantly, she peered down first one aisle, then another. Catherine stood behind a high counter, talking with a squaw. Louisa walked quickly toward them.

It was easy to see why Doc Maynard had married Catherine Simmons Broshears. She was a tall, pretty woman with dark, soft hair caught behind her neck. Her skin was smooth, like cream. Her eyes were dark lights in her face. But it wasn't just the way she looked, Louisa realized, as she watched her patiently show a squaw different buttons she might sew onto her buckskin jacket.

"You do that so well," she said when the squaw had gone.

Catherine's face lit up, her eyes an invitation. Louisa remembered her eyes, always inviting friendship. "How are you, Mrs. Denny?"

"Oh, please, call me Louisa."

"Very well, Louisa then. May I show you something?"

"Oh, no! I mean, I mean yes." Sudden nerves dried her tongue. She forgot what she was supposed to say. It only made her more nervous, and she clutched the basket until sweat from her hands made the handle slippery. "No...what I mean is...do you want to buy some of my eggs? I thought I would give you first choice," she rushed on, "seeing as how it was Doc Maynard who gave us the chickens in the first place. You could sell them to the new folks in town. And David tells me Mr. Maurer is thinking of building on an eating house. You could sell them to him."

Catherine laughed. "He's going to open up his eating house right here. In the summer, I guess, he plans on putting in his own store across the street."

"Here? But I thought...what about...."

Catherine laughed again, with music in the sound. "That Dr. Williamson has just about put my husband out of business."

"Oh, I'm sorry. Then I suppose you won't be wanting to sell my eggs."

"Oh, no, on the contrary, my husband and Mr. Maurer are going to go into partnership. We're going to need those eggs. So your chickens are laying, are they?"

"Yes." She set her basket up on the high counter, feeling better. "We've had two broods of chicks already. David said it was time we quit making chicks and start seeing some profit."

"Men and their profit! Well, I've certainly been hearing the same thing."

"I want to keep this a secret, though. I'm saving for something special, and I don't want David to be asking about it. Do you have one of those catalogues from San Francisco?"

Catherine pulled out a badly battered book. "Like this?"

"Yes!"

"What do you want to look up?"

"It's a secret. Do you mind if I look through it myself?"

Catherine laughed gently.

"You won't be telling David, will you?" asked Louisa, suddenly afraid that it might get out.

"Oh, I won't breathe a word. Here, you look while I set out the eggs." Catherine opened the cloth. "Why, Louisa Denny, what a clever idea! Packing them in moss!"

"I got the idea while ripping it out of my garden. It helps to keep them cool, too."

"Then I'll just transfer them to another basket. Just a minute, I'll be right back."

Louisa flipped quickly through the pages....12 dollars and 75 cents...such a lot of money. But the bunting was so pretty. And it was pure lamb's wool. It would be so warm. "I don't know how much or anything—for the eggs," she said when Catherine returned. "Arthur says they're selling for a dollar-fifty a dozen in Olympia, and you'll be needing to take your share—"

"My share? Don't be silly! They're *your* eggs!"

"But it's *your* store."

Catherine's large smile splashed all over her face. "I suppose it is," she said, and they both laughed together.

• • •

"David!"

He had come to meet her! She called again, "David! Over here!" She jumped off the bottom step, then remembered too late and walked slowly to make up for it. He saw her, waved, then broke into a run. He looked wonderful, his blue shirt-sleeves rolled up, his skin dark, the late sun bouncing off his hair—hair that had grown so long it hung in light brown curls over his collar and onto his shoulder. She blushed to think he belonged to her, that she might possibly—

"Where have you been!"

Startled, she looked into his eyes. They were cold. Stung, she stumbled back a step. The whole wonderful day collapsed. "I, I left you a note. I . . ."

"I've looked all over for you. Don't *ever* leave the cabin again without telling me." He caught her arm at the elbow and started walking her back toward the mill. She stiffened and yanked free. She had seen Dobbins do it to Anna once. It was insulting—the way a father grabbed a naughty child.

"Louisa." He grabbed her arm again.

"Hey, what's the matter?" A stranger leaned against Doc Maynard's brand-new blacksmith shop, a bottle of Jack Daniels in his hand. "What's the matter there, Denny? Your pretty little wife running away, is that it?" Doc Maynard stuck his head out the door. "You sure are pretty when you blush like that, Mrs. Denny!"

"I got home and you weren't there!"

Her attention snapped back to David. He was *yelling* at her! Actually raising his voice—out here in the street! Where everyone could see and hear! "I didn't know where you were or what had happened to you!"

"I left you a note!" She threw her shoulders straight. "And since when was I supposed to stay at home? I didn't know I was a prisoner!"

"Thar she goes! Hey, Denny, you give 'er the buckle end of

the belt!" the drunk hollered. "Show 'em who's boss!"

"Louisa!"

Wiping her eyes blindly with the back of her free hand, she leaped over the last puddle onto the dry sawdust by the mill. He had no right, no right at all. He had ruined the whole day. Everything was ruined. Everything. All her plans for tonight, the—

She stopped so quickly that David slammed into her, nearly knocking her over.

"*Louisa!*" He caught her before she hit the ground. But he let her go quickly, his arms hanging heavily at his side. "I'm sorry. I shouldn't have done that."

Her heart pounded as if a stone spun chaotically inside. Why didn't he take her in his arms and say it properly if he was really sorry, the way Pa did to Ma when he had been unfair? The way Arthur even did to Mary? Why did he just stand there?

"Let me take you back home. I have the canoe."

They walked with a foot of distance between them, and a silent wall.

"Is Salmon Bay Curley coming for supper?" she asked when they got to the beach.

"I forgot to ask."

She had known he would. She had even planned on it. But now it didn't matter. The sun slid to bed, a soft yellow ball pulling up the jagged mountain covers. *I will lift up mine eyes unto the hills . . .* The Psalm seemed to speak. Yet David stood quiet.

"David? Didn't you see my note?" she asked quietly. She didn't want to fight. And *saying* you were sorry had to count for something, didn't it?

"What note?"

"I left you a note. Right in the middle of the table."

He glanced sideways at her, then stuck out his lower jaw so that his beard bristled. He looked quickly away.

"David!" She reached up to turn his face. "You didn't look on the table, did you?"

"Liza. I wasn't looking for a note. I was looking for you."

12

April 25

"The frightful 'statalth,' or 'stick siwash'. . . haunted the great forest."

—Emily Inez Denny in *Blazing the Way*

Statalth. Stick siwash. Giant spirit ghosts, and David could almost feel them as he paddled back to the mill in the dark of night. They seemed to follow, these giant spirit ghosts of a long-ago race of savages. Legend was that the *statalth* were tall and dreadful and fond of chasing people out of the forest on dark nights. He glanced furtively to the left, to the silent, dark woods. Each paddle stroke took him further from Louisa.

But it wasn't the notion of *statalth* tearing after him in the dark that put the worry heavy in his mind. It was what he had done to Liza. Two weeks had passed since he had raised his voice to her in front of the blacksmith shop, and despite his apology, nothing was right. She had withdrawn and the quickness was gone from her smile. When he came home each noon he could see that it was hard for her to smile, to greet him well. He would catch her watching him all the time, as if wondering. Wondering what?

He liked to think it was simply due to the fact that no letters had come from Illinois, and that it was making her sad. But he knew that this wasn't all of it. It was him. He had raised his voice to her.

Why? Did he think that to shout, to bully, might have stopped the strange, uneasy fear that had come to him when he had come home and found her gone? The same strange, uneasy fear that had come the day he had seen the cows so close to the house? It was a nameless fear, a dread inside that wouldn't go away. He couldn't explain it, and so he had yelled at her instead of admitting he was afraid.

He was sick with shame. . . to the core, yet powerless to mend, to heal, to kiss away what he had done, for there was no excuse. He had used her as a shield to protect him from this irrational fear, as if to blame her for nothing might deaden the stirring of unrest inside.

That's what was wrong. He had violated something precious to their love, that sweet trust of safety always in the other's eyes. And, despite his apology and despite her attempt to forgive, something had come like a plug to stop a drain. There it was, a pillow of reproach, suffocating him and separating him from her as surely as if James had come to step between and take her from him.

James.

He hadn't thought of his brother for a long time. James had stayed in the Willamette with Pa because he loved Louisa; two brothers could not live in the same town when they loved the same woman. James had burnt umber hair with thick brows and temper to match, but he would never have raised his voice to Liza. His eyes were the color of a robin's egg, and it was through his eyes that he spoke to Louisa—tender and gentle and always full of good. The sick in David's stomach turned, and he grew hot. No, the *statalth* weren't the ghosts of long-ago savages, they were the ghosts of today's sin. And they pursued, crying.

The mill whistle blew. It was a welcome relief to see the men, shadows with form. "Hey, Dave!" Dobbins hollered. "You look like you've just seen a ghost!"

"What?" He jumped onto the platform. Other men waited to get started. Blue light shadowed their faces. Dobbins pulled on a pair of protective gloves. John Hanford took one end of a board and helped Dobbins move it off the platform. "I don't know," David said. "I think I'm getting spooked." He laughed. "Thought I imagined those *statalth* or *stick siwash* after me tonight!"

Everyone laughed. Arthur slapped his back and Dobbins called out affectionately, "Ah, out in the woods too long!"

"You been listening to too many of those Indian legends!" hollered Joe Foster. "Maybe you ought to think about moving in—and keeping the company of *decent* folk!"

David shrugged, grinning now. That was it—too many Indian legends. "Don't laugh! I've thought of it! But Louisa won't hear of it!"

"No, I suppose not! She's gotten kind of attached to it out there, hasn't she?"

"It's her garden, Dobbins. Keeps waiting for that sweetbriar to come up, you know."

"Just as well!" someone else hollered. "You'd have to give up your claim!"

The men guffawed and Arthur threw on the switch. He took his place behind the saw as it roared into action. This night couldn't be finished fast enough. He needed to get back to Louisa.

• • •

Morning crept upon the sound. The men stopped for breakfast and then went back to work. David kept watch on the sun, impatient for it to reach its height.

"Hey, look! It's Moxlie!" someone hollered. The saws died and everyone rushed for the beach and the newly appointed mail runner. David followed, hoping that Pamelia had written. It would be good to take a letter home. Trying to picture Liza's face if only he might hand her a letter from Illinois, he wasn't aware that anything unusual was happening until Arthur snatched his hat. Bob Moxlie was bellowing, "*All's well that ends well! All's well that ends well!*" He tossed mailbags onto the beach near the Indian canoes.

"Dave! This is it!" yelled Arthur. David leaped after him, jumping logs and seaweed in duet. Men shouted and hollered and sang, congratulating each other with wild thumps across the back. Newspapers flew into the air. David grabbed his own copy, excitement in his lungs. There it was: "ALL'S WELL THAT ENDS WELL!" Arthur whacked him across the back, pitching him forward. "We did it, Dave! We did it!"

"Let me read the paper, for heaven's sake!"

> *It will be seen by reference to our columns of today that a bill has been passed establishing a Territory Government for Northern Oregon under the name and style of the Territory of Washington.*

"WASHINGTON!" he yelped. "What happened to Columbia?"

"*Washington?* Here, let me see that!" Arthur snatched the paper and began to read out loud.

> *It is reported that an anonymous Congressman was concerned that the name "Columbia" might too easily*

> *become confused with the "District of Columbia" and*
> *thought a more appropriate name might be "Washing-*
> *ton"—in honor of George Washington. It seems that no*
> *one considered the fact that a territory and city of the*
> *same name might be equally confusing. But even if the*
> *name "Columbia" had our preference, we would not*
> *care at a name when principals are at stake.*

David scanned the article for details. The Organic Act. Passed March 2 by President Pierce. Nearly two whole months ago.

"YA-HOO!" Someone shoved close. "Ya-hoo! You did it, Arthur Denny! By God, you did it! You and McConaha got that bill through!"

David could not stop the grin on his face. Arthur for once didn't know what to say. Pleased, yet trying to hide his pleasure, he looked for all the world like Pa. Others rallied round, and before anyone knew what was happening Arthur was riding high, buoyed up on the shoulders of John Chapman and David Maurer. Someone started screaming "For He's a Jolly Good Fellow" and Doc Maynard was yelling that the drinks were on him.

"Hey! hey! Wait a minute! You got a letter! Who you know in Washington D.C.?" Bob Moxlie pushed through the noisy, swarming crowd. He held up a large envelope with an official seal, and Arthur glanced at the envelope.

"*It's from the new governor!*" The men carried him to the cookhouse, and David trudged along after. Boy, did he wish Pa were here now!

• • •

Whiteface bawled outside the window, and when Louisa stuck her face over the sill she saw that the cow was all muddy. "Whiteface! What happened to you?" She dashed outside, rubbing the flour from her hands onto her apron. "Where's your calf?"

Far off in the forest she heard the calf cry. Something was wrong. For a moment she debated. Should she go see? But what if— No, maybe the calf was stuck. The cows frequently got stuck in a root tangle or fell into soft ravines. She pulled a coil of heavy rope off the side of the cabin, slung it over her shoulder, and started off, taking the trail that wound around back to the out-house and Chodup's shack, a tiny, tumbledown cabin a few hundred yards away.

• • •

David leaned over the table in the cookhouse. Arthur sat on the other side, sorting documents. The cookhouse was a log build-ing, 25 feet square, set along the north side of the mill. It was where the millhands ate and sometimes slept. It was also the place where men gathered to boast and tell stories, and where Henry Yesler paid his men—rectangular brass checks worth a dollar to the whites; smaller, square brass checks worth 75 cents to the Indians. The men pressed against David's back, crowding from behind, pushing, shoving, anxious to hear, to know the news. He had to brace his feet to keep from falling forward. "Go on," he urged. "Read it!" Arthur glanced up, his eyes wide all around and terribly blue. There was a bit of fright in those eyes, the sort of fright that comes whenever dreams are realized. Doc Maynard slammed a hammer against the bottom of a tin bucket, and there was an instant, shocked hush. "Go on," he urged again.

Arthur focused on the sheets of parchment, the tight scrawl of black ink. "Washington, D.C., April 18, 1853, To A.A. Denny, Esq., Dear Sir:" He paused. The men grew impatient.

"Go on."

He began to read in a loud, steady voice. He sounded just like Pa, and David was proud. Arthur had done it! Arthur had *really* done it! He had pulled them loose from Oregon! And who cared if it was to be named Washington and not Columbia? Oh, couldn't he just hear Pa laugh!

> Herewith you will find a printed copy of my instruc-tions from the secretary of war, by which you will see an exploration and survey of a railroad from the headwaters of the Mississippi to Puget Sound is entrusted to me. To avoid the delay such expe-dition might occasion in the organization of the territory, Colonel Anderson, the marshal, will take a census preliminary to an election for members of the

legislature. He will be found to be a very worthy gentleman, will consult with his fellow citizens on all subjects of interest to the territory, and for him and his brother officers I bespeak your good offices. A military road is to be built from Fort Walla Walla to Puget Sound. Captain McCleallan, distinguished for his gallantry in Mexico, has command of the party who will make the exploration of the Cascade range and the construction of the military road. His undertaking of the task is a sure guaranty of its accomplishment. I expect to pierce the Rocky Mountains, and this road is to be done in time for the fall emigration so that an open line of communication between the States and the Sound will be made this year.

Desire to know your views on these and kindred topics, inviting your consideration of a proper location of the territorial capital.

I am, Yours Truly, Isaac I. Stevens.

Bedlam broke out. A railroad! A military road! Paid for by the government! It was too good to be true. "Wait'll Henry Smith gets back!" David yelled. "Wouldn't he crow!"

"Some people know God is alive!" someone shouted. "But only Henry knew about the railroad!"

"Where is Henry, anyway? Ain't he back yet?"

"Heard he's due next month."

"Who says it's going to terminate in Seattle?" someone bellowed.

John Holgate hollered, "It's going to terminate in Puget Sound, ain't it?"

"Don't mean Seattle!"

"Where else would it end?"

David grinned at Arthur. His brother sat dazed, sweat pouring off his brow. "You know what this means, Dave?" Arthur said, shaking the daze off. "It means we're going to get that pass opened up and pioneers are going to come pouring in just like we planned. It means the railroad..."

"Hey, you all right?"

"All right?" Arthur jumped to his feet. "I've never been more all right in my life, Dave!" He straightened the papers and dropped them back into the envelope. "Dave, this means we've *got* to finish the Steilacoom road! Once that military road goes in we'll have a direct link all the way from The Dalles. Not just the Willamette, but The Dalles! The Dalles, Dave! And it's going to be done by fall! The emigrants can come to *us* this fall—they won't *have* to go to the Willamette!" They pushed their way past the drinking, boisterous men. "They're going to let loose tonight," said Arthur under his breath, glancing back over his shoulder. He set his arm over David's shoulder. "We're going to make it, Dave!"

It was rare that they had their affectionate times, and David enjoyed them when they came. "You mean you had your doubts?" he teased.

"Of course I had my doubts. You did, too. Come on, we've got to find Dobbins and bring out those maps we started last spring. It's time to make this a real town! Hey, Dave," Arthur planted his feet suddenly, "I'm counting on you to straighten Maynard out."

He was talking about the worst of the disagreements between the two men—how they were going to lay the city streets. Maynard insisted on going by the book, running the roads directly north/south and east/west. Nobody could get it through his head that it would look better to put the roads at a slight angle so they lay perpendicular and parallel to the shoreline. It meant that Yesler's strip of land, Skid Road—and the division between Maynard's and Dobbins' claims—was going to have to absorb the chaotic mismatch.

"If he *has* to be right," said Arthur, "at least he could be right and have his lousy roads run *into* Dobbins' streets. But no, he must prove a point. You can bet the last of that booze of his that forever after this town is going to have to put up with the ridiculous inconvenience of streets jogging off-course half a block and running different directions."

"I'll do what I can. But you know him . . . when his mind is made up."

"I'm counting on you, Dave. Hey, Seattle is going to get on the map! The railroad guarantees it! First thing, though, Dave, I better go tell Mary."

Liza. He had forgotten all about her. What time was it, anyway? And how much time had he wasted with this new-territory nonsense?

13

Louisa met him at the door. "You were right, David. There *is* something wrong with the cattle." It took a minute for the words to register. He was still caught up in news of Separation, going through in his mind all that it would entail: the arrival of the new governor, the establishment of a territorial seat, the appointing of judges. It probably meant that the Methodists would be more inclined to send out a minister now, too. "I heard a calf bawl," she was saying, "as if something had caught it, and Whiteface came up all muddy and distressed."

"What?" A roar came to his ears as sudden alarm slipped like a noose about his neck, stopping his breath. He knew again the intensity of his earlier premonitions. "You didn't go see what it was, did you?"

"I started to, but came back."

The room tilted. A grateful prayer got lost in the constriction of his throat.

"I thought I heard an Indian shout, and even looked out the window expecting one to come down the trail, but I didn't see anything at all. I got a little scared. Whiteface has been bothering the chickens all morning with her worry. I think something has happened to her calf."

"Guess I'll go see what I can find."

"Shall I come with you?"

He couldn't help but laugh, it was so obvious she didn't want to. "No, you just stay behind the locked door. If you hear me scream, you come running!"

"Oh, stop," she scolded, and he laughed again, tension between them finding escape.

Not many yards from the cabin he found the remains of the calf. Large tracks all around the carcass told the story, and he shouldered his gun grimly. Why hadn't he figured it would be something like this? *What if Louisa had followed?*

Tom Mercer edged his thoughts; it wouldn't hurt to have somebody cover him in case the gun misfired. No, he could take care of it himself. Suddenly it was important to him to take care of it himself.

The ground was soft with the spring rains, outlining the retreating trail. He followed it easily into thick timber, then heard something scratch and run up a tree. A fir log ran across a narrow gorge and he jumped up onto it, walking along perhaps 50 feet, ears straining, gun in hand, searching out the boughs of the giant cedar tree straight ahead. He was ready, but nearly slipped when he finally saw the great, savage, yellow eyes of the largest cougar he had ever seen. It took his breath. The forearm was easily the size of a horse's leg above the knee joint, and mentally he figured his chances if it jumped. Sheer weight alone from that height could be enough to crush him.

The cougar glared through the crisscross of cedar boughs, crouching motionless except for the incessant twitching, to and fro, of the tip of its tail. This is what he had sensed. This is what had unnerved him so badly. It was a good feeling to know that it would soon be over and life could go back to normal. No more looking over his shoulder.

Right in front of him, attracting attention, was a large limb that had fallen and stuck to the ground. It stood alongside the log he balanced on, and he swung his gun onto it, but it sank into the soft earth from the weight and he quickly drew it up, aiming at the chest of the cougar. The tail still twitched.

The gun misfired.

The cat snarled and pawed the air. David backstepped quickly along the log, took a pin out of his coat, picked out the tube, poured in fresh powder from his powder horn, and put on a fresh cap. Yellow eyes watched him.

Advancing, he fired again. The bullet struck. Blood spurted from its chest. The cat bolted up the tree. David's fingers trembled as he loaded the gun again. Powder spilled. He prayed through gritted teeth, forcing a calm to his hands. *Good. Another bullet rammed home in the old muzzle loader.* He aimed again.

The cougar held on by its claws stuck deep into the bark of a top branch, head resting over the limb. A second bullet crashed into its skull and the cat let go. It hurtled downward, bouncing off a limb. It struck the ground with a thud. David lost his balance and slipped, skinning his shin, landing in the deep gorge—and a patch of devil's club. For a minute he lay dazed, breath knocked from his lungs. Then stinging prickles danced all over his body.

Zing! Zing! Zing! Three successive shots meant that Tom Mercer was to come on the run. It wasn't long before David could hear his new neighbor crashing through the trees, calling his name.

"Over here!" he yelled, still tangled in the mesh of devil's club and blackberry vines. He lay still, weak with giddy relief. It was over—nothing to be afraid of anymore. Tom's thrashing grew closer.

"Denny?"

"Tommy! Over here!"

He squirmed to better see Tommy's face. From where he lay he knew Tom wouldn't be able to see him, just the cat. He wasn't disappointed. Tom's eyes bulged. Then Louisa was there, peering over Tom's shoulder, and he watched as the color drained from her face. So that's what she would look like if ever he were dead.

"David?" she called, a sweet tremor in her voice.

"Over here!" he yelled, poking the gun barrel out of the devil's club and swinging it in a circle so that they might spot his brutal nest.

"Where?"

"I fell in the gorge!"

She stepped cautiously over the huge cat, gathering her skirts and jumping clear, then scrambled up onto the fallen fir.

"Be careful," he warned.

"Oh, David! You're alive!"

"Of course I'm alive. Liza! Be careful!"

She slipped and nearly tumbled.

"Never mind. Guess I better come after you." He struggled to rise, to pull himself out of the large leaves and up onto the fir. He felt bruised and disjointed all over. The itch burned, and he forced his way carefully back down the log, desperate to claw the skin from his arms and legs and neck and scalp.

"Are you all right?"

"Yeah...I think so. Itch like crazy, though."

"You fool. What did you do, jump in?" Her smile was quick, and he laughed. So this was how to fix it--shoot a cougar and fall into devil's club! They jumped off the fir together and he threw his arm about her shoulder, glad to feel her quick response. "Let's go take a look at the thing that's caused so much trouble."

Between the three of them they managed to get the cougar home. They staggered under the weight, even the short distance it had to be carried. "How long do you think that thing is?" Tom Mercer asked, shaking his head slowly from side to side. He was an older man, about 40, with thick, gray side-whiskers that grew ten inches long from both sides of his face. He had soft, sorrowing gray eyes. His wife had died at The Dalles, and his four motherless daughters were waiting for him in the Willamette to finish his cabin, plant his garden, and come for them.

"Eight feet?"

"Naw...got to be ten at least. You got a measuring tape?"

"Yesler's got one. Think maybe I ought to skin it? Louisa, would you like a nice cougar rug in front of the fire?"

"No, I would not! I want that thing taken out to sea and dumped, or buried deep in some hole. It could have killed you, David."

"Well, we can thank the Lord it didn't, Mrs. Denny. Although they don't usually kill people—unless you go after their young," said Mercer in his slow, ponderous voice. "Well, now, think maybe I'll mosey into town and get that tape from Yesler. You going to let me take your canoe, Dave, or are you going to make me walk?"

"Canoe's yours, if you want." David leaned against a tree and rubbed up and down on the bark. "But it's just a cougar. No sense in getting excited."

"Biggest cougar I've ever seen. People are going to want to see it."

"Not today they're not."

Tom's eyebrows went up, and he turned around in the path.

David grinned. "They're already celebrating. Separation. We got it, Tommy."

But everyone came anyway. They just brought the celebration out with them. And Yesler brought his tape measure. It was an old yellowed and stringy rope, frayed and chewed along the edges. Someone spread the cougar out flat, and one of the new millhands, Seth Lambert, the brother of Lambert and Smith of Alki, held the end of the measuring rope to the cat's nose while Yesler made a big production of running the rope along the cougar's sleek back. "Made sleek by dining off fatted calves," someone laughed.

David shivered and glanced at Louisa. She was serving tea with her new dishes, substituting the old coffee kettle for the broken teapot. So Tommy thought cougars wouldn't attack people, did he? Well, he'd heard stories. He certainly wasn't going to say anything to Louisa, though. He had seen the relief in her face.

"Nine feet! Top to tip!" Yesler declared. David shoved his hands into his pockets, fists clenched to keep from scratching. He walked around the cabin seven times for something to do, nodding politely when one or another congratulated him. It was odd how he had known...one day chopping trees, then the sudden dread, the cold sweat. Now a nine-foot cougar. He better get that straight—things were never the way they seemed. Trouble was always ready, elusive, hiding—like a cougar in a tree.

"Hey! You are quite high-toned here!" Yesler hollered. He had his head stuck through their doorway, examining the interior of their cabin. "I see your house is papered!" Everyone laughed. But it didn't strike David funny at all, and he didn't laugh.

"What did Louisa use for the pretty border around the ceiling?" Sally Bell asked him. Pulling his eyes off the leering, empty grin of the cougar, he answered, "Blue calico—I think."

• • •

For awhile it had been all right between them. They had laughed. But now that everyone was gone, it was just the same as it had been for two weeks, and Louisa sat on the front stoop wondering what had happened. David had retreated again. He had gone to bed brooding, hardly aware she was there. So while he was off to bed she sat on the step needing to cry and not wanting him to know. She had begun a letter to Pamelia. The paper sat in her lap. The ink bottle sat at her feet. Absently she read over what she had written.

April 25, 1853
Seattle, Territory of Washington

Dear Pamelia,

David killed a big panther today. It killed a calf in broad daylight a few hundred yards from the house. The Indians say that they are not afraid of them, that they never attempt to kill a human being, but we don't know what they would do if they had a chance and were hungry.

Oh, she had been scared. Two shots with eternity between. Then the three-shot signal for Tom. She had vowed to God and herself that she would try even harder to forget that David had yelled at her. And all during the time that everyone was here, admiring her tea set, consoling her over the broken pieces, and asking how to fix the newspaper so it wouldn't peel from the logs, she did forget. But now...how *could* she forget when he reminded her of it every time he looked at her, and she saw how careful he was when speaking to her?

A tear leaked, and angrily she brushed it aside. Why didn't he just take her in his arms and tell her he loved her? Why? Why didn't he tell her again he was sorry—the way Pa always did to Ma when Ma was hurt? Didn't he know that she had to know all over again? Didn't he know he had to say it again and again? Didn't he know that she needed his gentle words right now?

Maybe he didn't love her. The thought put a cold pain to her head. Oh, why was such a silly thing as being yelled at so difficult to bear? Goodness, Arthur had spoken sharp enough a time or two and she hadn't seen Mary Ann dissolve into tears for it.

A quiet wind blew off the bank, touching her damp cheek. The sun had lost its strength. The forest was quiet, as it always is when it sighs and falls asleep. The chickens fussed restlessly. She thought of her money in the white jug, a little over a dollar, but it brought no secret pleasure. She started to cry then. She hadn't heard from Pamelia for so long, months and months, and tonight it seemed just too much to bear.

I have had no news from Illinois. I look and look for letters from my friends until I begin to think that I have none, or that my friends have forgotten me. I have written several letters, and as yet I have received but one besides yours last fall. But I do not believe there has been none written. I think that they have been lost or miscarried. Perhaps there will be one this week.

It is time to go to bed, so I can't write a long letter.

L.D.

P.S. Our sweetbriar is planted. Maybe your long-lost letters will come when the sweetbriar grows.

Part Three

Summer 1853

"Spring quickened into a prosperous summer. Nearly every brig and schooner that came into the Sound brought a few immigrants, some for Seattle, others who were planning to found settlements elsewhere. . . . This was undoubtedly one of the busiest summers in all Seattle history."

—Roberta Frye Watt in *Four Wagons West*

14

July 8

"I should like to omit one event of this summer of constructive activity, for it mars the splendid record."
—Roberta Frye Watt in *Four Wagons West*

"You staying on for dinner, Dave?" Arthur hollered above the saw's buzz. Sweat dripped from his face and ran into his sandy beard, trimmed short for the summer.

"That baby of yours born yet?"

"Haven't seen Kickisomlo come running!"

"Princess Angeline," David corrected before feeding another tree into the large, circular saw. Giant teeth bit and choked, and the buzz rose to a whine. Joe Foster on the far end guided the boards. George Frye stacked the boards in measured rows.

"Angeline then!" hollered Arthur. "Whew! It's hot!"

"Quittin' time!" bellowed Joe. He swore and looked to the sun. "July and already it's hotter 'n blazes!"

The whistle blew. "Turn 'er off!" shouted Arthur. "Noon!" And for five minutes the earth was quiet.

The noon-to-midnight crew arrived and the saw started again. David stepped off the platform and walked north alongside his brother, following the worn trail of Front Street toward Arthur's new board cabin, one built closer to town. "What are you going to call him if it's a boy?" he asked.

"Don't know yet."

David mopped his hair back and replaced his cap. Sawdust fell out. "Don't remember it being this hot last year. Guess I better not complain, though. Beats winter. Sure been peculiar, though."

"What?"

"The weather. The whole year's been odd. That bitter winter and then the blazing spring beating back the snow. And now it's so hot."

"You staying on?" They were nearing the new house.

"I don't know. Think I might be in the way. I'll just pick up Louisa and get on home. That two miles never gets any closer."

"Nonsense. Mary won't mind if you stick around. If she's still in labor she may even want to see you. She. . ." Arthur left the sentence unfinished, but David knew what he was about to say. Mary Ann counted on David in a way she didn't with Arthur—she drew strength from him, his quiet acceptance of things. Arthur felt it, David knew, although, as now, they never talked about it.

David thought about that—about his quiet acceptance of things, and how it wasn't so quiet anymore. There was a part of him these past few weeks that stood back to dare, calling into trial his old perceptions and ideas, and it left a disturbing sense of disquiet.

They stepped into the house, leaving their shoes on the outside step. Mary Ann liked to keep her new board floor clean. It hadn't mattered in the old log cabin. You couldn't add dirt to dirt.

"It's awful quiet," said Arthur. He tossed his cap onto a pile of crates stacked just inside the door—FROM THE PORT OF SAN FRANCISCO stenciled onto each in black ink. "Wonder what's happened? Where is everybody?" He moved quickly to the closed bedroom door and gave it a tight knock.

"Shh!" Doc Maynard hissed, peering over his spectacles between door and jamb. "She's sleeping."

"Where's Louisa?" David asked.

The doctor slipped out and quietly shut the door. "Sent her out with Princess Angeline."

"What about the baby?" demanded Arthur. "Boy or girl?"

"Boy."

"Then come out and have a visit with us."

"Got any Blue Ruin?" Doc Maynard polished his round glasses on the tail of his black doctor garb. "Could stand a good stiff one right now."

"I'm surprised you didn't bring your own. David—put the kettle on and make the man a cup of tea. I'm going in to see Mary and the baby."

"Don't waken her," cautioned Maynard, settling wearily into a table chair. He glanced back at the bedroom. "Sometimes I don't understand that brother of yours, Dave, my boy," he sighed, when the door was safely shut. "Him and his high-totin' *principles.* Can't even have a drink on the happy occasion of a baby being born into this wonderful world. Look at it out there, will you? God's good earth and not even a drop to celebrate. What's the use of having a baby if you can't celebrate, I say."

"A drink's a drink," said David, lighting the stove and setting the old kettle on a black plate. "It's the harm it does, not the good."

"Now that's what I can't figure out," said Maynard, leaning over the table and stabbing a finger at David. "I never mind those high-totin' principles when they come out of *you*, but when they come out of that brother of yours, why, I'd like to—" He lowered his voice. "Kick his teeth in, if you know what I mean." Suddenly Maynard laughed, breaking the quiet that held the cabin. "Don't know why that is, either. Enough to puzzle a man."

"Where'd you say Louisa went?"

"Berry-picking."

"Thought she wanted to help Mary Ann with the birth."

"Not with Angeline and those daughters of hers hanging around the place! Couldn't stand the din. Mary Ann screaming, Angeline and her daughters—what are their names?"

"Mamie and Betsy."

"That's right. Sticking tubers and camas root under the sheets, they were, chanting some fool spirit song. I sent them packing. Told Louisa to take the whole kit and kaboodle. She's a good woman, Dave." He sighed. "Ah-h...if I didn't have my own wife—"

David laughed. "She wouldn't have you, sir."

"Ha! That's the pity of it. Ah, you're a lucky man, my boy."

"She talk to you at all?" he asked, looking through the pantry for sugar. Doc Maynard liked three spoons with his tea.

"Why should Louisa talk to me? By jingle, what a beautiful day!" He leaned back in his chair, arms spread behind his neck, and stared out the window. The sun bounced off Elliott Bay.

"I think she's in the family way."

Maynard looked up sharply. "So soon? Hey—you ain't scared?"

David found the sugar and spilled in the three spoons.

"Babies get born every day, Dave. You quit that, being scared. You'll scare Louisa, and I won't have you doing that, you hear?"

"I've seen Mary, Doc. She doesn't ever have it easy—and they're sisters."

Maynard fixed his blue eyes on David, pinning him with their intensity. "I *know* they're sisters, but Mary Ann's a whole different constitution! And that trip across the Oregon Trail her last time didn't do anything to make it strong in there, you know. Besides..." He relaxed and winked, breaking the tension. "Besides that, she's married to *Arthur*. Louisa ain't got that handicap. How far is she, anyway?"

"Don't know. She hasn't said. I don't even know for sure."

"Then why don't you ask her?"

"Figure she'd tell me when she's ready."

"Been sick mornings?"

"How would I know? I'm always down here, working that saw."

Maynard whistled and shook his head. "You don't waste much time."

David set out two cups and poured the tea. He sat across the table and raised the cup. "To Mary and the baby."

"To Mary and the baby."

Maynard was the sort of man who loved life, and perhaps that was the reason David liked him so well. He was of medium build. His eyes were blue. He had a square forehead, a strong face, and black hair that curled when he let it go long. He overflowed with generosity and his own humor. He gave away anything within reach and was full of extravagant promises—even if they weren't in his power to keep. Most of all, he loved the Indians. People like Arthur and Henry Smith respected them, even thought highly of a few, but Maynard was hopelessly in love with them all—even the scoundrels. He delivered their babies in filth and squalor, bandaged their knife wounds, handed out trinkets for any show of game, spent hours smoking with Chief Seattle down in the Indian camps. Maynard knew how it was with the Indians.

The door bounced in the frame. "What the—" Maynard swung around. Salmon Bay Curley knocked the top of the door open. "Jim—Masachie Jim!" he wheezed, slipping the bottom bolt and letting himself in. He stumbled across the floor, and sawdust from the lagoon dropped off his bare feet. "Masachie Jim, he—he..."

"Come, come, spit it out!" said Maynard.

"He killed his klootchman! He got drunk! He got angry! Very angry! And he—"

"*What's this?*" Arthur stood at the bedroom door, hand still on the knob. "And be quiet about it," he ordered.

David was already pulling on his shoes. He threw Arthur's to him. "Sounds like trouble, Arthur. Curley says there's been a murder. Masachie Jim got ahold of some booze again."

• • •

Louisa sat along a low bluff just north of town. A narrow beach hung inches from her bare feet, then tideflats stretched to meet the sound. The Olympics appeared closer than usual, their jagged fissures defined clearly by the blazing sun, and she thought that the lingering snow of their peaks dripped like cream against the sky. She swung her legs off the sandy bank, shoes and stockings close by. She wiggled her toes, glad to feel the cooling wind.

Katy, her nine-year-old niece, played along the sandflats, shrieking as she splashed water over her berry-stained cheeks. Nora, the four-year-old, hung back. Anna's daughter, Gertrude, sat quietly, thinking deeply, as she did so much of the time, and Louisa wondered what her youngest niece thought of. She was so serious for three.

"Come here, Gertie," she called. "Come let Auntie clean your face!" and she took the edge of her petticoat to Gertrude's solemn round mouth.

"You think baby come yet?" asked Kickisomlo, or Princess Angeline, as Catherine Maynard had begun to call Chief Seattle's daughter. Angeline watched as she dabbed the child's mouth, swinging her own feet over the edge of the bank, her feet thick with calluses and half-inch cracks.

"Maybe."

"Then we go back. Our berries go flat."

The berries sat in five tin buckets, fat and shiny black, sweet with sunshine. But Louisa remembered Doc Maynard's exasperation. "No," she said, although she longed to see if Mary Ann was all right. She remembered when Rollie had been born—at the end of the Oregon Trail. It had nearly killed her sister. "Let's wait," she said wearily, feeling suddenly alone and a little frightened.

Angeline sighed and lay back, flopping her arms over her head and resting them against the warm earth. She shut her eyes, and Louisa, glancing back, was startled to see that her Indian friend looked almost happy.

Angeline rarely looked happy. Harsh living had left scars, deep lines that laced her square brown face like pen scratches. Although she was only 45, she looked 60. Her eyes were dull, her front teeth worn. But she had a smile that belonged to a child, and it was hard not to love her. There was compassion in Angeline, and a trust that couldn't be violated. She wore the red handkerchief that Louisa had given her last spring, and impulsively Louisa leaned to tuck a strand of loose hair under the kerchief. Angeline turned to give Louisa the child-smile.

Mamie and Betsy, Angeline's grown daughters, played with Rollie further up the bank, and she could hear his giggles. *Acha-da, acha-da, memaloose, memaloose!* had been the cry a year-and-a-half ago. *Too bad, too bad, he die, he die.* But now he giggled. Nearly two, fat and bright, with thick red curls, the Indian women thought of him as their own, for they had saved his life when he was only eight weeks old. Mary Ann had been too sick to nurse and they had spooned clam broth for milk into his mouth.

Louisa couldn't understand some of the new settlers' attitudes about the Indians. People like Joe Foster. She shivered and glanced up the bank to Betsy.

Poor Betsy. She was Joe's *klootchman*. He beat her, and even though Betsy tried to run away, he always found her and brought her back. And now Betsy was pregnant, due any day.

"Goodness!" Louisa exclaimed, suddenly conscious that time had passed while she daydreamed. The sun had just begun its descent and the tide had washed in. "Did the mill whistle go? Is it noon yet?" Waves rolled over the rocky shore, nearly touching their toes, cutting off the path back to Seattle. Angeline sat and squinted, then drew up a foot and picked at a sore, unconcerned. "We have canoe," she said.

"*Ac-c-hc! The canoe!*" Up the beach Betsy was scrambling to her feet. "Ac-c-hc!" she shouted again, discarding her moccasins while way out their canoe bobbed on the water.

"Angeline! How could we let this happen?" Louisa cried. "Katy! Nora! Gertie!" she called, scooping up shoes and stockings. "Angeline! The canoe's way out there! We're stranded! How are we going to get home? Oh, Betsy!" she hollered. "*What are you doing?*"

Angeline's daughter had dived into the cold, icy water. Louisa watched as she swam with strong, sure strokes. In just a few moments she reached the canoe, then dove to pull up the stone anchor.

"Betsy?" One shoe fell. "Betsy!"

"Now she's gone," said Angeline flatly.

"*Betsy!*" Louisa screamed, dropping the other shoe and sliding over the bank into the shallow water. But just then Betsy's round, black head broke the surface and the Indian girl flung the anchor into the canoe and clambered in.

"Oh, Betsy!" Louisa exclaimed, laughing and crying at the same time, throwing her arms about the poor, drenched pregnant girl when she reached the shore. "You scared me! You scared the living daylights out of me! Oh, Betsy! You should have told me you could hold your breath so long!"

Betsy laughed, a pretty face streaked with water. "I should have taken off dress!" she giggled, staggering under the weight of the wet cedar bark. Louisa hauled up the canoe, hardly able to do it for laughing at Betsy falling and tripping and shaking water. Angeline came down and took the baby from Mamie, and the little girls tugged on their shoes. "Auntie!" Nora cried before they shoved off. "Mama's berries!" Katy dashed back after them.

15

"A murder, which had a far-reaching effect on pioneer history, was committed by 'Masachie Jim' (bad Jim), an Indian."
—Roberta Frye Watt in *Four Wagons West*

Doc Maynard and David left Arthur with Mary Ann, and followed quickly after Salmon Bay Curley. They jogged south across the Sag and onto the Point. In front of Doc Maynard's Seattle Exchange they turned east and descended into the lagoon, a thick swamp of mucky tidewater speckled with water striders and other bugs. Rotting seaweed and salt air hovered over the marsh. "This lagoon can't be filled in soon enough to suit me," said Maynard. They all piled into a rowboat, and David pulled back on the oars.

"Over there!" Curley yelled, pointing where to land on the opposite side. In two minutes they pulled alongside Tom Pepper's shack, a miserable shanty with wild roses growing over cedar slabs. A trail opened into the forest, and death wails led the way as they plunged deeper and deeper into the woods. The sun was hidden and the way grew dark. David shivered in the growing dampness.

Twenty-five Indians congregated around Masachie Jim's cabin, a tiny log building with no windows. Some wailed, some just stood. "Where's Masachie Jim?" Doc Maynard demanded in Duwamish, plunging through the crowd. David was glad that someone else besides him had bothered to learn the native tongue; he doubted he had the presence of mind right now to take control. Jim and George Seattle stepped forward. "Inside," they said.

Polysyllables and the guttural sounds of the Dunwamish language flew about like weighted wings. "Firewater," said one.

"Traded it from a Boston for two buckskins!"

"Klootchman snored in her sleep when he came home!"

In a drunken rage he had struck her, with the end of his musket—the way he had always done when he'd gotten drunk.

But this time the musket had gone off, blowing a hole through her neck.

"You'd better come in with me, Dave, my boy," said Maynard. David followed, fighting the numbness that stole over his limbs and mind, a numbness that tried to deny what was happening.

The world fell away when he stepped through the open door. Like a foul cave, the blackness was instant. A putrid stench reached out with grabbing hands to choke.

"A-cgh!" Masachie Jim snarled, leaping out of the filth, and David instinctively stumbled backward, recoiling. Jim Seattle bellowed and the Indian slunk to a smelly cot. David took a cautious step back inside.

The blackness broke into chunks and the chunks took form. Two beds. Boxes. Clothes strewn over the floor. Baskets hanging. Masachie Jim huddled in a corner. The numbness snapped, heat bursting through his veins, and he found that every detail came to him now out of the fog. Time slowed. Any fear he had had now fled. Compassion rushed in, beating stronger in his veins than his own blood. "Masachie Jim?"

The man cowered on the bed, and the compassion rose up in David like a pain. "Who sold you the firewater?" he demanded, hard put to keep the shout from his voice. Masachie Jim didn't hold the guilt alone. They shared it for selling liquor to a people who had no tolerance for alcohol. Liquor was a key that loosened demons, and Masachie Jim was a man caught, trapped in a power bigger than himself. David ached to understand. He clenched his fists, needing to strike out. A rage against his race came in a fury. A rage against God followed swiftly as Curley's words came to mind. Perhaps God after all was choosing the white man over the red.

"Who sold you the firewater?" He stared into the man's face— the dark, swollen eyes. The black night of the cabin was not dark enough to hide the Indian's fear. It jumped from his eyes like a rabbit's when caught, knowing its doom.

"They said the Boston with the liquor had a canoe with blue drilling sails," sighed Maynard wearily, rubbing his head. "Come on. We best get her out of here."

"What about Masachie Jim? What's to be done with him?"

"They'll take care of him. It's Seattle's jurisdiction, not ours."

Seattle would take care of it—an eye for an eye. There was

nothing he could do except find the whiskey trader.

Four of the Indians wrapped the murdered woman in a blanket, as was their custom, then picked her up and headed outdoors. David followed. "Let me know what happens, all right?" he said to Jim Seattle. "Has someone gone for your father?"

"We sent Yoke-yakeman."

They had all laughed together as friends once, and hunted together. They had helped each other out in what now seemed days gone forever. "Let me know what happens," he said again.

"I will." In an uncommon gesture of friendship Jim put a hand to David's shoulder.

They returned to the settlement in a hush. It was agreed to put the woman in the toolshed by the mill until morning. Seattle, when he arrived, could decide where he wanted her buried. "Amazing how a day can turn on you," said Maynard, standing outside his defunct store, bankrupt now from the competition and his own generous impulses. His sign, "The Seattle Exchange," clanged over his head from a gust of wind. "You wake up and deliver a baby. Then you declare a squaw dead and go to sleep waiting for the funeral. Days sometimes spill faster than a pot of beans. Well, guess I better go see what Catherine has to say about this."

David nodded and said goodbye. He retraced his steps, picking his way over the sawdust and mudholes, dragging his feet as if lead soled his boots. The men on the noon-to-midnight shift at the mill stood huddled in conversation. Bad news traveled fast. Luther Collins raised a hand. David waved back. He tripped over a stump root and hurried on. How was he going to tell Arthur? With Mary and Louisa and the children all around?

• • •

"Where's David?" Louisa asked Arthur for the fourth time. She pulled the biscuits out of the oven. "Nora! Go get some pretty flowers for your mother! Please! Where *is* he, Arthur?"

"I told you. He and Doc Maynard went off somewhere."

Louisa sighed. "That doesn't tell me anything, Arthur. Here, you put the dinner on—I'm going to see how Mary's doing." She handed him the tea towel, wiped her hands on her apron, and gave him a you-don't-fool-me-Arthur-Denny look before going in to check on her sister.

Mary Ann was asleep, propped against five or six pillows in the large bed. Her head had fallen to the side, and her cheek rested against the top of little Orion's bald head. The baby was asleep too.

Sometimes Louisa felt very protective of her older sister. She did now. She tucked in the counterpane, one that she and Mary Ann had made years ago. The bright colors had long since faded and holes had worn right through in spots. She felt Mary's forehead to see if there was a fever. Doc Maynard had said to be sure her skin was cool.

She tiptoed across the room, a nice, airy room with a window out to the sea. Mary Ann was lucky to have such a nice new house. Poor Anna had been so jealous. Louisa pulled the shutter to block the evening breeze. The baby's diaper was dry. Finding nothing else to do, she softly shut the door.

"David! You're back! Where have you been? Arthur wouldn't tell me."

"Shh-h," he whispered, kissing her cheek quickly.

"David?"

"What's for supper?" he asked, ignoring her. "Katy? Nora? Is that blackberry pie I smell?" He kicked off his shoes and set them on the step. "Let me wash my hands first and I'll pick you up then, okay, Rollie? Arthur," he nodded, plunging his hands up to the elbows in the bucket of warm water that sat on the back of the stove. He grabbed the bar of soap.

"We were just about to sit down," said Arthur.

"Where's Mary Ann? Is she all right? The baby?"

"They're both asleep," said Louisa. Something was wrong—horribly wrong. This wasn't David's normal preoccupation about things. He was *deliberately* ignoring her. And he and Arthur kept looking at each other. Her hands trembled when she poured the little girls' dinner into bowls. "Katy? Nora?" she called. "Time to sit up."

"Where's Gertie?" whined Nora. "I thought you said Gertie could stay for supper, Auntie."

"Hush!" said Arthur sternly, bowing his head over his plate. They all did the same. When he was finished with the blessing they all said amen, and David leaned over like he used to and kissed Louisa. She tried to hold him with her eyes, but he looked quickly away. Then Rolland cried to be put on his lap.

"Auntie?" Nora whined, her eyes large and wet. "I thought Gertie was going to stay for supper."

"Shh, she'll be here. After supper."

"Is Aunt Anna going to spend the night then?" Katy asked.

"To help with the new baby, Katy."

"Oh."

The men talked of nothing. The little girls told what they had done that day and laughed softly about Auntie Louisa getting so scared when Betsy didn't come out of the water.

"I was beginning to think she was gone," said Louisa, remembering her fright. Then the conversation went back to nothing. The new baby woke with a squall and Louisa gratefully excused herself, glad to have something to do. She changed the diaper and cleaned the umbilical cord the way Doc Maynard had instructed, washing it with a cotton ball dipped in whiskey (it was the only alcohol Doc Maynard had had). She dressed the baby in a gown she had made herself, and then helped Mary to sit comfortably enough to nurse. Outside the door she heard David clearing the dishes and talking softly. To the children? To Arthur?

"What's the matter, Liza?" Mary Ann asked. "You look so nervous."

"Do I?" she said with a forced nonchalance.

"All right. Don't tell me. I don't want to know anyway."

"Are you in pain, Mary? Can I do something for you?"

"No. I'm just tired."

"Can I get you a glass of water? We had clam chowder for dinner. Would you like me to get some of that for you?"

"Louisa, would you *please* sit still!"

"I'm sorry." She sat, forcing her mind off David and Arthur. "Mary? Was it hard this time?"

"It always is." Mary laughed softly. The brightness had come back to her eyes, and she stroked the baby's cheek with the backs of her fingers. "But it's worth it, don't you think? Look at him, Liza. Such a fine little boy. Now I have two girls and two boys!"

"But wasn't this one better?"

"What do you mean, better?"

"You nearly died with Rolland."

"I didn't nearly die! I did just fine."

"You nearly died."

Mary Ann turned away. "When is Anna coming? Isn't it time you and David got on home?"

She had gone too far in making Mary rude, and she ought to have known. Mary didn't like to think about death. "I'm sorry, Mary," she blurted. "I'm being a worry to you. I'll go get Anna now if that's what you want."

Mary wouldn't look at her.

"Mary, I didn't mean to worry you—I'm just not feeling myself these days. It's so hot, and...of course you didn't nearly die," she added, stopping the ramble.

"No, of course I didn't."

Louisa reached across the bed and turned Mary's face to hers. Mary had a round face, with bright eyes, and hair that was always just a little messy. She saw Ma in Mary Ann's face. "Mary?"

"Liza? Is something wrong?"

"Oh, Mary...I'm going to have a baby!"

"A baby!" Mary Ann slapped her fingers to her mouth, smiling, her anger forgotten. She didn't even notice Louisa's quiet. "Oh, Liza, is it true?"

"Yes," said Louisa, feeling forlorn and uncertain. "I haven't told anybody—not even David. I thought maybe I might tonight..."

"So that's what this is all about! No *wonder* you're acting so oddly! Why, Louisa, I think that's wonderful! How far?"

"Three months."

"That far! How come you haven't told anyone? How come you haven't told David?"

Louisa hung her head. "I don't know, Mary Ann. I guess I was just waiting for the right time. He's so busy, you know. So preoccupied, always at the mill, talking politics, and... Well, I guess I just like keeping secrets," she finished lamely, not wanting to sound like she was complaining.

"You and your secrets," Mary laughed, and Louisa was grateful. "You're not going to be able to keep it to yourself forever, you know."

"I know."

"Have you been sick?"

"No. Not yet."

"You should have no problems, then. It'll be like shelling peas. You just wait and see."

"Oh, stop." Now she was laughing. Goodness, but things switched quickly on her these days. "Come in!" she called, and David poked his head around the door.

"David," beamed Mary Ann, obviously glad to see him. "Have you come to see your newest nephew?"

"I came to see you, Mary."

"Well, I'm certainly nothing to look at. Here, take a peek at Orion."

"So that's what you've named him, is it?"

Louisa watched in pride as David gently lifted the small bundle out of the bedsheets. He gave Mary a pat. "You did a fine job," he told her. He kissed the baby's forehead and held him up to the light, grinning. When he glanced at Louisa she wanted to cry again. Embarrassed, she mumbled something about going to get Anna and slipped from the room.

• • •

It was only a short walk between the two cabins, but Louisa and Anna, with four children in tow, took their time returning to Mary's, enjoying the evening and watching the children scamper between the trees, playing catch and discovering wildflowers. "Are you going to come in before you go?" Anna asked when they finally arrived back.

"No, I think I'll just wait out here for David." She kissed the children good night with promises to be back in the morning, and when David came out he looked sad, even old. He sat on the stoop to pull on his boots, and he laced them slowly. "Liza?" he said without looking up. "Mary says to be extra good to you tonight." She was startled by the sound of pain in his voice. "Do you think I'm not being good to you?"

When he looked up the pain had shifted to his eyes. "Oh, no, David! That's not true! Oh, David! She only meant . . ." She rushed to sit next to him, close so that he could put his arm around her.

"Liza, I know it's been a little strained these last couple of months, ever since that business in town. I told you I was sorry. I guess I just don't know what else to do." She watched him, his fingers in the laces, not knowing what to say. "*What's that?*"

he suddenly demanded, sitting up.

"What?"

"That shouting. There's something going on in the settlement."

She listened closely. Yes, there *was* something. Shouting. Arguing.

"Louisa, maybe you better go down to the beach and wait for me there. I'll pick you up on the way out. Arthur?" he called, popping his head back in the door. "Walk down to the mill with us, will you?" There was urgency in his voice, and panic jumped upon her with sharp claws; she felt the scratches along her arms.

"David," she whispered, going cold. "Tell me what's going on here, and tell me right now!"

"I don't know."

"You do too! I can see it in your eyes. You and Arthur have been acting strange all evening and now you're positively agitated. Where *were* you this afternoon? Look at you! I can see it! Now what is going on?"

"All right, Louisa. If you want to know. Masachie Jim murdered his wife this morning."

So matter-of-factly. Like "Maynard lost his glasses" or "Have you seen my hat?" It took a second to understand, and then it was hard to think beyond the words. Arthur marched past. David hurried after him and she ran to catch up. "Who's Masachie Jim?" she called. "What happened?"

"Louisa! Go back!"

"No! I'm going with you!"

"*David!*" ordered Arthur.

David sprang after him. She followed. The din grew louder. The words separated and she recognized Luther Collins' voice. "String 'im up! The only good Injun is a dead one! Dirty Siwash!"

"Arthur! They're lynching him!" David yelled. He shot forward, leaping stumps and brush. Arthur broke into a run. "God Almighty! I *knew* something like this would happen!"

Lynching? The hair along her neck crawled. Skirts gathered, she hopped and ran, tripped and scrambled, heart pounding behind her ears.

A block and tackle had been set up just outside the cookhouse, not far from the toolshed. Five or six men stood around and Luther Collins hollered "Now!" Then there was a gasp. Arthur and David burst into the gathering and Luther Collins fell over backward. Another man went down and Louisa screamed. David rolled into the dirt. Dust flew.

"David! *David!*" she screamed, flying down the hill. "*David!*" she screamed again, throwing herself between him and a tall man she didn't recognize.

"Get your brother," he wheezed through clenched teeth. "He's the sheriff. *Get* him, Liza. *Now!*"

"But—"

"NOW!" He scrambled to his feet as the big man took another swing. It was Mr. Maurer, the man who had started the new eating house at Maynard's. David ducked, turned, then lunged for the guard. Louisa tried to run—but couldn't. Right in front of her, at eye level, was the knotted rope that Masachie Jim used for a belt. The Indian bounced with desperate and futile exertions. His feet, tied at the ankles, jerked in quick, tight circles.

"NOW!" yelled David. She felt wind as he lunged a second time. Finding her feet and senses at last, she took off, fleeing down Front Street, praying and screaming as she went.

"DOBBINS! DOBBINS! DOBBINS!" She veered through the woods when she got to the narrow path that Dobbins called Cherry. "DOBBINS!" He met her at the turn, pulling on his boots as he came. When he passed she stood against a tree, winded, panting hard, the world turning gray, then dark, then gray again. Then she was sick.

16

"He [Masachie Jim] killed his 'klootchman,' and a few white men in Seattle took the law into their own hands and lynched him the same evening.

"Not only was the hanging a lawless thing to do, but an unwise one, for it loosed a stream of hatred."
—Roberta Frye Watt in *Four Wagons West*

Gradually Louisa heard the birds and insects, and looking up saw that the air was yellow. She wiped her face on her petticoat and spit. It was all sandy from the beach. She could see the berry stains from where she had washed Gertie's face.

I'll go wait for David, she thought. The sun had slipped low and was dropping out of the sky, melting like butter. A snake slithered out of the grass as she made her way down the cliff. Across the water the Olympics stood in the bath of the yellow light, the snow looking golden and warm now. A wide path of yellow sparkled across the bay, and she found a log to sit on so that the yellow ended at her feet.

What was happening? Over and over the question stabbed. *What was happening? To their city? To them?* She closed her eyes, burying her head in her arms, shutting out the world, the fright, the confusion. But it didn't go away. Mr. Collins had hung an Indian! This wasn't Mr. Low pulling a hatchet off the wall. *Oh, God*, she prayed, opening her eyes and staring at the dying sun and the gold rim of the mountains until her eyes burned. *Don't let them retaliate. Don't let them hurt us.* Suddenly she thought of her brother. Dobbins was the sheriff. It was up to him to keep law and order. *Oh, Dobbins, what are you going to do?*

What *could* he do? The governor hadn't come yet. There were no courts. There was no law and order, not really. There wasn't *anything* Dobbins could do. Oh, *why* had Mr. Collins done it? He was a county commissioner! He was their friend! And Mr. Maurer? And all those people standing there watching? Why? Why such a stupid, cruel thing? Why did they do it?

She wondered what Jim and George and Princess Angeline

thought. Were they angry? Did they feel betrayed? And Chief Seattle? What would he say?

Seattle. Of course he wouldn't let harm come to them. He wouldn't let anybody get hurt. He and David and Arthur and Doc Maynard would all sit down and talk.

The mountains glowed bright with the final setting of day. Lavenders filled the sky. Gold edged the mountain rims like burning, scalding, fiery liquid, and out of the dying beauty God seemed to speak. *The sun shall not smite thee by day, nor the moon by night. The Lord shall preserve thee from all evil; he shall preserve thy soul. The Lord shall preserve thy going out and thy coming in from this time forth and even for evermore.*

Do You mean it, God? she asked silently. Then quickly, *What do You mean?* The gold turned dark, bleeding into the shadows. The yellow path over the water thinned and spread, and was swallowed by the night-gray sea. She shivered and looked down the empty beach. Where was David?

She could see the pilings where Mr. Yesler had begun to build a wharf. She waited a long time. When he finally came, he paddled up so quietly that it startled her.

"You don't look so good," he said.

"You don't look so good yourself." His nose had been bleeding; she could see the dried blood in his beard, even in the growing dusk. Already one eye was puffing shut.

"You should see Arthur," he said, trying to grin.

She was afraid to ask. He shook his head slowly and she stared at the seaweed by her feet.

"Come on," he said gently. "Let's go home."

• • •

Dusk was strong when they climbed the hill to their cabin, arms around each other, tired, quiet, resting their heads one upon the other. They nearly collided with two Indians, but exchanged quick hellos and goodbyes in Chinook before going on.

"David...that's my collar," Louisa whispered, pulling him to a stop as the image of the Indian finally registered in her troubled mind.

"Your collar?"

"He had it tied around his neck."

"Are you sure?"

"I think so," she said, glancing over his shoulder to where the Indians could still be seen near the bottom of the trail.

David turned, saw them, then jumped to life. "Hey, wait! Wait a minute!" he hollered, rushing after them, cap flying. "Where did you get that?"

'He gave it to me," answered one belligerently, shuffling his feet.

"And where did *you* get it? It belongs to my wife. And this ribbon. It belongs to her too."

Their cabin had been broken into. . . . The realization blurred across her mind as she stumbled up the trail. The door sections swung open, adrift in the dusk, but the sound of chickens squawking without restraint brought a measure of reality to the nightmare. She stood a moment to catch her breath, then tripped over the step.

Inside it was a mess.

The coffeepot lay on its side near the door. The rooster, one leg raised and curled, cackled from the top of the stove. The hen clucked from inside the tipped flour barrel. One panel of the pink cattice on her pantry was ripped loose. The steel engraving of the little girl on the gate was knocked off the wall.

Her clothes! She flew across the room to the other side of the bed and gasped. All over the floor—even her undergarments. "Oh, David," she moaned when he came in and softly shut the door. "They even went through my undergarments. . ."

He shooed the chickens outside and shut the door again.

"David?" He stood with his back against the door, watching her. "Did you get my things back?" she asked, not liking the look in his face.

"Were they something special?"

She nodded and bit her lip. "Ma made the collar for me."

"And the ribbon?"

"A gift from James."

He pulled himself away from the door and began to set up the chairs. It was all bad enough without having to add his brother's name to the heap. Why was it that James always popped up in times of trouble?

"David?"

There was a whimper to her voice, but he didn't care. He hung his coat on the back of the door and set his cap over the nail. When she called again he pressed his forehead into the cool clothes, unwilling to face her.

"David...my mirror..."

He spun. It lay upside down on the floor across the room, a small piece of glass poking from beneath like a thorny nest. He felt sick. He wanted to offer comfort, but he couldn't. He just stood empty, watching her quiet tears. All those white lies, all that sneaking, all that worry each time the covered wagons had to be lightened when coming across the country... At last he walked toward the mirror and, dropping to his knees, hesitated before touching it. He glanced back. She stood white and silent, the tears still dripping. When he slowly turned the precious wall mirror in his hands he heard her first sob...and the awful tinkle of shattered glass.

His reflection startled him—a distorted, twisted version of his face; scraggly beard, tight jaw, eyes hard and cold, his whole face broken and mismatched in countless pieces. The entire lower portion of his left cheek was missing where a large chunk had fallen through to the floor, and looking past the hole to the floor he saw a reflection of his throat where his cheek should be.

He grew cold. It was a picture of his mind. Everything out of place. All his ideas knocked and shattered. Just pieces of things now. Nothing making sense. All broken and loosely joined, with outright holes in places. Bear and Ant. Masachie Jim. The hanging. Nothing making sense. Now this. He set the mirror aside and stood slowly. "I'm sorry, Liza," he whispered, not knowing what else to do.

"It's all right...it's not your fault."

His eyes burned at the sound of her voice. He needed to take the sorrow, to pluck it from her heart. It was all she had of her father—it was her treasure, her gift to him. "Liza, come here." She slid into his arms, small and frightened, and he wanted to crush her, to hold her so tightly that they might dissolve into one and not fear the marching unknown. Her tears wet his shirt as he felt the rise and fall of her shoulders. He could hear her stifled sobs, the sigh of the wind outside. For some strange reason the scent of salt and sea breeze was strong tonight, and he rested his chin over the top of her head, rocking her gently, breathing in the scent he had grown to love, praying with whatever strength was left inside that he might somehow understand, that he might somehow put the pieces together again, that he might somehow, once again, have the old quiet acceptance of things. But even as he prayed he sensed no easy answers, no easy solutions, and he finished his prayer by simply asking for courage, and forgiveness for such doubt.

"David?"

"Yes, Liza?" Her voice was small, muffled against his chest. "Yes, Liza?" he said again tenderly, lifting his chin from the top of her head to plant a kiss.

"Do you love me?"

"Do I love you?" he asked, startled. "Of course I love you!"

"No, no you don't. You. . . you're so quiet. You never talk to me anymore. . . you yelled at me, and you. . . " Gently he brought her face to meet his, and for a long time each tried to read the other's eyes. Finally he kissed each of her eyes and she closed them under his lips, leaning close. "Oh, Liza, I do love you. Did you think I didn't?" He kissed her quickly now, taking her face in his hands, desperate for her to understand. "Yes, Liza, I love you, I love you, I love you. . . "

She started to cry again. Was this what was wrong with her? Was this what Mary Ann had hinted about? That Louisa somehow thought that he *didn't* love her anymore? Not loving Louisa would be the end of life! Didn't she know that? How could she think anything different? How long had she doubted? How had he let it happen?

"Shh-h," he whispered as she tilted her head to accept his kisses. "Shh-h. . . " Her arms came round his neck as he lifted her onto their bed. He brought the warm comforter over their faces, sealing themselves in the secret darkness.

"Oh, David, I'm sorry to cry so," she said.

"It's fine." He brushed her hair from her cheek and smoothed a tear with the back of his fingers.

"I didn't know anymore. I tried to believe you did, but. . . "

"Liza, my heart is so full of you, I think it might burst. I sometimes don't know what to do, it's so full." He prayed she might forget her mirror, the hanging, and all the troubles outside their door. He loved her tenderly, just as Mary Ann had said, and when she at last fell asleep, her breathing coming in regular, deep intervals, he cradled her still.

17
July 9

"There was a worthless fellow here on the Sound who owned a sloop with blue drilling sails. He made it a business to sell whiskey to the Indians."

—Arthur Denny in his memoirs

Louisa woke with a dull ache in the small of her back, and an ache for her broken mirror. But she was strangely happy. David loved her, and nothing else mattered. She lay quietly in the wakening sounds of morning, the cluck of chickens, the birdcalls. She was comforted by the sounds, comforted by the tender words of last night. She stared at the roof, her gaze resting directly overhead upon the 18-inch cedar slabs, then following the line of supporting fir poles to where they met the wall, then down to the place where her mirror had hung. Finally she turned her eyes to the empty frame, propped against the wall by the door, and quickly to the largest of the glass pieces propped on the mantel. "We have to have some kind of mirror, Liza," David had said.

A gull screamed beyond the roof. A sudden burden of grief rushed to her heart, and she groaned and turned to bury her face in her arm as it all came to her. Her mirror, the hanging, the awful tension that had come upon them all. Masachie Jim kicked. The knotted rope-belt swung, his eyes bulged black and glassy like a bug's. "David..." she whispered, and wished he were there.

The cabin was lonely and empty as she ate her breakfast, then gathered the things she would need for the day. She was glad for the excuse to be gone. Every noise was loud, making her start and drop things. If only David were here. But there was no sense in thinking about it. He had to work at the mill—at least until Thomas Mercer got back from the Willamette with his four daughters and team of horses. Then they might blaze a road through the forest to town, where they could sell timber to Yesler instead of having to earn it by working the saws. But for now he was stuck. Flour was 20 dollars a barrel, sugar 20, butter (when you could get it) 2½ dollars a pound. They were just going to have to put up with the awful hours. But still . . . no, there was no helping it, and she wasn't going to waste time wishing. If wishes were true, beggars would ride.

A shadow fell over the floor, right by her feet. Whirling, she saw two Indians. They passed the clearing, but stopped, then turned. She slid along the back wall, putting the bed between herself and the open door. But they passed on.

Whew . . . what a silly, she thought, sitting weakly onto the bed. Just Indians. Since when did she ever get so unnerved by Indians walking past?

Masachie Jim's knotted rope-belt swung like a pendulum in front of her. *Stop it!* she told herself. *Just stop it! Everything is going to be all right. David will take care of it. There is nothing to be afraid of. David and Arthur and Doc Maynard will talk to Seattle when he arrives. They'll explain, they'll . . .* But when she stood, her feet behaved like wooden blocks and she had to coax them around the end of the bed. She took her basket, the one Betsy Foster had made. Would somebody break in while she was gone? She shut the door carefully and almost ran down the trail to the beach. Her back hurt, and she slowed, turning south.

Halfway into town a large, smooth log, washed clean by long days at sea and stripped so clean that it glistened as if waxed, sat at an angle across the beach, confronting her. One end reached into the woods, lost in the tangled growth of underbrush and blackberry bushes, while the other end endured the cold, wet licks of the sea. She sat squarely in the middle and swung both legs over the log.

Sudden pain took her breath. Her basket dropped to the sand and she sat crouched, waiting for it to pass. When at last she was able to look up she saw a couple of large war canoes paddling toward Seattle. She eased to her feet and forced herself forward.

• • •

"*Louisa?*" Anna yanked open the door. "No, Mary! It's only Louisa! *Louisa!*" she hissed, "you're as white as a ghost!"

"I think something's wrong. My back . . . and a pain inside," she breathed, easing into the rocking chair. Katy looked up from the table by the window where she sat working sums on a slate, but seeing Louisa's face got busy with the chalk again. In a lot of ways she was like Mary Ann. "Where's Nora and Rollie and Gertie?"

"Outside somewhere. Running wild—like the Indians, as likely as not. It isn't the baby, is it?"

Louisa looked up sharply. "Mary Ann tell you about the baby?" For some reason she didn't want Anna to know. Not yet.

"She did."

"Well, I don't want you telling anyone. I haven't told David yet."

"I suppose it's one of your grand secrets again, is it?"

"I'm waiting for the right time," she said defensively. "I was going to tell him last night, but somehow it just didn't seem right. Not with the hanging and everything."

"For heaven's sake, Louisa Denny! Since when were you superstitious?"

"Superstition has nothing to do with it. There just *never* seems the right time."

"I expect you're going to have to *make* the right time, Liza Denny. Dobbins told me what happened last night. You shouldn't have been running in your condition, or didn't you think? You've brought on a miscarriage is what you've done."

"I have not!" Louisa shouted, half-rising from the chair, but pain zigzagged through her middle and forced her back. "Don't you say such a thing, Anna Boren..."

Anna swung on her heel and went to the stove. She had gotten so thin on the Oregon Trail, but was plump again. She was rosy in her cheeks, too. "Katy," she said, "take your sister and cousin down to the mill and get your Uncle David." Katy lost no time, grabbing her bonnet from a spike on her way out, red braids flying. "And get Doc Maynard too!" Anna called out the door.

Tears pocketed behind Louisa's eyes. "No, Anna, please. It'll be all right. Don't tell David. There, see? The pain, it's not so bad."

"He has to know, Liza. And it won't hurt to have the doctor take a look at you."

Louisa concentrated on the little things in the quiet, fighting the panic. Anna's hem was frayed. There was a pie on the stove. Arthur's desk was crammed full of papers and letters and ink bottles and crumbs from a slice of bread. There was a new posting tacked onto the wall over his desk.

A.A. DENNY.
U.S. POSTMASTER.
SEATTLE, TERRITORY OF WASHINGTON.

It wasn't the baby. It couldn't be the baby. Sweat dripped down her back. It was so hot. She felt sticky around her ribs and chest and under her hair. No, there wasn't anything wrong. It was just the weather, the upset last night, her broken mirror, walking into town too quickly. No, there was nothing wrong with the baby. Of course there wasn't anything wrong. She had her promise, didn't she? She had her Psalm.

But the dull soreness inside, and watching Anna bustle about, tidy and efficient with her grim, round face, wasn't making it easy. Lots of terrible things happened. Lots of terrible things *were* happening. All the old arguments came back, making fun of such simple faith.

Anna smacked the kettle with the backs of her fingers impatiently, then took a furious broom to the floor. "There you are," she said when the tea was ready, handing Louisa a hot mug.

"Thank you." Louisa tried a frightened smile.

"Oh, it'll be all right," Anna said with a sudden kindness. She pulled over a stool and sat down, propping her chin in her hands, elbows on her knees. She smiled, and for an instant Louisa saw the old Anna, the old, happy Anna from Illinois. "I didn't mean to scare you," Anna said. "Doc Maynard'll know what to do. Louisa? Are you all right?"

"Yes. Yes, I am. Anna?" she whispered, leaning forward. "Are you sorry we're not in Illinois anymore?"

Anna's chin came up. "What? Illinois? I never think of it." She put the stool back by the hearth, then went over to crack the bedroom door. "Mary Ann, I was just getting Liza a cup of tea. Would you like some?"

Louisa stared at a barrel of molasses, listening to the hum of conversation in the bedroom and the buzz of a fly somewhere, trying not to think of Illinois, of the old farmhouse and apple trees and church on Sunday and her schoolchildren and Pamelia. Was Pamelia pregnant? The letter last fall said she was married. Would they have babies together?

"There's nobody at the mill!" The door flew open and the children tumbled in, crying out at once. Anna hurried to help with the boots.

"You couldn't find Uncle David?"

"No, there's nobody there," said Katy, panting. She sat back-ward on the step, tugging on her shoes, all muddy and caked with sawdust.

"What about your father? You didn't see him?"

"No. Dutch Ned said they were all at the cookhouse."

"But we were too scared to go in," added Nora.

"Maybe I better go find out what's going on. Will you be all right here by yourself, Louisa?"

"I'm fine now. And Katy is a big girl. She can help."

Anna tied on her bonnet, setting her grim face. "Well, once again," she said bitterly, "it looks like it's Anna." She left without saying goodbye.

• • •

David stood near the back of the cookhouse, back pressed against the logs. Through the crowd he could see Maynard, presiding over the informal court hearing. George McConaha, a Democrat—and the only attorney in town—sat beside him. Henry Yesler as county clerk sat on the other side. Where was Arthur?

Boy, this was a fine how-do-you-do, he thought, seeing Luther Collins near the front. A county commissioner lynching a man . . . He looked about for David Maurer and William Heebner, the other two men who had helped hatch the plot. Maynard stood. He took off his glasses and began to painstakingly polish them on his suit coat, rubbing the black cloth in slow circles over the lens. He did the other lens too, first puffing air over it, then rubbing and rubbing, slowly rubbing. When he was done the room was quiet. You could hear the breath of the man next to you. It got so you could almost hear his thoughts. Jim Seattle and Salmon Bay Curley stood beside him, their thoughts and feelings a mystery.

"It's a ticklish sort of thing we've got ourselves into," Maynard began, setting the glasses onto his face and looping the wires about his ears. "Masachie Jim, in Chinook, means Bad Jim. He did not get his name for playing the part of Little Red Riding Hood." David glanced at the Indians. Still their faces revealed nothing. "It has been brought to this unofficial court hearing," Maynard went on, "that the White River settlers repeatedly warned Masachie Jim not to beat his wife. He took no steps to alter his behavior. Now we're dealing with a murder. If the situation had been left to normal circumstances, we can all be assured that the good Chief Seattle would have taken care of it according to Indian custom—if you know what I mean." His eyes focused through the crowd, picking out the few Indians in attendance, and coming to rest on Jim. David felt the brave stiffen. "A-hum. As it is, we— or Luther Collins, David Maurer, and William Heebner, the three men directly involved in this unfortunate little episode—have spared the good chief the distasteful decision by going ahead and exacting the due punishment for such a dastardly crime."

David could hardly believe his ears. They had *hung* a man without trial! They had usurped the Indians' right to conduct their own affairs! They had been responsible in the first place for allowing liquor to be sold! But then what had he expected Maynard to say? What *could* he say?

"The ticklish point we are faced with is not," Maynard announced, "did Masachie Jim receive an unjust end—for we know it was the only end for such an action—but rather, was the law violated in meting out the end? What *is* the law?"

The room was unbearably warm, the air close with sweat and dust. A muscle next to Luther Collins' left eye twitched, and David realized he had been holding his breath. He let it out in a long, slow wheeze. "We have only begun to bring law and order to the wilds," Maynard was saying. "Our governor for this brand-new territory has not yet arrived from Washington D.C., and as Mr. Collins duly pointed out, he knew there was no system as of yet set up for trial, by which to try Masachie Jim.

"And as our fellow pioneer and attorney friend, George McConaha here, pointed out in the findings, what we are dealing with is *mal*feasance versus... What'd you say it was, George?"

"Misfeasance."

"*Mal*feasance versus *mis*feasance! Performance of a wrongful act versus improper performance of a lawful act! There *is* a difference. Let me repeat myself. Performance of a *wrongful* act versus improper performance of a *lawful* act!" Arthur pushed past, his face granite. "We are not dealing with performance of a wrongful act," Maynard hastened, seeing him, "but rather the *improper* performance of a *lawful* act. And as such, I see no need to unduly chastise our good friends. So. Under the circumstance I think it best to offer our apologies to Chief Seattle and his elders for the unfortunate way in which justice was handled, and admonish our good friends, Mr. Collins, Mr. Maurer, and Mr. Heebner, that it is not to be done again.

"Furthermore," he added, raising his voice in counteraction to the commotion Arthur was creating. "I propose we put an end to the whiskey trade on the sound, for *that* it is the real violation of our laws. In way of recompense to the Indians I suggest we lay in wait for the fellow with the blue drilling sails and offer him a piece of our primitive justice, thereby putting an end to this whole unpleasant business."

"You're a fool! All of you are fools! You think this is going to do it?" Arthur hollered, finally reaching the front, his eyes cold and terrible in the heat of his anger, pinning them all to their spots as he looked over the room. "Where's Seattle?" he demanded. "Don't you think this calls for sitting down and talking with him? You're treating our Indian friends as though they had no position in this mess! As if—"

"What else can we do?" Maynard interrupted, ice in his own eyes. "Call for a real trial so that as soon as Governor Stevens arrives we can be hanging our friends on order of men who know nothing of this country? I tell you!" he hollered, waving a hand at Luther Collins, nearly hitting him in the nose. "Is that what you want to see, Arthur Denny? An outstanding man, your friend and fellow commissioner—if I may remind you—hanging from a noose over an incident that would have ended exactly as it has been done? *Mis*feasance, Mr. Denny! Not *mal*feasance!"

"Poppycock!"

"Are you saying that the letter of the law be carried out? Though it mean your friend be hanged until dead? Are you saying—"

"I'm saying nothing of the kind and you know it, you two-bit huckleberry doctor!"

"*Court dismissed!*" Maynard swung the gavel and slammed the table so hard the table cracked.

"Objection!"

"Objection overruled! *I* am the Justice of the Peace! *Court dismissed!*" The gavel hit the table again with a resounding blow and Arthur beat his way to the door, grabbing David on his way out. "*Fools!*" he hissed as they made their escape. "Jim! Curley! Over here!" he yelled. "So that's that, Dave. The whole thing dismissed. I can't believe it! What's Seattle going to say? Jim, where's your father? Dave, translate, will you? I want this done in their language, so we don't start getting loose communication around here."

"DAVID!"

Anna was running toward them, out of breath, cheeks flushed, bonnet askew. "David, it's Louisa! She's not feeling well—can you come?"

"What's the matter with her?"

She stood panting, eyes darting quickly, as if she was about to flee but first looking for the danger. She seemed to want to say something, but was not ready. "Oh, nothing...just a little stomach pain. But I thought..." Maynard strode past, not looking one way or the other, slapping his heels into the sawdust.

"Well, if it's nothing," said Arthur, "tell her David will be along shortly. We've got troubles down here. Tell her to sit tight. Give her a hot-water bottle or something. Come on, Dave."

David hesitated, torn inside out. Maybe he'd better go back. At least see if she was all right.

"Dave! We need you to translate! Step on it!" Arthur yelled. Still he hesitated, unsure.

"Oh, never mind," said Anna. "Go on. Men always have more important things to do than worry about a bit of stomach pain."

"Anna, if it's something serious—" He could hear Arthur yelling for him as Anna marched back up the trail toward the dark woods. "Anna! Tell her I'll be there as soon as I can!" But Anna kept marching, not looking back, and he turned slowly to follow Arthur, knowing in his heart of hearts that he had made the wrong decision.

● ● ●

Maynard hurried down Commercial to his blacksmith shop. How *dare* Arthur interrupt! Him and his principles! It was about time that that man learn a few things—like life is never so easy! *God*, he moaned, half-praying, what a mess. What a *nightmare* of a mess.

Well, one thing was sure, you didn't go around setting your own men up for the noose. Yes, he was right, he decided, thinking it over, turning and dropping his thoughts like a farmer his soil. He had done exactly what had to be done. Thank God McConaha was around. Malfeasance, mis— whatever the heck that was. Nice to have a few legal words to fling around. It had been a long night, tossing and turning worse than a patient burning with fever, wondering—no—*worrying* how to get out of this one.

But they weren't out of it yet. The Indians. . . . He shook his head. Well, he'd have to keep his fingers crossed and pray for the good Lord to work one of His miracles. It wasn't so miraculous at that, though, he thought. What Arthur didn't reckon into anything was the sway he had with the chief. Chief Seattle was a real corker with the Great Spirit. Besides, Seattle was his friend. They understood each other. It was almost like they were blood brothers.

He smiled, his confidence coming back. What a lucky day that was when the Catholic Church sent their bishop to these parts! When tempers had a chance to cool, and if that blasted Arthur Denny stayed out of it, he would be able to soften up the old chief by appealing to the converted side of his heart. Given enough reason, Seattle would turn the other cheek.

It did the trick every time.

Thank God.

18

"Lots of people now do not know this story because the people were forbidden to tell it unless they were from the family. Then they were to tell it only to members of the family. Taqwseblu asked if she had permission to write the story for others to hear. The answer was yes. March 5, 1975."
—Dora Soloman in *Huboo*

There was someone who knew that a flood was coming. He told his people to get ready and make canoes because there would be a flood.

• • •

Tzee-tzal-ahe-itch had never known the name of the one who had known the flood would come. Some stories said it was Beaver. But all Tzee-tzal-ahe-itch knew was that the mountain which did not flood was the home of thunder, and that the Great Spirit had given him, the son of Schwaebe, the voice of thunder. His spirit powers tied him to the story, and always he wondered—who had told that the flood would come? What had been his name?

Tzee-tzal-ahe-itch was a warrior, allied chief of six tribes, and at 52 winters he stood with his friend, Leschi, Chief of the Nisquallies, listening to the King George man speak at Fort Steilacoom. The King George man was dressed in black, with white about his neck. An ornament of crossed bars hung from his neck—and he spoke about the flood.

How did this King George man know the story, when only family members knew such things? Who had told him? Who had told him that two of every animal had gone on a boat? Who had told him they had found safety at the mountain where thunder lived? Who had told him that after the flood everything was just scattered bones? Who had told him the name of the man who told that the flood would come?

Tzee-tzal-ahe-itch strode forward, a head taller than the others who congregated. Son of nobility, he had not had to paddle his own canoe and so his legs were straight. They had not bowed, and he towered above his people.

"Tell this again," he demanded in his own tongue, using Leschi to translate his Duwamish into the lesser tongue, Chinook. The black-robed man explained over and over, pointing to a cedar slab, the Sahali Stick.

It was six feet high and eighteen inches wide. Each century was painted with a mark. Each year, a dot. Dots, one above the other, showed how long a man called Jesus had lived on the earth. Other marks stood for the centuries since the flood.

Tzee-tzal-ahe-itch stared at the round peg that marked the flood. "How do you know all this? How do you know what he is called— this one who knew the flood would come? How do you know he is called Noah?"

"It is here, it is written in this book—Sahali Tyee Yaka. This book has the words of the Great Spirit."

Words of the Great Spirit? The Great Spirit told him, this King George? Through words in a book?

Tzee-tzal-ahe-itch brought the elders to hear Bishop Demurs tell all the words. Bishop Demurs told all the old stories and new ones, too. He told them about the son of the Great Spirit, this man named Jesus, how He had come to earth to show how much He loved His children—white men, red men, and even the slanty-eyed men the stories told of.

"This we know," Tzee-tzal-ahe-itch said, and his elders agreed with nods: "We know the Great Spirit has love for all His children. We have this in our stories. Why did this son of the Great Spirit, this Jesus, come to show what we know?"

"Because He wanted to teach us to love each other with the same kind of love."

"The son of the Great Spirit said this?" Tzee-tzal-ahe-itch said, brooding. Was it possible to love as the Great Spirit did? He thought of the skirmishes between tribes, and then of the fierce Haidas to the north, and of the raiding and slave-taking. It would be better to live in peace—everyone knew this—but...was it possible? Without being destroyed?

"His name was Noah," he mumbled, shaking his head. "This man who knew the flood would come." It always came back to that, and he couldn't shake the wonder from his mind.

Then came the thought—like an unexpected wave thrown against a dry stone—the Sahali Tyee Yaka had to be the words of the Great

Spirit! How else did this King George know such things, when only family knew?

Thoughts followed like other waves, one upon the other. If that were true, how very big, how very powerful the Great Spirit must be, to tell all the people of this story. How much better, too, to have a book of His words than just words passed down through the elders, who grew to be old men and forgot such things as names. And if it were the Great Spirit's wish to live in love with the Haida, and the Kliticat to the east, then. . .

Tzee-tzal-ahe-itch looked to the sky, then all around, where the Great Spirit lived and breathed in every living thing. "What do you think?" he asked Leschi.

"I think we should hear the stories. I think we hear great words of the Great Spirit."

Tzee-tzal-ahe-itch and Leschi were baptized the same day, and Bishop Demurs put words in a book that said "Chief Noah Seattle, 1938."

"su · · · ?usukwutab kwi dsya · · yacid.
"ha ha ha?u ha? hi? · · ·
"ha hu · ?i · ha hu ?u ?u ?u"*

Seattle's spirit song shattered the break of water. At 67 years of age he still stood a full head above his people, face square and strong, forehead unmolested by the custom of being flattened as a baby. His eyes were intense, seeing beyond the simple to the complex. They reflected keen intelligence. They brooded, mirroring thoughts. They darted, searching; they grew dark, thinking. Superior intellectually and physically, he saw and understood what his people could not, and he bore the understanding heavily.

Understanding gave him the bearing of nobility. But nobility was not merely a coat he put on and off like a Hudson Bay blanket, worn and abandoned at will. He took the responsibility seriously, more seriously each year as he saw the decline of his people. Inside he questioned, torn by conflicting dreams, but always his spirit powers whispered of the peaceful, loving ways of the Great

---

* All Duwamish sentences are only approximations of the Lushootseed Indian dialects.

Spirit. To love as He loved was the only answer for men at war with each other. One must die so that both might live. In the end there could be no other way, and so he cried out his sorrow and lifted his arms. His cry came from his soul, an outpouring of his questions riding the voice of thunder, blessed by the sea gull over the lagoon. His cry was in Duwamish, a frightening cry to even himself.

> "su · · ·?usukwutab kwi dsya· ·yacid.
> "ha ha ha?u ha? hi?· · ·
> "ha hu· ?i· ha hu ?u ?u ?u"

• • •

Doc Maynard dropped yet another new nail into the bucket of water by his fire, heard the quick sizzle, and stood gratefully. Seattle was here. It was time to go. Time to get all this wretched mess ironed out. The four blackened walls of the smithy stood round him, thick with smoke and heat and nothing to say. But sunlight charged through the open door, and he grabbed his raccoon tail off the smoky walls and headed for the sun.

"Whoa!" he bellowed, sidestepping and twisting his ankle in his rush out the door. It was Anna Boren, and he apologized quickly. "I'm sorry. Didn't see you." Confounded ankle throbbed under his weight. No matter. He started on his way. He could see Seattle a few hundred yards to the south, standing along the shore by the lagoon, his left arm stretched over the crowd like a benevolent grandfather. A few of the white men had mingled with the crowd. That was good. Showed they weren't scared. Others had gathered along the Felker House porch. That was stupid. Isolating themselves like that.

"Doc Maynard! Please!" Anna caught him by the sleeve, and he slowed, trying to hide his impatience. A woman at the wrong time was hard to take, even a pretty woman like Anna Boren. "It's Louisa," said Anna. He came to an abrupt halt.

"What's the matter with Louisa?"

"She's not feeling well. I tried to tell David, but he's too busy."

"She's not ill, is she?"

"I went back to Mary's—that's where she is—and she's in worse pain. Worse than I thought. I thought maybe if you could come, it would ease her mind."

"Why didn't you say so in the first place? Good Lord," he muttered, reversing direction and breaking into a trot, ignoring the shooting pain in his foot. Why did everything have to happen at once? He rubbed the back of his hand over his forehead. Wet. Whew, it was hot.

• • •

David shifted his weight and glanced uneasily at Arthur. He should have gone to see Louisa. What if something was wrong? Really wrong? He tried to imagine what it could be, and he went over everything that was said last night. Well, this was a fine way of showing he loved her—running off when she needed him.

They stood with some of the other men on the porch of the Felker House, the brand new hotel that Captain Plummer was building on the southwest end of the Point, still not finished and only half-painted. "What's he saying, Dave?" Arthur asked. "He's raising the hair along the back of my neck."

David didn't answer. He pretended to concentrate on the chief, but he was staring across the empty lagoon to the wild roses crawling over Tom Pepper's shack. It was a veritable tangle of brush and thorn, the soft, pink petals daring the neglect. Louisa's sweetbriar had finally come up, frail green shoots, without blossom.

> "su · · · ?usukwutab kwi dsya yacid.
> "ha ha ha?u ha? hi? · · ·
> "ha hu · ?i · ha hu ?u ?u ?u"

Seattle cried again, creating thunder to pour from his soul. *Ha ha ha?u ha? hi?* He stood naked, the sun too hot for the usual musty-blue Hudson Bay blanket that draped his shoulders. He stood naked and vulnerable, yet powerful, imitating his thunder with rumbling yelps. David wondered what was going through the man's heart. Was it being torn in two directions, as his was? What *did* a man do when torn between wife and responsibility? Between a nation and changing times? David fidgeted uncomfortably, needing to leave this gang of men and gathering of Indians.

"Dave! What's he saying?"

"He's singing a spirit song."

Arthur shook his head. "I don't know. I don't like it."

"So what the deuce does it mean?" someone asked.

David translated. "My people are blown about in their sailboat." He hung over the railing, envious of the man's imagery, the way he spoke so you could see it inside your head.

"What's thunder got to do with anything?"

"I think it must be a word picture. Haven't you ever seen a piece of driftwood get bounced around in a storm?"

"Of course I have, Denny."

"Then figure out for yourself what he's saying. It's clear to me."

"Whoa, listen to Dave Denny!" shouted Joe Foster.

"Shut up, Foster," said Arthur, taking his defense.

"Shut up? Hey, just waiting for that brother of yours to tell us why his Injun friend don't say what's on his mind. All this chanting and speech-making. Enough to give a bloke the willies."

Seth Lambert was leaning against the wall behind them. "For centuries his people have paddled these waters," he said quietly. "Now suddenly they got people of another world snatching their men and stringing them up on a pole. The thunder just fell out of the sky and it's tipping their old world upside down."

"You ain't going to tell me that Siwash didn't deserve it! He *killed* a lady, didn't he?"

"Don't you think the Indians are the ones to handle it?" Seth asked, and David turned to hear the young man, pleasantly surprised.

"We're the ones that's law and order!"

"And I suppose last night's episode is considered law and order."

"We ain't got no courts around here!"

"We could have let the Indians handle it."

"You saying Collins was out of line? Is that what you're saying?"

"I'm saying we have to be careful not to rock the boat around here. That's what I'm saying."

David listened, warming toward the young man. So there were a few of the newcomers who understood. Maybe Seth could explain to Joe that if Seattle so much as breathed retaliation they were all dead. Why couldn't men like Foster understand that? Not that Seattle would ever go to that extreme. But why couldn't they see that it was going to take cooperation from both races to live in coexistence with each other? A give-and-take on both sides? *They*, after all, were the trespassers—at least until treaties could be negotiated. Couldn't Joe see that they lived and breathed by Seattle's grace? Couldn't he understand that? David smote the railing with his palms, welcoming the slap of pain. When was that governor going to get here, anyway? None of this would have happened if they had a governor to lay out the ground rules. Or a minister. This town was getting too bawdy, too cocky and wild, thinking they had no authority to answer to. He wished he had gone back to Louisa, more now than ever. But then, who was there to translate? He *had* to stay. Arthur was right. There was no one else until Henry Smith got back—except Maynard, and he was nowhere around. Where *was* Maynard?

"Shut up," said Arthur suddenly, motioning the men to silence. "I think he's starting his speech!"

David struggled to hear as the bickering fell away and the men lined up along the railing. "Translate, Dave," said Arthur.

Seattle looked old, even defeated. But his voice held unmistakable power. The thunderous oration carried the wind, sending it across the Point. It drowned all other sounds, and David, knees trembling, began to translate. *"Day and night cannot dwell together!"*

Curley's story flew out from the back corners of his mind, words beating like eagle wings. Bear and Ant. Night and day. Eagle wings descending out of the sky to fasten upon their prey. *Day and night cannot dwell together.*

19

"Day and night cannot dwell together. The Red Man has ever fled the approach of the White Man, as the morning mist flees before the sun."

—Chief Noah Seattle

David's knees grew weak. He wanted to be gone from here. He wanted to be with Louisa. Somehow he kept on, though, repeating the words, putting them into English. "Day and night cannot dwell together. The Red Man has ever fled the approach of the White Man, as the morning mist before the sun. Their people are many. They are like the grass that covers the vast prairie. There was a time when our people covered the land as the waves of a wind-ruffled sea...

"I will not dwell on, nor mourn over, our untimely decay, nor reproach my paleface brothers with hastening it, as we too may have been somewhat to blame."

Relief rushed like a fresh wind.

"Youth is impulsive. When our young men grow angry at some real or imaginary wrong, and disfigure their faces with black paint, it denotes that their hearts are black, and that they are often cruel and relentless, and our old men and old women are unable to restrain them. Thus it has ever been. But let us hope that the hostilities between us may never return. We would have everything to lose and nothing to gain. Revenge by young men is considered gain, even at the cost of their own lives, but old men who stay at home in times of war, and mothers who have sons to lose, know better..."

David bowed his head while Chief Seattle admonished his people to seek a better way. He preached the gospel of forgiveness, of forbearance—even when wronged. It shamed David to be a part of men who knew such truths but did not see them so clearly.

He ought to have known. Maynard had.

• • •

147

"Louisa?" Sally Bell stood hesitantly on the threshold, Indian basket in hand. "May I come in?"

Louisa hastily pulled herself into a sitting position. The exertion left her weak; blood pounded behind her eyes. "You caught me napping," she said, brushing quickly at the wrinkles in the bedclothes and smoothing the counterpane. "I'm sorry about the mess," she added when she saw Sally's eyes rove about the neglected room, "but I'm not to get out of bed."

"Mr. Bell told me only this morning you've been confined."

"I'm just being lazy," said Louisa, still embarrassed. "But, please, do come in."

"I'm not disturbing you?"

"No. I'd like the company, eight days in bed all by yourself. . ."

"The baby? Mr. Bell says that you might have lost the baby."

Louisa rested her head against the wall, glad that her friend had come, that there was someone to talk to. It had been awful. Poor David. He hadn't even known, and then they had nearly lost the baby. It had nearly made him crazy. She should have told him weeks ago, when she had first suspected. But she hadn't, and he'd had to suffer through the dreadful shock. And now *she* was going crazy, isolated, unable to get out of bed, David silent about what was going on in town. He wouldn't talk about it. He said everything had blown over, but he seemed preoccupied even more than usual. Maybe it was her punishment for keeping the baby a secret.

"The baby?" Sally asked again.

"The baby is fine. Please, Sally, don't worry about those clothes. Just throw them on the floor."

"But they'll get dirty."

"They *are* dirty."

Sally carefully set David's pants by the potato crate. "Looks like you need to hire a squaw, too," she said, brushing aside the dried mud from a chair. She perched on the edge, basket in her lap, hands folded over the handle. Her breathing came in quick, wheezy spurts. "You really do need help, don't you?" she said when her breathing eased a little. More relaxed, she was like a bird—frail, ready for flight, not really firmly fixed to the world around her. "You should ask David to get you a squaw."

"He told me last night he's thinking about getting Betsy Foster. It would do her good to get away from Joe. But of course the money would go straight to him, and I don't like that thought. But I haven't been able to do a thing, and Doc Maynard said to stay in bed. I don't know when..." Her voice trailed. Doc Maynard didn't know when it would be safe to do anything. "So Princess Angeline is working out all right for you? She was so happy to know you wanted her help."

A quick laugh and Sally set her basket onto the table. "She scrubs the shirts until there's holes in the center, Louisa, but then she leaves the dirt along the collar. Squaws just don't understand about corners, I guess. She sweeps the middle of the floor but doesn't look under the table or behind the pantry! The baby, it'll be all right?" she asked suddenly, anxiously, eyes dark and unsure whether to push.

"Doc Maynard says to stay in bed. And no more frights."

"It must have been quite a shock, that lynching. It's all over town how you saw it and everything."

"I see it sometimes still," she said quietly.

"It's a pity; I'm sorry. But it should be all right now. Chief Seattle apparently just wants peace."

"Then it really is fine?"

"Why, yes. Didn't David tell you?"

"I kept thinking he just didn't want to worry me, that..."

"Oh, heavens no. Now don't worry about a thing. Everything's just fine. Why, those Indians act as if nothing had ever happened. They're working the mill, and wave and holler just like they did before it happened. I do say, Louisa, we're lucky that Chief Seattle is such a good man."

"What does Princess Angeline say about all this?"

"No one speaks of it anymore, Louisa. It's like it didn't happen."

"Oh."

"Louisa? Now there, I've gone and worried you."

"No, no. It's just that I've been lying in bed all week wondering and worrying."

"Louisa, don't cry! There, there, it's over and done." She moved to the bed. "Oh, I wish I'd known how it was with you. I could have come earlier."

"Oh, Sally, it's been so hard. All week I've worried and fretted. Sally, I've been so untrusting. I don't know how you do it. So ill all the time, and you never doubt God, do you?"

"Shh. I doubt God all the time, and of course you've worried and fretted. You're pregnant. We all worry extra when there's a baby."

"Really? Is that all it is? I'm not losing my faith or anything?"

"God knows how it is with us. That I'm sure of. If we worry, or get irritable, or even do silly things, He only loves us more for our weakness. But you know that, don't you? Here, I've brought a surprise for you."

"For me? Really?"

"Look. See? Mr. Bell found them this morning."

Louisa dried her face and peered into the basket. Three pheasant eggs sat carefully on top of Sally's knitting. "Oh, Sally! Thank you!"

"How would you like me to cook them?"

"Oh, Sally..." She nearly started to cry again. "Would you poach them?"

"Certainly. Now you sit back and rest. I won't plague you with my nonsense anymore."

Louisa watched her friend boil the water and stir in the eggs. She was a pretty woman, with fine features and gentle skin. Two bright dots burned high on her cheeks. "How are your lungs these days, Sally?"

"Better. I haven't had a bad spell for some time. And Dr. Smith, now that he's back, is a help. Did you know that boiling chamomile tea and breathing the steam is good? And he wants Mr. Bell to build me a cedar bathtub so I can take a very hot steam. Arthur said he would help him build it. That Dr. Smith really has some very different ideas about things."

"Dr. Smith's back?"

"Why, yes! Didn't David tell you?"

"No."

"He got back in the middle of all that mess with the Indians."

Just like David—forgetting to tell her the important things.

"Well, here we are. I'll just pull up a chair and we'll have a good visit before I go. Who shall we talk about?"

They talked about everybody. Sally did most of it while Louisa listened, resting in the cheerful chatter. "You hear that Charles Terry renamed New York, Louisa? Now that John Low is gone? He's calling it Alki."

"I read it in the paper. David thinks it's funny. Says it means by and by."

Sally laughed. "You read that Mr. McClellan's announced that the Cascades are absolutely impassable?"

"Who's McClellan?" Louisa asked, sleepy and comfortable.

"You don't remember? He's the man the new governor wrote your brother about last April. He was to find a mountain pass for the railroad."

She had forgotten about the railroad. Arthur would be disappointed.

"Mr. Bell is so disappointed. He talks of nothing else. It's such a waste, isn't it? And all those months Arthur had Mr. Collins cracking that whip of his, fining everyone, trying to get the Fort Steilacoom Road finished so there'd be a road all the way from The Dalles."

"But Patkanim goes through those mountains all the time," said Louisa, remembering the conversation between David and Arthur and the Chief of the Snoqualmies, the tribe that lived in the mountains. "There are *two* trails—one from Natches Pass and one from Snoqualmie. I'm sure of it."

"Well, McClellan's just some ignorant fool who can't find his own feet," declared Sally, pushing four knitting needles back and forth with her fingers. She slipped a few stitches onto a hairpin, turned the sock, and worked the heel. "But Mr. Bell says there's a man in Olympia who's put together his own surveying party. And they're going to pick up where the Steilacoom Road leaves off, and blaze it all the way through to Natches Pass! Show that McClellen what's impassable and what's not. How do you like that sort of spirit, Liza? Oh, here, let me fix those pillows. There? How's that?"

"Sally, don't look now, but there's two Indians. And they really don't look very friendly. They're lurking out by the stumps. *No!* Don't look!"

They came to the door. One stuck his head through and glanced furtively to the other. Whispers. One left, then returned. More conversation.

Sally knit quickly, the two red spots burning feverishly on her cheeks.

"*Kloshe mika potlatch wapatoes!*"

Sally's eyes widened.

"*Kloshe mika potlatch wapatoes!*" the Indians demanded again, slapping their hands upon the door.

"I'll get them," said Louisa.

"No! I will!" Sally got to her feet and slowly put down her knitting. She swayed a little. Louisa watched helplessly as Sally gripped the back of the chair, but when she turned, she was brave. Backbone stiff, face bright, her step firm, she marched straight past the strangers.

One followed her out and the other stayed, his eyes sharp and fixed on Louisa. She stared right back. She didn't blink and he blurred out of focus. Still she stared. *What was taking Sally so long? It was only a few potatoes!* The Indian came into focus again. Who was he? Why was he so menacing? She forced herself to narrow her focus, to look him in the eye. It frightened her. Just as she was about to scream and lunge for the rifle over the mantel, Sally was back.

"Bucket!" one of the Indians demanded. He pointed to Louisa's tin pail by the stove, and Sally straightened her apron into it. The potatoes tumbled over each other with tiny, uneven thuds. When it was done she handed the Indian the bucket and picked up her knitting. Without a word she began to knit again, furiously. She knit so fast that her fingers flew and the needles clacked. It made Louisa dizzy. *Make them leave, dear God!* she prayed.

The door slammed shut and Sally was across the cabin to drop the latch. She stood wheezing, back to the door, eyes shut. "Who were they?"

"I don't know."

"Are they gone?"

"I think so."

Sally pulled from the door reluctantly, as if without her there the door might burst open upon them. "I think," she said quietly, unable to take her eyes from the bolted door, "that it was a good thing I was here."

• • •

When David got home he didn't act worried. "Probably one of the northern Indians. They're always nasty—but mean no harm. How are you feeling today?" He bent over the bed to give Louisa a kiss.

He had never said a cross word about her keeping the baby a secret so long, although the shock of the discovery and the scare still seemed to cling to his face.

"I'm just tired," she said, wishing for some way to ease the far-away look in his eyes. "But no cramping today, so I suppose I'm better."

"That's good." He pulled off his clothes and slid in beside her. The bed creaked under his weight and she scooted to make room. "They caught the fellow with the blue drilling sails this morning. Your brother spotted him first, and we all lay in wait right behind Tom Pepper's place. They gave him a lashing he won't easily forget. Dobbins did it. Wish it had been me."

She had never heard him wish to do violence. It gave her an uneasy feeling. "Do you think the Indians are satisfied with the way Maynard blew everything over?" she asked, needing reassurance. "Those Indians this afternoon. They were so, so. . ." She couldn't find the right word. They had frightened her badly.

"Just belligerent, Liza. You can't act like it bothers you. You know that."

He was right. It was just like with Old Alki John last winter. They sometimes liked to throw their weight around. You couldn't let them know you were scared. "Your eyes hurt?" she asked. The roar of the saws was always in his head and the pain lurked around his eyes, never really leaving. He nodded and she patted the blankets. He moved over, resting his head in her lap, and she ran her thumbs over his closed eyelids, then pushed hard along his temples, over and over until she felt him relax.

"I doubt we'll see him again," he mumbled.

"Who?"

"The fellow with the blue sails. Good riddance. Now I feel like I can relax. We showed the Indians we meant business about all this. Oh. I almost forgot."

"Forgot what?"

"In my pocket."

She leaned over the bed and picked up his shirt and then slid her hand into the flannel. "Bob Moxlie was up today," he whispered, more asleep than awake as she pulled out two letters. One was from Ma, and the other was from Pamelia's mother.

"Read Ma's first," David said. But he was asleep before she could finish. Cupping his bearded chin in one hand, she read the other letter, the one from Mrs. Dunlap, and for a long time she rested against the pillows, David's head heavy in her lap, against the quiet heartbeat of her baby—their baby. She read both letters over and over until each word was memorized. Ma was coming for a visit. And Pamelia was dead. She had died in childbirth last February.

20
July 16

"A story of Louisa Denny and Mrs. Bell illustrates how entirely the women were at the mercy of the Indians in their lonely cabins while their husbands were away....

"One morning, Mr. Bell found some pheasant eggs which Mrs. Bell decided to take to Louisa as a great delicacy, since she was not well."

—Roberta Frye Watt in *Four Wagons West*

David didn't know what to say to comfort her. When she woke him with the news, her eyes empty and lonely, he shied from the duty. Quietly, methodically, he fixed supper instead, knowing as he set out plates and fried potatoes and boiled the water for tea that she longed for something else—strong arms and kind words, some sort of assurance from him. But he had nothing to give, and each went to bed lonely in heart.

He held her spoon-fashion, and he tried to smile, to recall the early days when they could still laugh in the midst of trouble. But it wouldn't come, and when she fell asleep he lay alone in the dark, thinking hard.

Life used to be so simple. You worked hard, you did what was right, and everything worked. Only now it didn't seem that way anymore. He tried to recall his verses from the book of James. He had memorized the whole book while coming across the prairie, and he was surprised to find he had forgotten much of it. All he could remember was the very beginning.

> *My brethren, count it all joy when ye fall into divers*
> *temptations,*
> *Knowing this, that the trying of your faith worketh*
> *patience.*
> *But let patience have her perfect work, that ye may be*
> *perfect and entire, wanting nothing.*
> *If any of you lack wisdom, let him ask of God, that*
> *giveth to all men liberally, and upbraideth not; and*
> *it shall be given him.*

> *But let him ask in faith, nothing wavering; For he that*
> *wavereth is like a wave of the sea driven with the*
> *wind and tossed.*
> *For let not that man think that he shall receive any-*
> *thing of the Lord.*
> *A double-minded man is unstable in all his ways.*

But how could a man ask in faith when there was so much that contradicted? And why had God let Pamelia die? He was power-less to work past that, and he fell asleep with his arm numb, holding Louisa but reluctant to let her go. Next thing he knew someone was standing over them, candle in hand, and he leaped from the bed and grabbed for his rifle. But it was only Chodups.

He sat back down on the edge of the bed weakly and bent over, elbows upon his knees, head down, waiting for his heart to settle and the fright to pass. "Don't ever do that again," he said, staring at Chodup's feet in front of him. Chodups was wearing Boston shoes, without socks. "What?" he said suddenly, jerking up, feeling the color drain from his face.

"You must take Louisa to Seattle. Two Indians—they nearly kill her."

He reached for his pants. There had to be some mistake. Even if the Indians did plan some sort of revenge, against Seattle's command, they wouldn't take a woman's life! Nevertheless his fingers trembled so violently that he couldn't jam the buttons into their holes. His shirt hung open.

"They see Sally Bell. They think you and Mr. Bell not far away, and decide no, no killing with men too close. They take wapatoes and tin bucket."

Louisa collapsed against the pillows and he cursed himself. Maynard had warned him severely about letting her get frightened.

"Who were they?" he demanded. "And you answer me in Duwamish."

"No. English," Louisa said weakly.

"Klitikats." Chodups bounced his gaze between them both.

"*From over the mountains?*" He stood rigid, shirt still undone, one sock on. It *wasn't* retaliation. It couldn't be. Not from Indians that far away. It had to be renegades. It wasn't as bad as he thought. Louisa crawled across the bed toward him, and he reached for her, catching her quickly. "Shh. It's all right. I have you," he whispered. "Liza? Liza? Chodups," he said, turning around, "would you go down and get the canoe ready? I'm going to have to get her into the village." The familiar sane control was washing out his initial panic, relieving him. He began to stuff her clothes into a pack, along with some of his own.

"She dead?"

"No. She's fainted."

"You sure she's not dead?"

"Yes, I'm sure! Please, Chodups, the canoe!"

Chodups shuffled out the door.

But they got only as far as the Bells. "She's cramping," he told William when the door opened. Sally made out the bed, and he waited only long enough to see that she was comfortable, then flew back out into the night.

• • •

"You might try praying if you're of mind—that baby is fighting to live," said Doc Maynard. The hour was very late, nearly morning, and David was exhausted. He sat numbly on a chair close to the bed. Every muscle in his body screamed from the abuse of paddling madly into town, then back. But Louisa was fine, which was a relief. She was in no danger—just the baby. Maynard had brought whiskey with him, with instructions to give her two ounces every quarter-hour.

"But she'll get drunk!" he protested.

"That's the idea, Dave. The alcohol will relax everything in there, enough to stop the labor."

"But you can't do that to a woman!"

"You want her to lose the baby? I don't know what's going on there, but this is your chance to put a stop to it."

She lay quietly against a stack of white pillows, her face as white as they. The flicker of a lantern cast shadows upon her face, outlining the hollow eyes and dark circles, turning her into a ghost. She seemed to have trouble keeping her eyes open, and David glanced quickly to Maynard. Did the man know what he was doing?

Nobody knew, he guessed. What mysteries were locked into a woman's body? How easy or difficult was it to lose a child? *He* certainly didn't know, and looking now at Louisa's face he wondered what torment he could exact of himself—to make up in some way for what he had done. He was the one who had done all this. He had started it all by sending her after her brother during the lynching—in her condition. She had denied, of course, that it had been his fault. How could you have known? she had asked. But he *had* known, hadn't he? He had suspected. And then he had left her home alone, knowing there were rumors of unrest. He had left her home alone, a pregnant woman unprotected. Well, one thing was certain—no matter what happened from here on out, he could never take her back. Joe Foster wasn't right about much, but he was right about moving in closer to town.

"Louisa, I don't think you realize the seriousness of the situation."

David sat up straight, biting the inside of his cheek to clear his brain, trying to concentrate on what Maynard was saying. Louisa struggled to speak, to keep her eyes open. "I understand it's serious," she said.

"As soon as it's safe to move you, I want you moved into town, where I can keep an eye on you. I'll speak to Yesler about some boards, and David can build you a fine little place—right beside your sister. Would you like that?"

He breathed a sigh of relief. She couldn't argue with Maynard. "What about my garden?" she wanted to know, drumming up strength from somewhere to argue. "And my chickens? I was saving for something special, something for the baby..." Her voice choked and she plucked nervously at the bedsheets. So that's what she had been doing with the eggs! She was selling them!

"Louisa." Maynard sat on the bed and took her hands in his. "No more gardening. Not for awhile anyway. And I'm sorry, but I can't let you take care of those chickens anymore, either. You're not to do *any* work for a long, long time. It's the only chance the baby has. You're going to rest, and when you're feeling stronger, take long walks. But no work. Can't I make you understand? We must take care of this baby."

David felt a stranger. He had no feeling for this baby, but Maynard did, and Louisa certainly did. Last week there had been feelings enough—anguish, despair, the thought of a child dying that he hadn't even known. But this week? This week nothing, and it separated him from them both—and from the Bells, who tried not to listen from the other end of the room. Maynard bent quickly to brush her cheek with a kiss. "Perhaps the good Lord will see fit to spare the child yet."

"I'm sure He will," she said calmly, and David felt a chill run through him. How could she say that, after all this, especially after knowing that her dearest friend had died? He glanced quickly to Maynard. Maynard stood in the door. The first of dawn lit the sky, a metal color of blue and gray. "What makes you so sure?" Maynard asked, and David waited, breath held, for her answer.

"Psalm 121."

Maynard snorted. "That's horse rubbish, Louisa, if you don't mind my saying so. I hate to sound so untrusting at a time like this, but an isolated verse out of an ancient book of songs hardly applies to you in particular."

Louisa's answer came quickly. "Of course it does. He sent Sally Bell, didn't He? I would be dead right now if Providence hadn't led her to my door."

A chill ran down David's back. He didn't know if he should feel sorry for her or envy her.

Part Four
Fall 1853

"New people arrived. The mill hummed. Gardens of the pioneers' own planting were beginning to produce. White picket fences enclosed flower gardens, and kept the children in and the cows out. The Indians were friendly, some working in the mill, others peddling clams, salmon, and berries. To be sure, there were rumors of discontent among some of the tribes, but these were not alarming, for Governor Stevens, Superintendent of Indian Affairs, would settle all of them."

—Roberta Frye Watt in *Four Wagons West*

21

September 30

"Young David built a second home, this time a small board one near Arthur and Mary Denny's. These two little homes stood near the 'big laurel,' as they called the great madrona that overhung the bluff near First and Marion."
—Roberta Frye Watt in *Four Wagons West*

"Liza! No!" David was sitting at the table in their new house, drawing a map for Arthur. The Governor had written from somewhere on his treck west with a request for a map of the Indian nations. "How many times do I have to tell you? We-are-not-moving-back-out!"

"Please, David."

She was washing clothes and cooking supper at the same time. Betsy Foster apparently hadn't come in today, and he worried. Maybe she had run away again. But no, her money was still there, tucked inside a small burlap sack on the wall. "I thought I told you I would fix supper as soon as I was finished here," he said.

"I don't mind. I'm going absolutely mad with nothing to do. David, when are we going back? I'm a lot stronger now. And Doc Maynard told me that the danger has passed."

Louisa's strength had indeed returned. The initial crisis had lasted a week—one long, dreadful week in the hottest part of July. Yet even now, 2½ months later, David could not rid himself of the image of her swollen, bloodshot eyes imploring him to make it all stop. But he hadn't stopped. Unmercifully he had kept on, feeding her the prescribed two ounces of liquor every quarter-hour, prevailing only upon Sally Bell when he could no longer bear it. He had slept with her in his arms, held her in the rocking chair, rocked her by the hour, sung to her, hummed, prayed when she asked. He had forgotten everything but her and doing what had to be done. He couldn't let the baby die. He couldn't let her heart break.

Arthur had been livid. Drunk for a week! A woman! And everyone talked of it. They *still* talked of it.

But it had worked. Maynard, of course, took all the credit, and when the baby began to move and stretch and kick a few weeks ago he strutted proudly about town like a grand peacock. But David watched Louisa's returning strength with uncertainty. It was the cougar hiding in the tree all over again. He couldn't shake an unnamed dread.

Chief Seattle had caught the renegades. That's all they had been, renegades—nothing more serious than that. But they had meant to kill her, and he could never take her back to their cabin, their little cabin with the newspapers and blue calico, the giant stove and mud floor. No, he could never take her back, alone and unprotected, no matter how much she begged.

He had built their new cabin where it was safe—set on the bluff just north of Arthur and Mary Ann's place, beyond a large madrona tree that for some reason they called a laurel. It was a nice house, too, made of sanded boards, and it had a wooden floor. Even without paint it looked like a house from the States. And out back was a henhouse. He took care of the chickens himself, taking the eggs into one of the new stores in town once a week, since Maynard's Seattle Exchange was out of business. He never saw the money; it was Louisa's. He did everything he could to make sure she was happy. But somehow it didn't seem enough. She wanted to go home.

Her consolation was Betsy. The agreement with Joe Foster was 25 cents a day, although David secretly paid her another 25 cents. It went into the burlap sack nailed on the wall behind the table, and Betsy knew that whenever she needed it, or wanted it, she could help herself. So Betsy came each day to wash and bake and clean, and to sit with Louisa. The two women became close, and often David came home to the cheerful sound of Betsy (and sometimes Mamie and Princess Angeline), cackling uproariously over some funny story or antic of Betsy's new baby, and sipping English tea through two sugar cubes pinched tight between their front teeth. Louisa particularly loved little Joe, and on the days that Betsy arrived late with a blackened eye or a gash along her cheek or a bloodied rag wrapped about her arm, Louisa bit her lip in silence and carefully made sure the baby was all right.

"It's not that I don't *like* it here," she said quickly, seeing David's face. "It's just that it's not home . . . where it's just you and me."

He was sick and tired of this subject, and he could feel his irritation mount. All right, they would end it—tonight. This was going to be the last time they would talk of it. "And wandering renegades?" he asked, tilting his chair a bit and catching his hands behind his back.

"Don't be silly."

Don't be silly? "I don't know about you!" he flared, "but if Indians came looking for *my* scalp, I'd think twice before going back out!"

"Seattle took care of them, David."

"I *know* he took care of them! *But doesn't it scare you that it might happen again?*"

She draped his clean shirt over the clothes rack to dry. "I suppose it could," she said slowly. "But I don't think so."

She was so pretty, but so, so naive, and it drove him wild that she could be that naive, blindly trusting, never considering the possibility of disaster. Just like the rest of the pioneers, she was utterly convinced in the rightness of what they were doing, confident that Providence would see them through.

Louisa wrung out another of his shirts and draped it alongside the first, then poured some warm milk into the potatoes and started to mash them. "Don't you see?" she said, and he shook his head. "Last winter I just about went mad being scared all the time. Scared you would get lost again, scared the ships wouldn't come in, scared we wouldn't get enough to eat, scared of the Indians, scared that John Low would do something stupid again. I used to make you *miserable* with being so scared all the time. Don't you remember? I was a regular crybaby, crying about trees falling on our heads and broken teapots."

He had to smile.

She smiled so sweetly in response that he wanted to jump up and hug her, sweep her off her feet, make her shut up for just a little while. "Don't you see, David? I'm not scared anymore. For the first time in a long time, *I'm-not-scared.*"

He couldn't understand her at all. If anything, there was more reason than ever to be scared. Rumor blew like soft breezes of Indian unrest in distant tribes. If Seattle's 4000 warriors appeared passive, forgiving of insult, it was only Bear sleeping. *But Bear would still eat.* Isn't that what Curley had said, *warned* him of?

"Remember when I planted my sweetbriar?" He nodded. "I told you it meant that God was with us. It's true! It was Providence that sent Sally to my door the day those renegades came!"

It would be cruel, but he said it anyway: "So where was Providence when Pamelia died?"

She blanched and quickly turned. The basin clanged against the stovetop, and she stood with her back to him, hands clutching the basin rim, slamming it up and down until water sloshed and spilled. Her hair fell in a black cascade down her trembling shoulders, and he longed to get up, rub the anguish away, ease the pain. But he stayed where he was, making her face it. Finally she spoke. "You think I'm going to end up like Pamelia, don't you?"

"What?" He shot out of the chair.

"You think I'm going to end up like Pamelia." Her expression horrified him more than her question. Did *she* think she might die? It was foolish! He sat back down, feeling the hardness of the chair beneath him, something solid in the spinning room. "You do, don't you?" she insisted. "You're thinking I'm going to die, and—"

"I do not!"

"Then take me home."

"No. Here, let me do that."

"No, I can do it."

He knew better than to argue. She flung open the door to toss out the dirty water, and for a brief moment he remembered the time he had first touched her fingers, under soapy water in the shadow of Independence Rock on the Oregon Trail. "I do love you, Liza."

"If you loved me, you would take me home."

He sighed in defeat, and began wearily to gather up his maps and sketches. "We'll talk about this again when Tommy Mercer gets back with his girls," he said, avoiding her eyes.

"All right, David. I won't say any more until then."

"Good. Let's eat. I have a political meeting to go to."

• • •

Some meeting, Louisa thought as she passed the cookhouse. Boisterous laughter erupted from the open windows and the chinks of the log walls. For a moment she lingered, delighting in the sound of men's laughter. *Political meeting.* It sounded more like a party.

The lingering laughter followed as she moved on, passing beneath the webbed overhang of tangled aspen and alders near the Felker House. The leaves had turned golden, and spots speckled them. A few leaves caught the evening breeze, dropping to the earth, falling like ancient used coins from a storehouse above. It was Indian summer at its peak, and when she rounded the back side of the hotel she paused, exhilarated, caught in the glory of fall. A hush had come upon the world.

Directly below, 16 feet down, was the gentle lap of gray-blue waves upon the clay bank. She stood mesmerized by the swell and break, the rolling in and draining out. The wind caught her skirts and tugged. She pulled off her bonnet to let the wind have her hair, and she stood chin raised, hand over her stomach, eyes to the sky, bonnet in hand. The uncertainty of last winter had no place here, nor the awful tension of summer. Even needing to go back home didn't seem so urgent either. All was at peace tonight.

The baby stirred beneath her hand and she sighed deeply. It would be a girl, she knew. Even Betsy thought so. It was the way she carried the child, a small round ball right in front. Boys made you bloat. David said it was silly, but sometimes silly things made sense.

Sometimes silly things made sense.

The thought repeated itself, over and over. It was why David couldn't understand, why she couldn't *make* him understand. It sounded silly to rest your life on simple trust while everything turned and tipped and seemed to slide out of control. It sounded silly to trust when your best friend died. But she would see Pamelia again, in a land where they would never be called to part. She had that comfort. Poor David looked for hard answers, but in the end all there was was simple trust; you couldn't live your life being afraid all the time.

"Auntie?"

Down below, along the narrow beach, Katy called.

"Oh, there you are!" Quickly Louisa tied the strings of her bonnet, letting the hat lie over her shoulders, and walked along the bank's edge in search for the trail down. "Your mother said I might find you girls out here!"

"Over there, Auntie! We'll meet you!" The three girls disappeared into the heavy foliage below. Louisa found the top of the path, a steep, narrow Indian trail. Two minutes later the girls burst from the shrubberies to greet her, laughing and giggling, arguing over who had gotten there first.

"Mind now, girls," she reminded them. "Don't pull. I have to be careful. We must keep Doc Maynard happy."

"When are you going to have that baby?" Katy asked.

"Christmas."

"Before or after?"

"Before."

"How long before?"

"Katy, I don't know. Babies make up their own minds."

"Auntie? What's that boat?"

They had reached the beach, and far out on the water, coming across from New York—Alki, was a large war canoe. Louisa raised her hand to shield her eyes from the late sun. It couldn't be Bob Moxlie. The mail canoe was smaller. "I don't know," she said slowly.

A woman stood, nearly tipping the dugout, and someone hollered, "Sit down!" A small child cried in fright. Who had come to Seattle? "*Sit down!*" The canoe bobbed precariously. Involuntarily Louisa took a step forward. Then Katy screamed, "It's grandmother! Auntie! It's grandmother! It's grandmother! And baby Reta!" The other girls took up the chorus. "It's grandmother! It's grandmother, and baby Reta!"

Ma? *Ma*? It *was* Ma! "Oh, Ma! MA!" Louisa yelled, catching her breath in a gulp and flood of prickles. "MA!"

The girls got to the incoming canoe first, racing into the water. They danced with the waves, dashing after them, then racing clear, trying to reach the canoe yet keep their feet dry.

"Ma! Oh, *Ma!*" The water caught her own toes, making her jump back. "Oh Ma! Oh Ma! Oh Ma!" she cried, grabbing hold of the boat and helping to guide it in.

They hugged before the canoe could slide into shore. Ma climbed right out into the water and Louisa pulled her onto the sand, out of the icy cold. Both of them were soaked, but no one noticed. Ma's skin went blotchy as she embraced Louisa silently, holding her close, and for a long time they held each other, patting the other's back.

At last Louisa pulled loose and took her little sister, marveling. The last time she had seen Loretta she had been only eight months old, and now here she was 2½ years old! "Oh, my," she exclaimed all over. Ma was here! Ma was really here! And here was her baby sister! So big now!

"Better give her back to me," said Ma. "She doesn't know you. And who are these little girls?" she teased in her kind, stern voice.

"I'm Nora," said Katy.

"And I'm Katy," said Nora.

"Go on with you."

"I'm Gertie!"

The three stood grinning, side by side, hands behind their back, pinafores wilted and stained and ruffled by the wind. Ma laughed and set little Loretta on the dry sand, where she stood shyly, hiding behind Ma's apron, thumb in her mouth. "I think I might take a better look," she said.

The girls began to giggle and Louisa dropped to her knees to better see the child that both she and David could call sister. "Ma! Loretta looks like me!"

"Well, that's what Pa says."

"Remember me?" asked a voice from a few yards away.

Louisa had been so caught up with Ma and Reta that she hadn't stopped to notice all that was going on. Several Indians were busy unloading plunder, hauling it up to the Point and mill. A couple of men in blue dungarees and denim jackets stood further down the beach, talking. One was pointing, obviously familiar with the village. But the man who had spoken to her stood pleasantly a few yards away, hat in hand, beaming, waiting for recognition. She studied his face—a round, massive face with clean cheeks and warts along the right jowl. He looked vaguely familiar.

"You were just a little girl when you saw me last," he said laughing, amused by her confusion.

"I'm sorry, I—"

"It's your Uncle Guthrie!" said Ma. "Do you remember my brother, Guthrie Latimer, from when we lived in Kentucky?"

"Uncle Guthrie!" Of course she remembered him—now! For hours he used to tell them stories, giving her and Mary Ann and Dobbins horsey rides all through the woods. He was the one who had taught them how to make maple syrup and how to sing "We

Are Climbing Jacob's Ladder." "So what are you doing in *these* parts!" she exclaimed.

"He came out to visit me," said Ma. "So I just brought him along."

"Well, it's a pleasure, I'm sure, to see you, sir." She stepped forward to give him a proper welcome.

"*Louisa?*"

Her heart skipped at the sound of another familiar voice.

• • •

David had left the meeting early. He thought maybe he would find Louisa on her walk. His boots thumped against the soft earth as he made his way to the beach. It was quiet. He debated which direction to strike out. North? South? Sudden laughter and excited calls caught his attention to the south.

• • •

"He wanted to come with us, to see how you were," said Ma. Everything seemed to grow quiet as Louisa looked from Ma to Uncle Guthrie, then down the beach to where James stood. His broad shoulders blocked the last of the sun's rays. His red, burnt umber hair shone in the reflected light. "James," she whispered. "It's James."

• • •

David stood motionless, a part of him seeing and hearing and knowing while the rest of him fought to deny. The water was still, hardly a ripple. It was like a great gray-blue mirror. Ironic, he thought, seeing it. He had finally gotten enough money together to order Liza a new mirror from the catalogue in Dr. Williamson's store. It was to be her Christmas present. He turned with effort. Once he got moving, he walked swiftly, north, past the mill and Indian canoes, past the trail that led up to Arthur's new house and their own new board house, past the "laurel" tree that hung out to meet the tide. Soft rustling along the bank arrested his attention. Two bear cubs frolicked, tumbling over each other and cuffing each other's ears. Their mother lumbered into view. They saw each other at the same time, each caught by surprise. But then she moved on, intent upon the whortleberries.

22

October 14

"Dr. Maynard and two or three kindred spirits very secretly represented to the Dept. that I was not in sympathy with the administration; in fact, that I was not only a Whig, but an 'offensive partisan,' and got me relieved October 14th, 1853, by the appointment of W.J. Wright, a little doctor."

—Arthur Denny in *Pioneer Days on Puget Sound*

A gust of wind whipped off the beach and up between two buildings along Commercial Street. "Indian summer is over, Ma," said Louisa, shivering and pulling up her shawl. The brim of her bonnet bent over her eyes. "You've come at the wrong time."

"We couldn't leave until Pa got the crops in."

Ma and James had been in Seattle two weeks. Ma was staying with Dobbins and Anna for now, and Uncle Guthrie and James had rented a room in Mr. Maurer's Eating and Boarding House—in his new building across the street from Maynard's. Since their arrival the weather had gradually turned cold, fall deepening and preparing for winter. Another gust pushed through a half-finished store. "Feels like it might even be working up for a storm," said Louisa, casting her eyes about the sky, looking for clouds. All around it was a bleak gray. Doc Maynard came out of his blacksmith shop.

"Good morning, ladies. And where are you off to on so cold a morning?"

"To buy some flannel to make diapers."

"You don't want Princess Angeline or Betsy Foster to show you how to make them out of cedar bark and moss?"

Louisa smiled. "You seem spry, Doc Maynard. Have you just sold another lot?"

"It just so happens I did. Sold the smithy. And was on my way home to celebrate."

"Such a nice young man," said Ma, watching him scuttle across the road. "Such a nice young man."

"You ought to hear him and Arthur sometimes. David says it

keeps the fiddle bow tight around here."

"He reminds me of James."

"Who? Doc Maynard? Doc Maynard reminds you of James?" Louisa was surprised. If anything, they seemed like opposites to her.

"Inside they're like glass, Louisa. Your Doc Maynard hides it behind his drinking. James hides it by pretending he doesn't care."

Now that sounded like David—pretending he didn't care that James was in town.

"How are you and James getting along?" Ma asked.

"We're getting along all right, Ma."

"And David?"

"He's fine." He wasn't, but she wasn't going to tell Ma any different.

"James talk to you?"

"He talks to me all the time. Why shouldn't he?"

Ma hesitated, then hurried on. "Where is this store you were telling me about?"

"Ma? Is something wrong with James?"

"There's nothing wrong with him."

"Ma, would you wait up? Now, Ma, there is too something wrong. I can tell by the way you're acting."

"Very well," said Ma, coming to a stop. "If you must know, he's missed you."

"Oh, is that all? I thought you were going to tell me he had consumption or something terrible."

"Louisa, it *is* terrible. You might as well know. Your Pa and I are afraid for him."

"For heaven's sake why? He looks fine to me."

"He misses you. Two whole years and he's still carrying the grief. He's a fragile person, Louisa. If you would just look, you would see it. When your letter came last winter saying you were married, he couldn't speak for weeks."

"But, Ma," she exclaimed, "When David went down last year and talked to Pa he said that James—"

"What else was James supposed to say? He *loves* you!"

"But he told David he would co-file with him so David could get the claim, so we could be married."

"He only wanted to make you happy. It's all he knew to do.

He still loves you, Liza. Why do you think he came up here when he heard you were pregnant?"

What was Ma saying? Did she still think she should have married James? But that was ridiculous. She was married to David. She loved David. "I think you're being silly, Ma," she said, defending herself by trying to remember all the times she had talked with James the past two weeks. He hadn't said anything, even *hinted* at anything. Or had she just been so worried about David that she hadn't noticed?

"He loves you, Louisa."

"So does David."

"David is a boy."

She was shocked and hurt. "I think we better not talk about this. I'm married to David. I'm carrying his baby. And I love him." She felt tears. What did Ma expect her to do? And what if David knew what Ma was thinking?

"I suppose you think I'm being unfair to David."

"I think you're being unfair to me. What do you want me to do? Chop myself in two and send half home with James?"

"Louisa!"

"I'm sorry, Ma, but you're upsetting me. If James is still pining away, which I don't think he is, for you to come up here and suggest anything different is cruel." Ma's mouth went into a straight line. "Here's the store, Ma."

Dr. Williamson's wasn't much of a store, but it was better than Charles Plummer's down the road. He carried only axes and hammers and broad saws, although neither was as good as the old Seattle Exchange. Ma frowned and peered at the shelves, examining the trinkets the Indians traded for and the price list for salmon and game on the wall.

"Hello, Louisa, Mrs. Denny," Dr. Williamson greeted, hearing the clang of the doorbell and coming out to see who was there. "Did you bring in some more eggs? Haven't seen you or David in awhile."

"Not today," said Louisa, dismissing Ma's concerns. She was not going to think about it anymore. "With Ma and James up, we've been eating them all."

"You won't be able to save any money that way."

"I don't need any more money. You ordered my bunting and baby hood, didn't you? Oh, Ma, you should see it! It's pure wool and has this wonderful little pink hat. I bought it out of my egg money, and I'm going to give it to David when the baby is born."

"Whatever is he going to do with a baby hood?"

"For the *baby*, Ma!"

"Maybe he could order you a new glass for that busted mirror of yours, Louisa," suggested Dr. Williamson.

"*What mirror*, Liza?" Ma was looking at her as if she had just been caught stealing apples. "Do I understand this gentleman correctly? That the precious wall mirror of your father's was broken after all?"

"So you *did* know I sneaked it across the prairies!"

Ma clucked under her tongue. "Louisa, you always were a trial. I suppose I should feel sorry for David." She hurried down an aisle, pretending to inspect hunting traps.

"Ma. The fabric is this way."

Ma set down a weasel trap. "All right, Louisa. Laugh at your old mother!"

They looked over the cloth quickly. "Is this all the fabric you can get? Five bolts? And the flannel! Why, Louisa, It's red!"

"Why do you think we all wear the same dress, Ma? Or hadn't you noticed?" Louisa looked down at her own dress, a faded calico with ivory and pale-blue forget-me-nots. "Anna has one just like this, only she put a piece of tatting from an old collar on her sleeves. And Mary Ann pieced hers differently in the front. The bodice has four panels."

"Oh, my," said Ma, shaking her head as she fingered the material. "But *red flannel*?"

"That's all we get around here. The Indians love red."

•   •   •

"*Offensive partisan! That confounded doctor!*" Arthur yelled, tossing a letter across his desk and slumping back in his chair. Mary Ann had invited the women to a sewing bee—to meet Ma and to help Louisa with the diapers. They sat around a crackling fire on boxes and crates, sewing and gossiping, spending a quiet day indoors. Yesterday's wind still blew, blustering the last of the leaves from trees, banging shutters against walls. Sally Bell, Ursala McConaha, Elizabeth Livingston, Sarah Yesler, Mrs. Butler, Anna, and Catherine Maynard had all come, and they all looked up simultaneously, stunned by Arthur's explosion. He was sitting at his desk in the corner of the crowded room, sorting mail and going through all his political correspondence. He snatched up the letter again and read out loud, giving them no choice.

"Honorable A.A. Denny," he read. "It is my unfortunate task to inform you that another Postmaster for the City of Seattle has been appointed, a Dr. W.J. Wright. It has been brought to my attention by Doctor David Maynard, Justice of the Peace for King County, and others, that you are not in favor of the present administration, and that not only are you a Whig, but an offensive partisan."

"Arthur!" warned Mary Ann, glancing quickly at Catherine Maynard. "We've got company."

But he kept on. " 'To expedite more readily the makings of government, I herewith relieve you of your appointment. Apologies are extended...' It's signed with President Pierce's stamp." He threw the letter aside again.

"I'm sorry," said Catherine quickly and quietly, keeping busy with her needle and thread.

Louisa dug her own needle into the red flannel and pulled up on the other side, feeling sorry for Catherine—and Mary Ann—and not knowing quite what to say or do to get past the incident.

"You know what that's all about, don't you?" demanded Arthur. "He's mad because I made such a fuss about that lynching last summer. He's trying to get back at me."

"Arthur...we have company."

"He resents the fact that I feel differently about law and order, and say so. But what sort of government is it that simply turns the other cheek to civil disobedience?"

"Now that David Maynard seemed like a nice enough young man to me," said Ma, and Louisa groaned. It was bad enough without Ma getting into the middle of it. "Isn't that what the Bible preaches, Arthur? Turn the other cheek?"

"The Bible, Ma?" Arthur asked. "I'll tell you who's turning the other cheek around here, and we're darned lucky he is, and that's Seattle. God help us when he gets tired of it. And he will, too, if we don't keep order. Dave says there's rumblings up the White River."

"Arthur!" cried Mary Ann, covering her ears and jumping to her feet. "I won't hear any more of this!"

"Aw, come back here, Mary."

"No more, I mean it!"

Louisa stared as her sister pulled on her hat and coat and headed for the door. Arthur grabbed her by the elbow. "All right, Mary, you win. No more." He grinned so comically that they all had to smile. Mary Ann slipped out of her coat and the tension eased. "You know what it is, Mary Ann, don't you? It's petty, political harassment. That's what it is."

"*Arthur!*"

"No, he's right, Mary," said Catherine. "That's exactly what it is. Petty, political harassment. But then, Arthur, you wouldn't know what to do if my husband left you alone, would you?"

"*Mama! Mama!*"

"Good heavens, what now?" exclaimed Anna as Nora and Gertrude and George McConaha Jr. tumbled through the door, banging it against the wall. Wind rushed in. "Mr. Mercer is back!" they hollered. "Mr. Mercer is back!"

"And he brought horses!" panted Nora.

Arthur scrambled for his boots, letter forgotten. The women, without a word, quickly began to gather up their sewing.

"Horses, Mama! He brought horses! A black one and a white one!" She danced up and down.

"Blast it all, where is my other boot?"

"Right here, sir," said George Junior, a strapping seven-year-old, handing him his boot from behind the stack of wood near the fire.

"You sure it's Mercer?"

"I'm sure. And, sir, he's brought his wagon. They came over your road, sir, from Fort Steilacoom!"

"Who is Mr. Mercer?"

"The man who has the claim just north of ours, Ma," said Louisa, slamming the lid down on her sewing basket and reaching for her bonnet. "He and David are good friends. Oh, Ma!" she exclaimed as the full impact of the news sunk in. "Maybe David will take me back home now!"

Ma's face wrinkled. "I should hope he has more sense than that."

23

The horses were magnificent Arabian thoroughbreds, the first horses on the sound. Tib was glossy black, and she pranced nervously in place, tossing her mane. Her mate, Charley, was a shocking, snowy white in comparison and stood quietly and patiently while men and boys examined his teeth and measured his height. Questions and answers flew back and forth as everyone took turns patting, rubbing, guessing, measuring, checking.

"Had double trouble getting these two across the country," said Tom, slapping Tib's glossy black neck and leaning to bring Charley's nose up for a kiss. The horse pawed the ground, straining against the reins. The wagon schooner in back bounced and creaked and the Indians jumped up, laughing.

"*Boston kaynim!*" they joked. "*Chik-chik!*"

"Whoa," laughed Tom Mercer, tugging tight on the halters.

Louisa stood spellbound, caught up in the excitement and general uproar, shivering in the wind. "Glad to see you made it," said Arthur, pushing forward and offering his hand. "Some of us were beginning to think you'd decided to stay in the Willamette for the winter." Others crowded in, shaking hands. *Where was David?* she wondered.

"No, sir. Whoa!" Tom hollered, slapping the horses gently.

"Nice team!" someone hollered. "I don't think I've ever seen a white horse like that before!"

"Don't come this way too often, that's for sure. Dexter! Come round here, let me introduce you!"

A young man and his wife eased off the wagon seat. "Dexter Horton and his wife," said Tom. "Dexter's come to help me in a transport business."

More handshaking and questions, and Louisa stood back, watching, imagining what it would be like to move back to her cabin. With Tom home, David would reconsider. He had said they would talk about it, didn't he? Surely he would have no more qualms about going back out there with Tom right next door. Did she dare hope?

"What's going on?"

She jumped, startled out of her daydreams. James stood beside her. "It's Thomas Mercer, the man who has a claim north of ours. He went back to the Willamette for his children and horses, and it looks like he's brought some new settlers with him." She spoke quickly, remembering Ma's words. She felt James' eyes upon her, but whenever she would sneak a peek he would look quickly away.

"Those his children?" he asked.

"Who? Where?"

"Looking out the back of the schooner."

"*Tommy!*" It was David's voice, and she turned, trying to locate him. There he was, working his way through the crowd. "Tommy! You're back!" he hollered, waving, breaking through at last.

"David! I've brought the children with me! I want you to meet them. Girls, come on out! And bring Rebeccah with you." There was an immediate hush as five little girls climbed out the back of the schooner one by one, shy, quiet, hardly looking off the ground.

"This one here is Rebeccah, Dexter Horton's daughter," said Tom. A little girl about Katy's age grinned, freckles sprinkling her nose. She giggled self-consciously and went to stand with her folks while the other four took their place in front of Tom, lining up in a row to await their introductions, pinafores wrinkled and stained, braids hanging loose, their bangs long. The oldest looked to be about 14, and she held the two middle youngsters firmly by the hand. The other, no more than three, sidled up close to her father, sucking on the frayed hem of her dress. "And these four are mine. Mary Jane. Susie. Eliza. And little Alice here."

"Oh, the poor dears," whispered Ursala McConaha, hugging her baby to her chin. "*However is he going to manage?*"

Oh, if only David would let her move back, she might be able to help. *Please*, she prayed.

"I wouldn't mind taking the oldest one," said Mrs. Yesler. "She'd be a help around the kitchen."

"I wonder if Tom would consent to letting us help by taking one or two," said someone else.

"Louisa?"

"What, James?"

"Where's their mother?"

"She died in The Dalles. Blue Mountain fever."

James winced. "Of all the rotten luck...to have made it that far only to..." He said no more, and Louisa strained to hear David through all the commotion.

"So you made it over my brother's road, did you? How was it?"

"He's complaining about the stumps," said Arthur.

Tom laughed hard. "David, you going to help me clear the trees behind us like we planned? Got to put a road through so I can take these little girls home. And put this wagon to use hauling our timber."

"Excuse me, James," she whispered, pushing forward. When she reached David she slipped her hand into his and he turned to look at her, smiling. She felt the pressure of his fingers tighten around her own, and she wondered if he had seen her with James.

"Why, hello, Mrs. Denny." She had never seen Tom so pleased. Having his girls made a difference in his eyes. "Been scaring off any more cougars?" he asked, smiling broadly. "And what's this? When is this one going to hatch?"

She blushed. "Christmas."

"Boy or girl?"

"Girl."

"Nothing wrong with girls, is there?" His smile was good to see, and her hope surged. Oh, surely, surely Tom could talk David into moving back out! "Well, David?" he asked. "What do you say? Put a road out past our places, start our own transport business? That way we can get our timber into town and—"

"I've moved into town."

Tom's mouth fell open. He looked quickly from one to the other of them, figuring out the point of disagreement quickly. "All right, David," he said quietly. "But does that mean you won't be helping me with the road?"

David's profile caught the darkening sky. Louisa was suddenly aware of the wind; it was really blowing hard. "Of course I'll help you with the road," David said, and she swallowed back her disappointment. He wasn't going to take her home! He hadn't even intended to the whole time! He had only said that to make her be quiet! A sudden clap of thunder rippled the sky.

"Looks like that storm is finally moving in!" yelled Doc Maynard as people began to run for cover. "Hey, Mercer!" he yelled. "Get those horses of yours out of the straps and in where it's dry! You can use the shed next to the smithy! Blast it all! I just sold that smithy! Wyckoff? You around here anywhere?"

"Right here." A tall, skinny man stepped up.

"Did I sell that shed of mine with the shop?"

The tall, skinny man laughed. "The name's Lewis Wyckoff. Mr. Mercer, follow me. I'll help you get them settled in."

Maynard shrugged. "Guess I sold him the shed."

"That's not all you sold," said Arthur. "You sold a post office, too. What I want to know is, how many pieces of silver? Come on, Mary, let's get out of this rain."

• • •

After the storm the Seattle men determined to put Tom's road through, and the rest of Ma's stay revolved around the "Mercer Road."

Tom was insisting on keeping his family together, and no one much liked the idea of him so far out, alone with the children, the only access to town being by canoe or by the beach at low tide. It was Arthur who had spearheaded the effort, but everyone had quickly fallen into the plot, and each night the men of the village dragged in from work too tired, stiff, and weary to do much more than eat and doze in front of their fires.

The Borens and Dennys fell into the habit of all eating together at one or another's house, and the women spent the evenings after dinner washing clothes, rubbing aching shoulders, fixing hot-water bottles, tucking children into bed, and sometimes falling asleep on the floor, sitting between the knees of their men before being pulled to their feet and taken home.

Sometimes Uncle Guthrie pulled himself away from the bachelors at Maurer's long enough to come up for a bit of cobbler or custard, and they all told old stories. Those were good nights. But through it all there was a standing barrier between James and David, an unspoken disquiet. And when Arthur and George McConaha left for Olympia the first week of November to wait for the Governor's rumored arrival, it grew worse. David had wanted to go, but he didn't, and Louisa knew it was because of James.

"Why does James bother you so?" she asked one night, tucked into bed beside him, feeling the warmth of his skin and the hard muscle of his arm against hers. She longed, even ached, to bring up the subject of moving back home, but she didn't dare. Not now, when he seemed so on edge.

But he didn't want to talk about James, either.

"We need to talk about it, David. It's getting really hard for me. I don't want him to feel unwelcome, and yet if I pay too much attention to him, you get upset."

"I do not get upset, Liza."

"You do too. You don't say anything, but I can tell. It's the same as on the Oregon Trail. I'm beginning to feel like some sort of booty, some sort of prize between the two of you."

She could hear him breathing in the dark. "I wonder," he said slowly, staring at the ceiling, "if the Governor's arrived yet."

She tried not to cry. He sighed and sat up, leaning on one elbow. "The baby kicking much these days?"

"All the time."

"Roll over and I'll rub your back."

She fell asleep with his hands taking out the ache in her back, but not in her heart.

24

November 25

"The new Washington Territory awaited the arrival of its first governor, Issac Ingalls Stevens.... No radio and not even a telegram announced the exact time of his arrival, but the little village of Olympia made preparations just the same."
—Roberta Frye Watt in *Four Wagons West*

Three weeks later a squirrel darted onto the Cowlitz Trail, then stopped, ears trained. A sudden swish of its tail, and it was gone. The earth vibrated with the thud-thud of marching boots. "Olympia straight ahead!" The cry shattered the forest glade. From a giant hemlock the squirrel scolded.

Olympia! A fresh burst of energy came to Isaac Stevens, and he marched with a quick step through mud and pine needles. He marched despite aching calf muscles and a dull throb in the small of his back, despite the snap of branches against his chest and the scratch of blackberry vines across his bared arms. *Olympia.* Here at last.

It had been a long, long trip—thousands of miles. First it was just putting them behind as they crossed the plains, but then, once they hit the mountains, it was retracing and circling back, mile after rugged mile, and over again. There were 11 Army officers, 76 enlisted men, and 33 members of the Scientific Corps, plus teamsters, packers, guides, herders, and voyageurs—240 bone-weary men altogether, searching out the best possible route for the Northern Pacific Railroad. Now here they were at last, on Saturday afternoon, November 25, on their final stint into Olympia, Territory of Washington, doggedly winding their way up the Cowlitz Trail.

It wasn't a good trail, although well-marked by rusted iron patches nailed to tree bark. It was muddy, slick from new rain, and steep in spots. Two mules had slipped and gone to their deaths.

The rain was miserable, a continual drizzle for three days straight, soaking their shirts and spirits and putting an ache into their joints. The only respite had been a brief layover with John and Lydia Low at Chamber's Prairie.

"We started the city of New York—before moving out here," said John, tipping his chair. "But I guess it's Alki now. Means by-and-by." He laughed, full of memories and regrets. "It was Luther Collins' idea of a good joke a long time ago. Guess Charles liked it. Heard he's made it official."

"Why'd you move?"

"Couldn't wait for the good old by-and-by . . . had to make a living." He quit laughing. He brought his chair forward, leaned over the table, and pushed the tobacco tin closer to Stevens. "Much as I hate to admit it, Governor, Arthur Denny and the rest were absolutely right about my New York—Alki. Getting timber outa there got to be a real headache and I didn't have the guts to move inside the bay. Something about telling Arthur Denny he's right sort of sticks in the craw."

"*Olympia! One hour!*" came the call again. Stevens pushed ahead, leaving the party behind. A hot meal without having to wait over a fire in this drizzle was too good to be true, and an hour later, exhausted to the bones, he stood heavily at the door of the first eating house he came to and leaned over his legs, hands on his knees, seat against the solid log wall. He took deep drafts of air into his aching lungs. This dampness could eat a hole through a man's lungs if he wasn't careful to air them out. When he straightened he could feel the pull down his back. Cautiously he pushed open the door. But a strong arm shot out of nowhere and knocked him sideways. He stumbled, hit the wall and landed on his seat in a mud puddle. A bald man showed himself from behind the door.

"Can't a man get a bite to eat?" he asked, too stunned and weary to jump to his defense.

"Not today you can't." The man cast a quick survey over Stevens, and he looked down at himself. A week's worth of mud caked his boots, his pants, his jacket, even his beard.

"I been walking over 3000 miles to get here," he said, "and I aim to eat." Somehow he managed to right himself. He wiped the mud from his hands on the back of his pants. His fingers were icy and throbbed unmercifully at the tips. He wanted to suck them, to ease the pain. "Get me the cook."

"See here, we are going to have doings here," the cook said

when he came to the door, "and we can't be feeding strangers until it's all over."

"I'm hungry! Can't you at least give me some of the scraps from the kitchen table?"

The cook thought a bit. "All right. I guess I could do that."

He ate his fill next to a piping-hot stove. It gave off the aroma of fresh bread and sweet things, and sizzled furiously whenever boiling water escaped the giant caldrons set on top. Potatoes, with venison gravy poured over them, sat in a steaming lump inside a cracked ironstone bowl on the table, and the cook dropped a scoop onto a cracked ironstone plate, dingy from use, and pushed it across to him. Stevens dove in with a sharp sense of gratitude. Then, with the edge of his hunger dulled and strength returning to his body and soul, he watched with fascination the bustling activity. Everyone was in a state of agitation, and it reminded him of an old story his uncle used to read of royalty.

"Time to get out," said the cook.

He grabbed a biscuit. The mud on his jeans crusted, and when he stood, it broke into chunks and fell to the floor. The cook was there immediately to sweep it up.

"You know when that there Governor is going to arrive?" a man asked the minute he stepped outside. Stevens blinked in astonishment. "Been hearing reports all day he's coming up from Chamber's Prairie. I tell you, the man is slower'n blackstrap—slower than one o' these here ugly things." He dropped a thick boot-toe over a slug and squeezed it between the plankings of the sidewalk. "Been all o' nine months. 'Tween you and me," he whispered suddenly, leaning forward with a hand beside his mouth so that his hoarse, throaty voice rasped directly into Stevens' ear, " 'tween you an' me, I'm hopin' he don't do his politickin' same as he marches!"

The "doin's" were for him! Stevens squared his shoulders. A sense of importance, of power, came to him—a different feeling, one that felt good. So this is what it felt like to be royalty in those old stories! "Then I suppose it's me you're looking for," he said, straightening and offering his hand.

The man took a surprised step back. "No!"

"Sir Isaac Ingalls Stevens, Governor of the newly formed Territory of Washington. At your service." The astonished man pumped his hand vigorously as the news settled in. Suddenly he broke free, dashed to the eating house porch, struck a discarded saw hung from a post, and yelled, "He's here! He's here!" with a voice that nearly outdid the raw clang. "He's here! The Governor is here!"

• • •

"It's really a lot more fun in July," said Louisa. "It's not as cold. Oh, look! There's one! Quick!"

James sliced the shovel blade into the wet sand, digging quickly. A fat clam flew off the shovel, and Louisa bent to pick it up. A sea gull shrieked.

"No, I'll get it," he chided, taking it from her. "I told you, I don't want you bending like that."

A chilling wind haunted the air. It tore at their clothes and made their noses drip. Louisa pushed her hands into the sleeves of her coat. November was nearly gone. Ma, James, and Uncle Guthrie would soon be leaving. The governor was probably here by now. And word had come that the new minister and his wife were finally on their way. Everything seemed to be happening at the same time.

"It's fun even in November," said James. He picked up the clam bucket and they walked on. Another hole spurted and he found another clam. "Beats chopping trees and grubbing stumps. How come you didn't tell me I could be doing this instead of working on Mercer's road my whole visit?"

"Guess we needed the road more than we needed the clams. And besides, the tides weren't right."

It was late Saturday afternoon and the tide was perfect. Several Indians and pioneers were out with buckets.

"It was a worthy endeavor, so I won't complain. You hungry yet? Should we head back?"

"I'm cold."

"Let's go sit on the beach for a bit. That'll warm you. Get you out of the wind."

She looked to where he pointed and realized they had come further than she'd thought. "James, my old cabin is just around the corner. You want to go see it?"

"Sure."

"Oh, phoo," she muttered, staring at the run of water by her feet, cutting her off from the shore. "The tide's come in a bit."

In one swoop he had her off her feet and was carrying her through the shallow water. Embarrassed, she tried not to look at his face, although she knew he was looking at hers. It was the same look he had given her when Mercer had arrived last month, and she remembered Ma's words. Was it true? *Did* James still love her? For the last six weeks she had gone back and forth, first making up her mind that Ma was wrong, but then wondering if maybe she wasn't. And David had refused to talk to her about it at all.

"I'll go back for the bucket. Wait for me."

The tide was low, but it had turned. Maybe they *should* go back. No, she wanted to see the cabin and her sweetbriar. They were so close.

For five months she had tried to picture it, to imagine how overgrown the trail might be, how her sweetbriar might have grown. But she was not prepared. "James, it looks so sad. So wild and gloomy."

He stood beside her, a larger man than David, and she felt small, despite her heavy pregnancy. "It doesn't look sad to me. *Or* wild and gloomy. I'd be able to tell this was your place even if you hadn't told me. No one else would bother putting stones around their garden, wanting it to look nice. What's this?"

So it had grown after all. David had come out once in a while during the summer to water and mulch it, and had even asked to transplant it for her. But it hadn't seemed right to move it. This was their home—it belonged here.

"What is it? Looks like some kind of wild rose."

"It's my sweetbriar. Pamelia and I . . ."

"That your friend from Cherry Grove?"

She nodded.

"I heard about it, Liza. I'm sorry." He wandered, hands in his pockets, looking at everything while she pulled herself together. She felt caught in a tangled web of emotions, snared with overwhelming sorrow for Pamelia, loneliness for her cabin, hesitancy over the tide, worry for David, and sadness that Ma and James and Uncle Guthrie were leaving, yet filled with anticipation that the new preacher would soon be here. Somehow it seemed that when he got here everything would be all right again.

James found the cedar slab nailed over two high stumps and

bent over it, testing it with his weight. Then he swung off his feet and looked at her upside down and through his dangling legs. "What's this?" he called, all red in the face.

"James!" she laughed. "Stop!" But he wouldn't. He just hung there, grinning.

"So? *What is it?*"

"My ironing board!"

"Your *ironing board!* Goodness, Louisa," He gripped the slab with his hands and slid further over the edge, flipping to land right side up the way it was done on an iron bar, only the board ripped loose and he fell with a crash headfirst. She was hard put to keep the laughter back as he sat and rubbed his head and face, groaning, and trying hard not to laugh himself. "Come on," she said, holding out her hand so he could pull himself up. "Let me show you inside. David designed it special."

He brushed off his pants and patted his hair. "Special? I was under the distinct impression that one log cabin was the same as another."

"That's where you're a bit ignorant, James Denny. He built *our* cabin to resemble King Solomon's palace."

He laughed outright at that.

"Song of Solomon, chapter 1, verse 17. 'The beams of our house are of cedar, and our rafters of fir.' "

"I always knew my brother was a little mad."

The door swung open with a squeak. It took a moment for her eyes to adjust as the gloomy interior came into focus.

"Hey, not bad," whistled James. "What'd you say it was built out of?"

"Fir and cedar. The stones are from Alki," she added when she saw him inspecting the fireplace. "That's where we first landed. He had the Indians haul them over on Luther Collins' barge."

"What'd he use to daub them together?"

"Blue clay."

His bottom lip came up and he stood with his hands in his pockets, nodding. "It's nice. It really is. I kind of like this place. How come you don't live here anymore?"

Her back was hurting and she glanced nervously out the window. The water was still way out. "Think maybe I'll sit down for awhile," she said. "My back...you don't mind, do you?"

He squatted in front of her, left arm braced on his thigh. The salt wind had put a ruddiness into his cheeks. "Is it serious?" he asked.

"No. It hurts all the time. It's just worse right now because of being on my feet so long."

"Then we shouldn't have come."

"No, Doc Maynard makes me walk just about every day. He says it's important."

"Does he know what he's doing?"

"Yes, he knows what he's doing, James."

She looked all around, seeing the cookstove, the empty shelves, the two bare nails sticking out the back of the door where their hats were supposed to hang, the faded and yellowed newsprint all over the walls. The silly story they had laughed at last winter hung over the empty bed. Nobody had ever noticed it; it was a secret they shared. But now it was all a skeleton of the past, and her emotions lodged thick in her throat, battling breath and tears. She mustn't cry.

"If you're going to sit, do you mind if I try to dry my socks? My boots must have sprung a leak."

She shrugged, unable to speak. He went outside and returned lugging in an armful of wood. She watched him lay the fire, kneeling and blowing quickly. It had been James who had always built the fires in Illinois. "Wood's wet," he muttered. But the flames caught and spit after a bit. He coughed and waved smoke out of his face. Thumps and bumps and short, high squeals came from inside the chimney. He sat back on his heels, staring wide-eyed at her. She stared back. Her first thought was a bird's nest, but then it was too late in the year for that. Suddenly a bat dislodged and dove into the room, and she ducked, screaming. Another bat joined the fray. "The broom!" she screamed. "Behind the stove!"

He grabbed the broom and started swinging. The bats dove and darted, wings outstretched like frightful nets, and she screamed again, hiding her face in her hands. "Go on! Git!" he hollered. "Go on, beat it! Git on there!" He went at them with a fury, striking the wall, the stove, everything but the bats. Twice she peeked, then quickly hid again. They terrified her. Ugly, filthy, foul things. "Oh, God," she whimpered, feeling one swoosh past her hair. At last it was quiet. Hesitating, she pulled her hands away.

James had flopped onto his back on the bare slats of the bed, bare feet hanging to the floor. "Whew," he sighed, turning his head sideways to look at her. "So tell me. *Why do you want to live out here?*"

25

"At first the forests were so dense that the only means of communication was along the beach at low tide."
—Emily Inez Denny in *Blazing the Way*

"So tell me again why you want to live out here?"

She laughed, but James insisted. "No, come on. Out with the whole story." He rolled off the bed, set a dusty chair in front of the fire, and made Louisa sit in it. He pulled up a chair for himself. "Nice of you to leave a couple of chairs. And the broom," he added. "Comfortable?"

"As well as can be expected."

"All right, then. Tell your good old brother, stepbrother, why you don't like living in Seattle."

"I didn't say that, James."

"Louisa, you don't have to. I can see that you don't."

"Your socks dry yet?" His socks, navy blue with red heels, were spread on the hearth. His rubber boots were propped so that the heat of the fire could dry the insides.

"Of course not. How come you don't want to talk about it?"

"James, the tide is coming in. I don't want to get stuck out here."

"You mean we could really get stuck?" he asked, jumping to his feet. "How come you didn't tell me?"

"I thought you knew!"

"No, I didn't know that!" He started to pull on his wet socks, tugging quickly. They kept sticking, and he tugged harder.

"That's one of the reasons they built Mercer's road. When the tide's in, the beach disappears. If you don't have a canoe, you're stuck." Even as she spoke she realized she didn't want to leave. The cabin was warming quickly, and if she closed her eyes, she could almost pretend she lived here again.

"You look wistful, Louisa. Why so sad?"

She bit the inside of her cheek and looked into his eyes, so blue, so different from David's soft brown eyes. Gone was the discomfort that she had experienced when he had carried her through the water. It really was just James again, her stepbrother and friend. All the things Ma spoke of were just not true. Or if they were, he was doing a good job of hiding them. And he could go on hiding them because she needed him this way. She needed someone she could talk to.

"How come so sad?"

"I'm not sad. I was just imagining I still lived here."

"Why don't you live here? Hey, did I ask you this already? Hold your right hand in the air if the answer is yes."

"Stop it, James. It's not funny."

"I guess I can see that. I keep asking a simple question, but I don't get any answer."

"He won't let me."

"Who won't? *David* won't let you? Now what's that supposed to mean?" He wiggled his toes in the wet socks and reached for his boots.

"He just won't, that's all."

"Maybe he thinks something might happen."

"That's ridiculous, if you ask me."

"Are you asking me?" He glanced at her.

"No, I suppose not. I just want to move out here, that's all. This is my home."

"But can't you see his position?"

"No, I can't. I *love* this place. It's mine. I have my garden, my—"

"You have a garden in Seattle."

"It's not the same thing!" She could feel herself losing control.

"It is a little isolated out here. Maybe that's what's bothering him."

"But they've got the road put through! I thought sure David would move back out here then! But he said no! And Mr. Mercer is only a mile away. And Dr. Smith—"

"No one is exactly next door."

"But this place is *mine*! It's David's and *mine*!"

"And your house in Seattle isn't?"

"No, it's not!" she cried. "It's Arthur's! Everything is Arthur's! The land, the house, the garden, the big laurel tree! Arthur, Arthur, Arthur! Everything belongs to Arthur! It's all his! Nothing's mine!" Pent-up frustration exploded, erupting like an infected wound, but she didn't care. James wouldn't hold it against her for sounding like Anna, for sounding selfish and unkind and stupid. "That's the way it's always been!" she cried, blinking back her tears. "Having to live with Arthur hanging over my head! Do you know he barged in here the morning after we were married? I'm getting so sick of Arthur I could scream! I can't get away from him! I can't get *David* away from him!"

"Wait, wait, wait a minute! Hold on there! Can't get *who* away from *whom?*"

"David! He's always with Arthur, doing what Arthur wants, listening to Arthur!"

"That's not fair. He didn't go to Olympia with Arthur, even though he wanted to. He stayed home for you."

"He did not! He stayed home to help finish that road! You don't understand how it is, James! You don't have to live with this like I do. You don't have to live with David!"

"Thank God."

Suddenly she felt ashamed, and she sniffed, rubbing her nose with her coatsleeve. That's the way it always was. No matter how hard she tried to bottle it in, it popped out sooner or later, like a cork flying off one of Doc Maynard's bottles, and everything that came out sounded so rotten. "How come you said David stayed home from Olympia for me?" she asked quietly, all her anger gone now, leaving her feeling tired and spent, and very sorry.

"Because that's what I thought. Didn't he?"

"Did he tell you that?"

"No, he didn't tell me that. He never tells me anything, Louisa, you know that. I just assumed it. How come you said it was for Tom Mercer? Is that what he told you?"

"I don't know!" Why *had* he stayed home? She didn't know; everything was mixed up. But what did it matter? She couldn't live here anymore; that's all she knew. "I'm sorry, James. It was unfair to bring you into this. We really should be going, too. That tide doesn't wait, and David will be wondering where I am."

He sat hunched over his knees, staring at his wet feet, boots still dangling in his hand. He said nothing for a long time, and she grew uncomfortable. Finally he looked up, his eyes penetrating and intense. "It's only fair to tell you this," he said slowly. There was something different about him—his voice, or was it his eyes?

"Don't, James. Please."

"No, Louisa, I need to tell you this. I came up here to make sure you were happy, and it's breaking my heart to see that you're not. I'd like to kiss you right now, but I don't think that would be a very good idea. This isn't like before. You're married now, to my brother, although in my book it doesn't count for much. He is, after all, five years younger than you. But for some bizarre reason you love him, so I'm going to take you home. But before I do, I want you to know that if ever you want to leave Seattle, for whatever reason, I'll be waiting in the Willamette."

She slid to her feet and pulled on her coat, heart pounding, not daring to look at him. Ma was right! He still did love her! *Oh, David,* she thought. James pulled on his boots and followed her down the trail to the beach. But the tide had come in. They were stuck.

• • •

No Louisa.

No note.

David knocked softly on Arthur's door, not wanting to disturb the baby, or Mary Ann if she was sleeping. But it was Mary who answered the door. "Is Louisa here?" he asked.

"No. Ma?" she called, turning back inside. "David's looking for Louisa. Have you seen her?"

Ma came to the door and looked David over. Sometimes he felt uncomfortable in her presence. He did now. "She and James went clamming today," Ma said.

What was she going clamming with James for? Animosity rose quickly, and he scrambled for something to say to cover it. "How long ago?"

"Well, I don't know. She was going to go out by herself. Said something about the tides. But I didn't think it was a good idea— not in her condition. So I sent James along."

He was angry that Ma had even let her go—with or without James. But there was no point in saying anything now. It wouldn't change anything. "When did they leave?"

"Right after lunch."

"Well, it's nearly dinner. Do you have any idea where they might have gone after the clamming? It's cold out there."

"No. As far as I know, they're still out there."

Mary Ann peered around the door. "Don't worry," she said.

"They'll be along any minute. Why don't you come in and get a hot cup of tea while you're waiting?"

He debated. If he went in he would have to listen to a bunch of chatter he didn't want to listen to right now. But if he didn't go in he would start getting furious and maybe do something foolish like go look for them.

"Come on in, David. Ma won't be here that much longer."

"I won't be bothering you?"

"Don't be silly," said Ma, smiling quickly. Louisa had Ma's smile. "I'll put the water on."

He sat in a chair that Mary pulled out for him, and tossed his cap onto a shipping crate. Arthur's commissary business was growing, crowding the space uncomfortably. "Hear anything from Arthur?" he asked.

"Got a letter today. One of the Indians brought it up. He says the Governor's somewhere on the Cowlitz Trail."

That meant the Governor was probably there by now. His disappointment in not being able to go had faded over the last couple of weeks. He couldn't figure out what he'd been thinking of in the first place to have even considered going off and leaving Louisa. *Where was she?* he wondered. Where could she be?

"Arthur said that the new minister was on his way too," said Mary Ann with a smile he hadn't seen in a long while. "Bob Moxlie's bringing him up right now so Ma will get to meet him before she goes back."

"You going back with Moxlie, Ma?" David asked, the news of the minister sliding away from him as he thought of James leaving soon.

Ma nodded. "But not Uncle Guthrie. He came over at lunch to tell me he wasn't going to go back." Somehow that news didn't surprise him. Guthrie had let spill a few of his thoughts.

"He wants to know if you or Arthur will donate timber so he can build a boarding house," said Mary Ann. "Says he'll let the new preacher use it for a church if you give him the timber."

"Where's he going to build it?"

"Dobbins gave him a lot near Front and Cherry."

"You think Arthur'll give him the timber?"

"What do you think?"

"I think he'll have to get it out of me."

Ma laughed. Sometimes he couldn't figure Ma out. *Where was Louisa?* Did she know any of this? No, of course not. She had been gone all afternoon.

"David? Didn't you hear me?"

"What? Uh . . . no, Ma. Thinking, I guess."

"I said, here's your tea."

"Oh. Thanks, Ma."

• • •

"We're stuck," said Louisa. All kinds of horrible thoughts passed through her mind. No dinner, Anna scolding, James uncomfortable, David hurt.

"We're not stuck. What about the new road?"

When she laughed, he said, "You forgot, didn't you?"

"Oh no you don't, James Denny! I saw your face! You did too!"

"Only for a moment." He grinned and led her back up the trail. "Looks like we forgot the clams, too," he said, seeing the pail sitting on the front stoop. He glanced quickly at the sky. "Think we'll make it home in time for supper?"

"I hope so. I'm hungry."

• • •

Sir Isaac Ingalls Stevens could eat nothing of the elaborate feast prepared in his honor. "I'm chock-full of scraps," he declared. Everyone laughed, and he took a deep breath, then glanced about the large room to the men who had gathered from all over the territory to hear him before plunging in with a three-point outline of what his responsibilities were to be. One, the railroad. Two, the establishment of the territorial legislature. And three, the settlement of Indian affairs.

Arthur was not impressed by the speech or the man: five-foot-five at best, with a voice that was slightly grating. Reminded him of the runt of the litter. He didn't like the swell in the man's chest, either, or the tilt of his chin as he spoke, or the way he stood on tiptoes, as if another inch might make a difference. Those were bad signs. And he worried about the man's focus of concern.

"What do you think, McConaha?" he asked when it was all over and he and George and the other men had retired to their hotel rooms for the night. He sat wearily on the bedspring and pulled off his socks, navy blue with red heels. He gave them a careless toss and they landed on the porcelain washbasin—one draped over the jug and the other lying in a heap beside the bowl.

"Let's wait until tomorrow. No sense in jumping to conclusions this time of night."

• • •

David laughed, tucking Louisa's head to his shoulder. "I figured there was no point in jumping to conclusions, Liza. Figured if you were going to run off with James, you'd have done it when he first got here."

"Don't tease, David." She was back, tired and chilled, and they stood just inside their door. James had just brought her home, and she leaned wearily and painfully against the pine slabs of the door, the latch catching her across the small of her back, strangely offering a measure of relief. "You weren't worried in the least?" she asked. Candlelight put sputtering shadows over his eyes and nose and mouth, and she drew a finger over his lips. She had expected to find him beside himself. It was a pleasant surprise to find him so cheerful.

He caught her hand and kissed the tips of each finger. "Now why should I have worried? I found your note."

"What note?" Then she saw the tease in his eyes.

"I'm sorry. I should have left you one, but I thought Ma would tell you."

"Oh, she told me all right." His eyes were intent upon hers. "You know, Liza, sometimes I think I will go crazy loving you."

"You do go crazy. David, why did you stay home instead of going to Olympia with Arthur?"

He pulled back, surprised. "To stay with you, Liza. Why?" He kissed her, lingering, playing his fingers through her hair. "Louisa? Why? Why did you think?"

She wouldn't look at him, but buried her nose in his shoulder, hiding from him.

"Louisa? What did you think?"

"I thought it was because of James."

"What?" he exploded. "Me sit around here with James when I could have been meeting the Governor? Are you mad? Ah, Liza, sometimes I wonder what goes on inside that head of yours."

For a long time they stood against the door, holding each other, the candle flickering.

26

November 27

"We came on some 25 miles down the Sound to Seattle—our Home. We reached Alki, a little place six miles distant across the bay, on Saturday, November 25, and as it was late in the day and the wind was high, we concluded to remain there until Monday."

—David Blaine in a letter

On Monday morning Betsy Foster didn't show up to help Louisa with the wash. It wasn't until all the undergarments were scrubbed and hung to dry, and three pairs of pants left to soak, and she was working on the collar of one of David's red flannel shirts, that Louisa noticed the empty burlap sack. *Betsy had run away*!

"David?" She sat on the edge of the bed, watching her husband sleep. He had taken the day off because the mill was closed. Suwalth had come over the day before with the news that the minister and his wife were in Alki. Bob Moxlie was going to be bringing them over this morning, and so Mr. Yesler had announced a shutdown of the mill. When the news had come, all the women had immediately set to work baking bread and cakes, stewing chowder, smoking salmon, and fixing pies. The men had gotten together to lay the foundation to Uncle Guthrie's new boarding house, where the services would be held. Everyone had been in a great state of excitement all day, arguing over who was going to get to donate a lot or two for the parsonage, and Doc Maynard and Dobbins fought over where the seminary ought to go—the Point or up north of the mill. So it had been a late night and a sleepy morning, a bittersweet kind of day today because in the middle of all the anticipation Ma and James were leaving. "David?" Louisa called again, touching his shoulder.

He jumped. "What...huh?" His eyes flew open, darting, then rested on her. "Oh..." he groaned, relaxing, rubbing his eyes and rolling over. He pulled the pillow over his head. "Time to go say goodbye to Ma?" he asked, his voice muffled and thick with sleep.

"No, David. It's Betsy. She's run away. She's taken all her money."

"What?" He pulled out and sat up, wide-eyed and awake now. "When did she do that?"

"I don't know. I didn't think to look yesterday, since she's not supposed to come on Sundays. Today I was in the middle of the wash when I finally noticed it."

• • •

A heavy mist shrouded Elliott Bay. It draped the trees and fell low between cabins. It settled over the Sound like a heavy, wet blanket. Caught in its damp folds, crossing the bay, was an Indian dugout. Catherine Blaine sat miserably in the middle, between her husband and Bob Moxlie. "This is not the life for a new bride," she said from her cramped position, packed in with plunder and mailbags and odd assortments of packages.

"Our life is not our own, but belongs to the Lord—wherever He sends us." Her husband of only a few months spoke without looking back. He sat hunched over the bow, trying to manage the awkward vessel in the choppy waves. Catherine, having to just sit still, shivered in the pressing, white dampness. The mist had begun to seep through her collar and she shivered. *If I don't catch my death,* she thought. But Mr. Blain was right—one mustn't complain when sent out under the direction of God. Thank God they at least had Mr. Moxlie to paddle them over to their new home. They had been spared the reeking stink of the Indians.

A gray, forbidding shoreline emerged out of the fog. At first glance she could see only a few buildings, all battered by wind and rain, none painted except for the place tucked just offshore, high on a bluff.

"That be the Felker House. Madam Damnable's place," said Bob Moxlie, speaking for the first time.

"Madam *who*?" stammered Catherine.

"Madam Damnable."

"She's *called* that?" Catherine asked, unable to believe her ears.

"It's what they call her, all right. Captain Felker just got her last week to run the place, and there ain't no pioneer, no sailor for that matter, what's got a temper and tongue as her. Swears up a storm, she does, and if that don't take care of things, she'll throw a block of wood over your head."

So this was where God had sent them. It was all so terribly depressing.

• • •

"David!" Louisa hollered, pulling muffins from the oven and turning them over onto the table. "They're here! The new minister and his wife are here! The girls are at the door!" She could hear Katy and Nora thumping furiously, knocking and calling for her to come and meet the Blaines down at the cookhouse. When she pulled back the latch they tumbled in. "They're here! They're here!" they cried.

"I guess that means we better go say goodbye to James," said David as the girls ran to him for a kiss. He picked them both up, as big as they were getting. "Get my cap for me, will you, Nora?" he said, standing close enough to the peg so she could reach out and stick it on his head. Louisa pulled on her coat and struggled with the buttons, trying to get them to meet around the baby. Then she set her bonnet on. But she couldn't tie the ribbons, her fingers shook so. "Oh, hurry, David," she pleaded.

"Hurry?" he teased. "I'm not the one who's got my coat buttons all done up the wrong way!"

• • •

Bob Moxlie, when he saw the fixings in the cookhouse, decided to stick around for a bit. That meant Ma and James got to stay on for the party, and Louisa, amused with the generosity of her feelings today, thought it was too bad Arthur was missing it all. He was the one, after all, who had been responsible; he had worked hard badgering the mission board, and now, finally, Seattle at last had a messenger of the gospel.

The preacher didn't look anything like she had expected. She didn't know what she had expected, but it was not this very short man with weak, blue eyes and thin, blond hair. He sounded like a preacher, though. "We're going to be needing a building," he said, "although I'm sure the Lord will provide."

"I'm going to let you have services in the Latimer Building, if

I can talk one of my nephews into giving me the timber," said Uncle Guthrie. "We've already got the foundation laid."

"How soon can you put your building up?"

"We'll have it up for preaching on Sunday."

"There, you see? The Lord really does provide."

David and Louisa exchanged glances, each trying not to smile. In this case they knew where the "provisions" were coming from.

"Catherine will sing a solo," said Mr. Blaine, planning it all out, and Louisa noticed that his wife lowered her eyes. Maybe she didn't want to sing?

Catherine was a tiny woman. She had complained of being cold, and so Mrs. Yesler had given her a dry, brown wool dress to put on. She sat in the corner of the cookhouse looking embarrassed, and kept apologizing for the dress that was too large. She didn't know yet that no one in Seattle really cared. Fashion did not rule in these wilds.

A sudden pounding at the door stopped everything, and for a moment everyone froze, caught in mid-sentences, coffee raised to lips. The door pounded again. "David Denny! You in there?"

Joe Foster! Louisa choked on her cake and sat forward. He had found Betsy! Oh, dear God, she prayed, let her be all right! David headed for the door and everyone let him pass, apprehension all over their faces.

"Open up!" Joe shouted. "I got my hands full!"

Through shoulders and heads and the partially opened door, Louisa could see Joe standing on the threshhold with something heavy slung over his shoulder. His face was mean and surly, a three-day growth thick on chin and cheeks, eyes bloodshot. "Brought you a present," he said, *"Injun lover."* He slung the burden to the floor at David's feet. "Don't worry," he said. "She's dead. Hung herself. Caught her yesterday just this side of Fort Steilacoom, and guess what I found on her! Almost 20 dollars! Now you tell me, Injun lover, where she might have gotten that kind of money!" There was a shocked, stunned silence. "I got it out of her last night, before she did this to herself," Joe went on in his cold, mean voice. "You been giving her extra pay, Denny. Well, she ain't gettin' no extra pay now, is she?" He left with one last sting. "You're the one that taught her she was as good as white!"

David dropped to the floor. When he stood he had Betsy in his arms, and Louisa saw the noose—and the bulging, black eyes, the choked, bleached face. It was Masachie Jim all over again. She moaned, a sickness rising up behind her eyes. The women rushed to get the children, and David backed out the door. But before he was gone his eyes caught on Louisa's through the still-stunned crowd, and she rose to go to him, for she saw his desolation.

The party dispersed, and ten minutes later David returned to the cookhouse. "Is she dead?" Louisa asked, anxious and sick, hoping against hope. David's eyes told her before he spoke.

"She's very dead, Liza." He sank into the closest chair and dropped low into the seat. "Maynard will take care of everything." He spoke softly, glancing about quickly to see who was still there. There was only a few of them: Ma and James, David, Mary Ann, Anna and Dobbins, the Blaines, Bob Moxlie, Mr. Yesler, Hillory Butler, a couple of the bachelors, and Uncle Guthrie. And the children.

"What are you going to do?" Bob Moxlie asked. "Kind of like to know so's I can report it to the Governor when I get back to Olympia."

"The Governor can't do anything." David stood, unable to sit, and moved over to the north wall, against a window, weight on one leg, arms crossed over his chest. He bowed his head long enough to rub his eyes with his thumb. "Joe didn't kill her. She hung herself. There was a note." He glanced at Louisa, then looked quickly over to where David Blaine sat, weary and deep in thought. "I'm sorry your first service has to be a funeral, sir."

"Do I understand correctly that this Betsy was not married to Joe Foster?"

"Common-law marriage."

"But not married within the law."

"That's right."

Louisa saw David tense, and she wondered what Mr. Blaine was getting at. Surely he wouldn't refuse to hold a funeral for Betsy. Betsy was at no fault. Joe had held her prisoner. He had purchased her like cattle, had abused and tormented her. Louisa recalled last summer, the day Betsy dove into the icy, cold water for the stone anchor when they had been stranded by the tide, and Princess Angeline had said, "Now she's gone." She shivered, feeling cold inside as the shock began to wear off. The same sorrow she felt for Pamelia was seeping in, taking root deep inside her heart.

"This has put us all into a very difficult situation," Mr. Blaine said sadly. "I can't conduct a funeral service for a squaw. The propriety of my position...well, it would give consent to their past manner of living to have her buried as other people, and—"

"You mean to say," interrupted David so sternly that Louisa was roused out of her sorrow, "that you won't even *bury* her?"

"That's what I'm saying."

"Then do you mind explaining yourself, sir?"

"The afternoon is late, and my wife and I are tired. And these good people, I understand, have to get a good start for Olympia so they're not caught on the water tonight. If it would be all right with everyone I'd like some time to rest and get settled. Perhaps I can deliver my explanation at service on the Lord's Day."

It was a dismal parting for Ma and James. No happy shouts, just sad faces and worry. James pulled Louisa aside. "You sure you want to stay? There could be trouble."

"Yes, James, I'm sure. Wish me well, and I'll do the same for you." She held up her cheek for a kiss.

"I love you, Louisa Boren," he whispered urgently. "You remember that."

"I will, James. Goodbye now."

She and David stood in the drizzle long after the others had gone on home, arms about each other, caught in shared sorrow and watching forlornly as Bob Moxlie's canoe grew small.

"Goodbye!" Louisa called when the mist took them from sight, hesitating, then waving anyway. It was little Loretta's call that came back through the fog.

"Goo-bye!"

27

"The governor was coming with three distinct and highly important missions: to start the machinery of the territorial government, to act as Indian agent between the races, and to make a report of his survey as to the best route for a new northern railroad to the Sound."
—Roberta Frye Watt in *Four Wagons West*

The railroad was clearly the Governor's consuming interest. He persistently downplayed concerns that Arthur raised regarding reports of Indian unrest along the back rivers. "Once we get the railroad in here, the Indians will very clearly see they're doomed," Stevens answered over and over. Arthur didn't like the word "doomed." "And we've got to fight for the railroad now. The Southerners are infiltrating Congress with outlandish obstacles—they don't want the railroad put through antislavery country. Now is the time to be sure our interests are served, or we lose our chance."

"I agree," said Arthur, swallowing that piece of news hard. The fight for the railroad was one he had long been involved in, and news of the Southern agitation alarmed him. "Nevertheless," he said, leaning forward to engage the Governor's eyes, "there are sporadic reports of growing unhappiness along White River. And Patkanim of the Snoqualmies has brought reports of unrest to the east."

"And who are the Snoqualmies?"

Arthur tightened his jaw. David had sent the map. The man was supposed to know all this. "One of the tribes that live in the Cascades. Patkanim, sir, is the man who reported the two passes. I wrote you last June."

"You ain't tickled with McClellan's report, sir?" interrupted Edward Allen from the far end of the long table. Close to 20 men turned to see who spoke. Edward Allen was the man who had almost single-handedly blazed the road from Fort Steilacoom out to Natches Pass in time for the Biles Party to make it over in the fall emigration—the same pass that McClellan had declared impassable. Ed Allen had the respect of every man in the room.

"No, Allen, I'm not!" Stevens came to life. "It's political nonsense. Another Southern ploy to defeat the railroad. *You* put in the road, and so much for his idiotic report. I've already given orders to Tinkham—a civil engineer in my tour—to get Indian guides and cross those mountains. What's your friend's name, Denny? Pat—"

"Patkanim."

"I want you to talk with him and investigate that pass of his— and Allen's. If we can go back to Congress with two viable routes, then the railroad—"

"I hate to interrupt," said Arthur, "but the Indians. We were discussing the problems we are immediately faced with, sir."

The sun had gone, leaving the surrounding hotel windowpanes dark, reflecting weary faces. Cigar smoke circled lazily above heads and a maid came in to turn up the lamps. Outside there was the sound of rain. Arthur had a sudden urge to be home.

"Yes, yes, the Indians," sighed Stevens, slumping back. "Go on, Denny."

"There are reports that even Leschi is expressing dissatisfaction. Settlers are moving in on his farmlands."

"But that man *gave* me 12 horses!" said Allen. "To blaze my road. He ain't feeling poorly toward the whites, I can tell you that!"

"That's just it, Allen," Arthur said, taking a deep breath, trying to explain. Why did he do this? Why did he leave Mary Ann to come down here for three wasted weeks, just to wait for some country bumpkin who couldn't tell the difference between trouble and a Sunday school picnic? "Leschi went out of his way to do us a turn," he said, playing the tips of his fingers against his water glass, spinning the glass slowly counterclockwise in its own puddle, "and look what he got for it—a bunch of settlers in his backyard, where *he's* farming. And Leschi isn't the only one. There's Nelson, too. He's always a hothead, but he has legitimate complaints."

"Thought he gave you folks in Seattle a canoeful of *wapatoes* last winter."

"That's precisely the point I'm trying to make! We were getting along until this past spring. But with all the new settlers coming in and upsetting the applecart, the Indians are starting to get a little alarmed. Quite frankly, I am too. Something's got to be done, and done quickly. There's the matter of those two Klitikats last July. Through the grapevine we learned that they'd intended to murder my sister-in-law."

"Grapevine, Mr. Denny," said Stevens wearily. "Grapevine. And when has there been a white man actually *killed* by one of these Indians?"

It was an obvious and calculated slur, and Arthur reeled. "Louisa is also my stepsister," he snapped, realizing the instant he said it that it only lent credence to the hysteria he was being accused of. "We're getting off the subject," he muttered.

George McConaha spoke up. "The basis for the discontent, near as we can see, sir, is that we're sitting on Indian land with no power of compensation. We're farming *their* land, clearing *their* trees, tearing up *their* hunting grounds, digging up the bones of *their* ancestors, building cities on *their* beaches—and we're doing it without payment of any kind. It doesn't strike fair to *any* man, white or Indian. And it makes it awkward for us as well," he went on, seeing that he had the Governor's attention. "We can't buy or sell property that isn't ours, and giving out deeds the way we're doing is going to get us in a legal tangle sooner or later."

The man was brilliant. Too bad he was a Democrat, thought Arthur. "What kind of authority do you have from Congress to negotiate with these Indians?" George asked. "What sort of compensation can we tell Chief Seattle and Patkanim and the others they can expect? What kind of appropriations do you have?"

"Ten thousand dollars."

"Ten thousand dollars!" shouted George, leaping out of his chair. "You're going to have to go back and get more!"

Stevens rubbed his face and stared blearily out of his fingers.

"We've been flying by the seat of our pants," said Arthur. "If we don't concentrate heavily on establishing mutual trust and goodwill, and I mean substantially so, while there's still a chance, all the mountain passes and iron rails aren't going to do us a blessed thing six feet under."

"I think," said Stevens slowly, "that these reports you keep hearing through the grapevine are wildly exaggerated. I repeat my earlier question. Have there been any whites actually *killed* by one of these so called dissatisfied Indians?"

• • •

Arthur sat hunched in the middle of Jim and George Seattle's long canoe, feeling like a bundle of cargo amidst his own plunder, wedged uncomfortably between a sleeping roll, sacks of flour and sugar, a box of books for Mary Ann, and other sundry bags and parcels. He sat cross-legged for as long as he could stand it, then shifted his legs straight for as long as he could stand it, then crossed them again.

It was a two-day trip, with lots of time to shift and think. He sorted through the progress that had been made—if any. At least some sort of law and order was being established. That had to go a long way.

"ACCH-C-C-C-C-*g-g-KG!*"

He whirled, heart slamming painfully against his throat, sucking the air from his lungs. The bloodcurdling Duwamish war cry came again, and George, in the stern, paused long enough to return the cry.

"What is it?" Arthur ordered, prickles dashing up his neck. On the far bank a war canoe was being put into the water. Excited cries and quick orders filtered through the mist. "What is it, Jim? Who are they? What do they want?"

Jim and George, hands over their eyes to keep off the drizzle, peered anxiously across the water and conferred in meaningless jumble. George hollered out to the approaching canoe and Arthur recognized his name. "What *is* it?" he demanded again, growing hot with fear as the shouts and his name bounced back and forth.

"Paddle!" he yelled, almost rising up on his knees. Jim threw his paddle into the water, arms churning, plunging his paddle deep into the water with such force that the canoe flew over the water. "They're gaining!" Arthur yelled, stiffening, clutching the edges of the skimming dugout with both hands. The wind tore at his hair. He leaned forward, willing the vessel to fly faster. "Hurry!" A knot of terror tightened in his stomach. The pursuers drew closer and closer, until at last he could see black and blood-red war paint splashed across their faces. Gun barrels lay across their laps. The gap between them narrowed and they drew alongside, reaching out to grab hold, but George made a wide sweep and the canoe swung out of the way.

A howl went up. Arthur bit his lip to clear the fright, welcoming the sting of blood on his tongue. Jim and George threw themselves into the work furiously, fueled by the cries. They paddled frantically, arms churning until sweat ran from their shirts and their breath came in ragged sobs. They didn't stop until they had pulled far ahead and around a bend. Only then did Jim speak.

"They want to kill you!"

Arthur looked back, heart throbbing. "Keep going," he ordered, forcing control into his voice.

"They want us to give you to them," Jim wheezed, raking his thick black hair out of his eyes. He held the bangs back, eyes wide underneath, sweat dripping off his temples. "They want to kill you for revenge."

"*What?*" He must have lurched sideways, because the canoe tipped and icy water spilled inside, drenching his feet and seat. "Revenge for what, for goodness' sake!"

"Some Boston kill Indian."

"What Indian? What white man? We're not talking about the lynching, and—"

"No, not my people," panted Jim. "No revenge for that. This other Indian nation. Nisqually maybe. Maybe Pullayup."

Sudden laughter erupted behind him, low and full and out of place. The sound jolted Arthur like a painful slap, and he turned to see George, helpless to even pull his paddle from the water. "Ah, ha! Ha-ha! Ah-ah-ah-ah! He-e-ee," he wheezed. "They say you *hyas typee*, great man, worthy of revenge! I paddle like *stick siwash* chase me!" George dropped over a mailbag laughing, shuddering, convulsing in his laughter. "Jim say—*Arthur Denny not so great as you think!*"

Arthur stared at the two braves, stunned. Chin to knees, arms about wet legs, he hugged himself tightly to stop the shake. The full extent of the danger that had just come and gone washed over him, leaving him sick. A hand squeezed his shoulder and he jumped. But it was just George. "We go to Steilacoom. Camp for night. You be safe there."

Lying under a giant cedar bough, the damp air touching his face with wet fingers, Arthur thought long and hard. The slow hiss of the dying fire kept the night awake, creating shadow and light. He tossed and turned. To have passed so close to death left him scared for the first time since leaving home. Really scared. How did Louisa manage it? It had happened to her.

He thought about the threat, too, and what it meant beyond just himself. There was unrest, all right—David was right about that. And anyone who denied it was simply putting his head in the sand. The camaraderie they might feel with the Indians, the sharing together to put through roads and find food, was just an illusion. By working together in the settlements and interacting with each other, a level of understanding had been worked out, but the Indians beyond the clearings, those Indians . . .

He groaned and stared past the branches of the tree. Moonlight lit the fog to veil the sky in gauze. Would it work out? Would there be peace?

Well, one comfort was that the new minister was here. After months of negotiations he had grown impatient with the delays and setbacks. As always, Arthur mused, God's timing was perfect. If ever they needed the strength of the gospel and the benefit of good men, it was now. It would be a difficult task ahead, bridging the gap between two worlds. They would surely need the wisdom of God. He fell asleep assured, and the fire went out upon three men snoring—two Indians and a white man. A white man who had just discovered that he wasn't as great as he had thought.

28

December 3

"These squaws are lower and more degraded than you can imagine, but little better than hogs in human shape.... The miserable creatures smell so strong of fish on which they live, and of the filth by which they are surrounded, one cannot approach them without disgust."
—Catherine Blaine in letters home

"It is the glory of God I desire to promote, by being instrumental in leading sinners to Christ, and persuading men to turn from death unto life." David Blaine stood behind a pulpit of fir and split cedar in front of the Latimer Building, the scent of sweet pine still strong in the walls. David Denny sat impatiently on a 12-inch bench while he droned on.

"What's the matter, David?" Louisa laid her hand over his thigh and he picked it up and held it gently.

"I'm just wondering when he's going to get on with it." Words. On and on—fancy, complicated words, but nothing that explained his position regarding Betsy Foster. It had been a dreadful week. David had tried to reason with the man, and when Arthur had gotten home late Wednesday night, the two of them had tried.

"In making choice of this holy calling," thundered Blaine, "I made a full surrender of myself and all that pertains unto me to God and His cause. I desire no higher honor than to be a humble, devoted, and useful minister of Christ. I would not have dared to advance without a conviction that my ways are directed by Infinite Wisdom. I feel no anxiety in reference to the course pursued. I have given myself and all my interests into the hand of One who never errs, and I rest there."

Blaine paused and looked over the crowd. When his eyes met David's, there was a clash of wills, and he hastened on. David followed his gaze as he scanned the room. They were all there: Tommy and his four girls, Arthur and Mary Ann with their four, Dobbins and Anna with little Gertie, the McConahas, the Yeslers, the Bells, and the numerous bachelors. Seattle, without exception, had crowded into Guthrie Latimer's brand-new hall to hear what would be said. Blaine glanced down at his notes and took a breath.

"But since coming to this post, to this isolated shore in answer to the holy call of God, that rest of which I speak has come hard, and I must remind myself of the hand of One who never errs. You came this morning to hear my explanations regarding the suicide of Betsy Foster, a squaw, on the day of our arrival this past Monday."

There was a sharp expectancy in the air. Women sat primly, hands folded, feet together on the floor. Men held hats or children on their laps. Almost all kept their eyes focused somewhere between the floor and far wall.

"A young man came to me this week," said Blaine, "imploring me to reconsider my position, reminding me that I am to love the coarse, filthy, and debased natives in order to do them good."

Memory of that conversation surfaced, stinging like the after-taste of bitter things, and David squeezed Louisa's hand. He had said nothing of coarseness or filth. It was amazing how your own words could be used against you. "Perhaps once I could have hoped to do them good, but alas!" said Blaine, his voice a mirror of ignorance to David's way of thinking, "they are almost undoubtedly beyond our reach. They are an abandoned, debased race, without redemption. They are but a remove above human-ity. Their ideas of a future state are indefinite. Moral feelings are blunted or blotted out, and they lie, gamble, steal, get drunk, and all other things almost as a matter of duty."

David's eyes burned; a fury against this man exploded in his mind. He was hard put to stay where he was.

"I believe that the situation we are faced with is that in your midst you have allowed a man to live with a squaw. He *bought* her a few years ago and has been living with her just as if she were his wife. A part of the time he has been unkind to her, yes, but since their child was born, he has, it is said, treated her well."

It wasn't true. Louisa's head was bowed. What thoughts passed through her mind? She had so looked forward to this day, had prayed for it, and had even asked that the preacher might arrive before the baby was born.

"Then sometime this past week," said Blaine, "for some trifling circumstance, she became angry, and when he had gone to his work she hanged herself, and when found, was dead. She never loved him nor wanted to live with him, and in fact had run away several times, but he had followed her and brought her back. This time she was beyond his reach. He was left in a rather peculiar position, the Indians claiming the body to bury among their own people, with their own ceremonies, and he unwilling to let her go, and seeking my consent to officiate the funeral. This I could not do. As a minister of the gospel of Christ, it was my duty to tell him that I could not sanction such sin. He saw the propriety of my position and did not urge the matter.

"Now, what a situation this man is in, with his little half-breed child, despised by the whites and hated by the Indians, who would kill him if they could get a chance, in revenge for her death. You may think me more severe and more scrupulous in the matter than need be, but the degradation that men bring upon themselves by their intercourse with the squaws is not one that can be tolerated. To be lenient is to offer encouragement for further activities of this foul nature.

"In conclusion, let me say again that it is the glory of God I desire to promote, to persuade men to turn from death unto life! Let there be a removal of Indian and alcohol, and this then would be, in most respects, one of the most delightful regions of the world. Nature has contributed bountifully to the healthfulness, prosperity, and happiness of you who inhabit this new country. But man—sinning, fallen man—has brought accursed immorality to these shores." His voice rose to a pitch. "*Man—sinning, fallen man—has brought accursed immorality to these shores!*"

●　●　●

"*We are not going back.*"

Louisa blinked. David, sitting across the table from her, blinked too, and she knew his own eyes stung. His mouth worked with tension. Lamplight flickered. Distorted shadows leaped on the far wall.

"We'll not step into that man's church again," he said. "I regret donating that timber to Guthrie. I wish I could tear the building apart plank by plank." He spoke slowly, evenly, watching her closely, articulating each word. She stared at the distorted shadows.

They had just come from Arthur's, where there had been a meeting with the new preacher. Several had been there; a lot hadn't bothered. Arthur thought that Mr. Blaine was just a greenhorn and didn't know anything, but that in time he would come to better understand how it was with the Indians. But David couldn't forgive.

"David," she whispered, choking on her disappointment, trying to bring hope out again. "I've waited so long. And the Bible does say that we are not to neglect the meeting of ourselves together." It was so feeble. Why did she bother? It was all so useless. David was right—they couldn't go to a church where the minister and his wife so clearly despised the Indians. So why was she badgering him, making him miserable, crying and carrying on like a denied child? Why did she fight? Why did the tears want to run and her heart break?

"The Bible also says that we are not to have respect for persons, Liza."

No, not again. . .not the whole unpleasant meeting all over again. She could not bear any more fighting over church. An early contraction pulled tight and she bent over her swollen stomach to lay her head upon her arms. The scratch of the puncheon logs of the table touched her chin and brought the musty scent of outdoors and the coming winter. The muscles tightening around her stomach frightened her sometimes—they were so strong, catching her in iron bands. But Doc Maynard said it was normal, the body's way of practicing. She would need iron-strong muscles when it came time. So she breathed in slowly, then let her breath escape as the tension eased.

"David," she said, not raising her head, "Arthur and Mary are going to go to church. And so is Mr. Nagle. They all joined today. Why can't we?" Now she raised her head, looking at him in the dim light, focusing on his right cheek where a scratch rippled his skin. "*Why can't we?*"

"*My brethren, have not the faith of our Lord Jesus Christ, the Lord of glory, with respect of persons.*"

She said nothing while he finished quoting the section from the book of James. She just waited for him to be done.

"*For if there come unto your assembly a man with a gold ring, in goodly apparel, and there come in also a poor man in vile raiment, and ye have respect to him that weareth the gay clothing, and say unto him, Sit thou here in a good place, and say to the poor, Stand thou there, or sit here under my footstool, are ye*

*not then partial in yourselves, and are become judges of evil
thoughts? Hearken, my beloved brethren, hath not God chosen the
poor of this world rich in faith, and heirs of the kingdom which
he hath promised to them that love him? . . . If ye have respect
to persons, ye commit sin.*"

"Arthur says we have to be patient with him." Why was she
doing this? Why was she putting him through it all again? She
knew how long he had agonized, and probably still was, unsure
whether or not he was right. So why couldn't she stop? Why
couldn't she just get up, sit in his lap, put his hand over the baby,
and put an end to this whole insane fight? "Arthur says Mr. Blaine
just doesn't understand," she heard herself saying in a voice that
didn't even sound like hers. "And as soon as he does—"

"*If* he does, we can sit there and listen to a ridiculous sermon
full of fancy words instead of one that tells us how to deal with
political squabblings, or how to trust God more firmly when we
hear frightening reports."

"That's enough," she snapped. Another contraction came. The
baby kicked, and she pushed down on the little foot to stop the
continual blows to her ribs. It was comforting to feel the wee
foot in her hand, but then the muscles tightened so completely
that they stole the foot from her touch.

"*If ye fulfill the royal law according to the Scripture, Thou shalt
love thy neighbor as thyself, ye do well.*"

"Don't quote James at me! I know what it says!" she half-
shouted, losing control of her ragged emotions. "David, we have
a responsibility to support the church and to see that the gospel
is firmly established in this town!"

He reached out to touch her hand, and ran his index finger
between each of her own, looking up now and then, his eyes
trying to speak. "What kind of gospel, Liza?" She looked away,
to the dark window.

"Arthur thinks it's all rather humorous. Really, David, try to
have a sense of humor about all this. Arthur—"

"Arthur!" he exploded, slapping his hand to the table beside
hers so that she felt the rush of wind. The slap rang in the air.
"I'm sick and tired of hearing about Arthur! He *has* to support
Blaine! He brought him here! He has him *living* in his home, for
heaven's sake! Packed in there with Mary and the children and
all those boxes and crates!" He jumped to his feet, jamming his

hands into his pockets. He stared at her before pacing madly back and forth.

"We need a church," she said as her arguments tangled and fell short. "I think Arthur is right this time. As Christians we need to stand together, right or wrong, and encourage each other to find the truth."

"*Mr. Blaine is no Christian. I will have no part of him.*"

His voice was cold, his eyes were cold. Alarm squeezed around her heart. He paced, hands in his pockets, back and forth, back and forth, face chalky, body tense and trembling.

"*If a man say, I love God, and hateth his brother, he is a liar; for he that loveth not his brother whom he hath seen, how can he love God whom he hath not seen?*"

"I suppose that's in James too."

"No. First John. And there's more. *Beloved, let us love one another, for love is of God, and every one that loveth is born of God and knoweth God. He that loveth not knoweth not God.* David Blaine does not know God." He swung to face her, eyes blazing, and she shrank back from his anger, but she couldn't stop.

"Don't you think that is a pretty strong accusation, David Denny?"

He stood before her, struggling. "Liza, you heard him," he said, his voice broken with pain and hurt and the terrible anger. "You heard him say the Indians were an abandoned race, degraded and beyond redemption!" He spun in a circle. He choked. "I cannot believe that! I cannot! I won't!" He slammed his fist into his palm. "God does *not* pick winner and loser! *God does not choose sides!*"

She started to cry. Great sobs broke loose as she wept, burying her face in her arms.

"Don't Liza. Don't."

But she couldn't stop. All she wanted to do was go to church. That's all. Go to church, and sing hymns, and have sewing circles and missionary suppers. She didn't want to fight. "I want to take our baby to church!" she wailed.

"*That's unfair!*" Don't you do that to me, Louisa Boren!"

"I'm Louisa *Denny*! And what am I doing to you?"

"You're using the baby!"

"I should have married James! *He* would have let me go to church!" She regretted it, but it was too late. "No, David! I'm sorry!" she screamed, leaping from her chair. He shook her off. "I didn't mean it! I didn't!" she cried, standing helplessly while he threw his arms into his coatsleeves, his face white, eyes pinched. "Please, David! I didn't mean it! I'm sorry!" She flung herself at him again, wrapping her arms around his neck, burying her nose against his cheek, but he pried her hands apart and pushed her from him. The door slammed.

"David!" She threw aside the sash. "David! Please! I'm sorry! I'm sorry! *David!*"

"You go to church, Mrs. Denny!" he yelled, staggering backward into the night. "You go to church! But just remember you can't take Betsy's baby when you take ours!"

Betsy. Dear, sweet Betsy. And where was little Joe?

Stricken, she shut the door and pressed her forehead to the splintery wood, and cried.

29

"Lines were drawn...on fundamental questions other than politics. Some of the settlers were puritanically religious men, strongly temperate, stern in their sense of right and wrong, others were more liberal religiously, not teetotalers, less exacting in behavior. The latter were unquestionably 'better mixers.' Both elements contributed much to the development of Seattle. Each fitted into the pattern. Later, when the need arose, they stood together as one man."
—Roberta Frye Watt in *Four Wagons West*

David followed the new road out to Mercer's with a raging pain in his chest, and dreadful thoughts gnawing to get into his brain. *James.* On and on he tromped, not knowing where he was, how far he'd come, blindly pushing forward, breathing around the pain and battling the thoughts.

The night was black; little light broke through the cut of trees. It occurred to him that he might easily lose the road and get lost. So he got lost. What did it matter? Louisa would rather be married to *James.* Everything paled next to that. The Indian problems, the new preacher. *James*—James, of all people!

He found himself at the old cabin, dark and empty. Why had he come out here? Starlight glittered on her sweetbriar. He winced when a thorn raked his fingers. Sucking on the sting, he let himself in. No fire in the fireplace, no crates with blue-down dishes. No counterpane, no mattress. He sat on the bare fir slats of the bed. Night moved restlessly about the empty room. Wallpaper peeled, mice scampered across the floor, and a cold draft sucked the corners and the walls.

He began to repeat the book of James. The whole book, out loud, from the first verse to the last—then over again, an exercise of mind to divert deeper, gnawing things of heart. But these verses brought no salve. Even the stars, visible through the open door, pulsed. A sudden need to be gone from this place drove him to his feet.

The night seemed darker when he ventured out. He could hear the forest breathe in its hiding. The wind came off the bay, bringing salt air to his nostrils, and he shivered. *I should have married James! He would let me go to church!* He reeled in the fresh assault of her words flying at him out of the cold darkness.

Where to go, what to do. The stars pulsed, giving no answers. They twinkled silently as he hurried back along the road.

It was a mild winter, but storms raged. Arthur and Maynard forever fussing. Democrats and Whigs always squabbling. Anna and Dobbins drifting apart. He and Louisa unable to understand, unable to break hidden barriers. Rumors of unrest drifting in and blowing on. Indians belligerent at times. Retaliation going on. He and Blaine. Joe Foster. Betsy. Tension tightening and loosening like fiddle strings. How would it all end?

A small cabin loomed out of the darkness, a black square in the night, and for a moment he stood stunned. It was Tom Mercer's place. How had he gotten so turned around?

The cabin was quiet, and his own knock startled him.

"Who is it?"

"David Denny."

The door creaked and his friend stood sleepy, lamp in hand. "David? Something wrong?"

"Got turned around. Can I borrow one of your horses? Been gone kind of long. Liza . . ."

"Yes, yes, of course! But what's wrong? You look beat."

"I'll explain tomorrow. I just need to get home."

"David?"

Tommy always knew, and David felt his friend's heavy, warm hand draw him into the cabin. "You had a fight over the new preacher," said Tom, and he nodded. One of the little girls called from the loft and Tommy answered, "It's only Dave Denny. Go on to sleep now." Turning to David, he said, "Sit down while I get dressed. I'll let you take Tib. She'll be better on a night like this. Knows that road blindfolded now."

"You go on to bed. I can saddle her up."

"Won't hear of it. You look beside yourself."

Bits of the story came out by the time Tib stood cinched and ready to go. Tom slipped the bit into the horse's reluctant mouth. David set the browband while Tom buckled the throatlatch. "There you are," said Tom, handing him the reins.

"Thanks, Tommy." He got ready to swing up.

"She didn't mean that about your brother, Dave. I think you know that."

He could feel the lump in his throat swell and cut off his air.

"Don't know a woman who loves her man more than Louisa loves you, Dave. You got to remember that when a baby's coming, women can say some pretty crazy things. You got to be extra kind." He opened his hand, set a sugar cube onto it, and pushed his hand under Tib's nose. "Dave, she wanted to go so badly."

The need to cry broke, and he stifled back a nervous laugh. He pressed his fist against his forehead and looked away from the bulky shape that was Tom. Of course she didn't want James! James wasn't the issue. He had just hung his hurt on that hook to hide the deeper issue, to cover the chasm that was widening between them. It wasn't even really Blaine. It was Liza. Her determination to ignore reality, to live in a fairy-tale world. "I shouted at her," he said, feeling the need to confess his part in the breach. "I shouted at her, Tommy. A pregnant woman, due any day, and I shouted at her." Again that urge to laugh.

"Don't be hard on yourself. She knows you love her."

"What do I say when I get home?" he asked helplessly. "I can't take her to church, you know that."

Tom didn't answer. The horse snorted impatiently.

"I am right, aren't I?" he asked, feeling a shadow of doubt. It frightened him. Tom's silence frightened him. "*I am right, aren't I?*"

"Maybe it's not a matter of right. Maybe she just *needs* to go to church right now."

"*Needs* to?"

"It won't hurt her, David. Maybe she needs to know just how contradictory the gospel can get, twisted by weak people who must use the twisting to support their fear and weakness. But here, I'm rambling."

David swung up on the horse and stared straight ahead, listening. But the words filtered past him, getting lost in the woods out there somewhere. "So you think my brother is right?" he asked, struggling to understand.

Tom's chuckle warmed him unexpectedly. "Arthur? Arthur's *always* right! Thought you knew that! No, David, if it's one thing I've come to learn in life, it's that each person must determine his own idea of what is right." He spoke slowly. "You know what's right for you. Your brother *always* knows what's right for him. But what about Mary Ann? What's right for her? And what's right for *your* wife?"

It was confusing. He fought harder to understand because somewhere there seemed to be a glimmer of truth, an answer.

"Maybe you're going to have to let Louisa work things through for herself. She's a grown woman, with thoughts and ideas and dreams of her own. Who are you to organize them and stack them up the same way you might stack your own?"

"You mean *let* her go to church? *Let* her sit under that man's poison?" But even as he spoke, he knew Tom was right. Who was he to force his will upon her? Maybe that was the problem. The more he fought to make her understand his side, the more she had to prove her own. And so the chasm widened. Soon they would not be able to hear each other for the distance.

He clucked his tongue and dug his heels into Tib's flanks. "Giddyup!" Tib galloped into the forest.

"David!" He reined in and swung around.

"Go with God!"

• • •

He found her in bed. When he climbed in she threw her arms about his neck and he sank against her softness, cradling her, rocking her, holding her tight. "I'm sorry, David," she cried, burying her face in his shoulder. "I'm sorry..."

"I know." He kissed her carefully, softly, planting flower kisses over her face and tears. "Shh," he whispered, brushing back her hair. An unreasonable terror swept over him, an icy blade against his heart, and he found that he held her with a sense of crazy desperation. He wiped her cheeks with his own. "Shh..." She had suffered more than he.

"I didn't mean it. I didn't mean to be so mean. I didn't David, I didn't!"

"It's all right, I know you didn't mean it. I know you love me. You just wanted to go to church, that's all."

But she kept sobbing, clinging to him. "Look at me," he ordered. *What would he do without her?* The baby moved between them, and he felt threatened. He thought of Pamelia. "Look at me, Liza."

"No." She dug in further with her nose. He could feel her breath against his neck.

"Liza, *please* look at me." He had to see her face, her eyes, touch her mouth with his.

"No," came the muffled cry again.

He sighed and stroked the back of her head, Tom's words in print behind his eyes. His awful fright ceased as she relaxed and grew quiet, and when her fingers softened, releasing him from their painful grip, he whispered, "Liza?" He knew she was still awake. "Liza? If you want to go to church next Sunday, you can. I was wrong to stop you."

"Oh, David, I can't go. I know that. I knew that all the time."

He jerked himself back into the pillow. "What?"

She raised her head from his shoulder, and lovingly he touched her face with the backs of his fingers, feeling the silkiness of her skin against his knuckles. She leaned into his touch, kissing his fingers. "It was mean, I knew it all along. But I couldn't stop." Her voice caught and she was crying again. "I just wanted to go so badly . . ."

"I know, Liza. I know. So did I . . ."

He loved her sweetly. It seemed that angels sang when she looked into his eyes, and he fell asleep in the joyful amen.

30

December 23

"I have just seen the Governor. He came to Seattle last night; is expecting to go up our river to visit our coal mines and make arrangements for the exploration of our country back to the pass in the Cascade range, with a view to ascertaining the most feasible situation for the terminus of the Pacific Railroad. Many in this territory are very sanguine in the opinion that this terminus will be at some point on Puget Sound."

—David Blaine in a letter

Two-and-a-half weeks later David shivered outside the cookhouse, hands in his pockets, feeling the lint in the seams. It was still morning, but the world was dark. Fog blanketed Seattle, blocking the sun and lying so thick upon the ground that it seemed you ought to be able to kick it aside with your boots. He stomped his feet, and inside his pockets clenched his fists, trying to warm them.

Thirty or 40 men had gathered to meet the new Governor. Stevens had come up from Olympia on the *Sarah Stone*, an open sailboat, to inspect the sound, and to everyone in Seattle nothing was quite so important as to toast the Governor and boast the latest discovery of coal. Not even Christmas, two days away, mattered.

Through the small windows David could see Bigelow, Tobin, Eaton, and Fanjoy busy with their explanations of their new Duwamish Coal Company. Stevens himself was indistinguishable, blending into the sea of red flannel shirts and unshaven beards.

David hated to go in. Maynard would only shove him aside again. So he stood alone, hesitating. Somewhere in the village a piano was being played, and children were singing Christmas carols. He imagined them making decorations, maybe even stringing popcorn. A sudden ache pushed him forward.

"Maynard, please just come take a look at her," he said finding the doctor with a nearly empty bottle and pink skin. "There's something wrong, I think. It's been hours."

"I saw 'er, Dave, my boy," he slurred. "Be a lo-o-ong time yet. Now, Dave, don't you worry none. It's considered a sweet thing fer you to get drunk at a time like this. Come, fellows, pour him one on me . . ."

Disgusted, David shoved away.

"How is she?" he asked when he got home. Mary Ann shook her head and he hurried to the bed. Dropping to his knees, he looked down into the sweaty, pale face and glazed eyes that were supposed to be Louisa. "Liza?" he called, touching her cheek. She jerked away and he yanked back his hand, terrified at what he had done.

"Your hands are probably cold," said Mary Ann.

"Oh." He was relieved. "Louisa?"

"She can't hear you. The pain has driven everything from her mind." Mary Ann made him get up and helped him to the chair. He half-dragged it, half-carried it over to the bed. "I take it Maynard's too drunk to be sensible about any of this," she said. He nodded, wondering if there was any sense left in *him*. He couldn't think—he couldn't even see anymore. Everything was out of focus, pulsating to the chaotic beat in his temples. What was he going to do? He had to get help.

"David."

He blinked, trying to clear his head. Mary stood over him, stern like Ma. It sobered him, and he sucked in his breath. Had she asked him something? No, she was talking. "Arthur's gone to get Dr. Smith," she said.

Henry! Of course, why hadn't he thought of it? Henry was a doctor. He relaxed in relief's embrace.

"They should be here before the hour, and when he gets here I don't want you looking the way you are. You go over to my house and take a cold bath. The tub is behind the bed. You know where it is. You shave and comb out your beard. Don't worry— the children are at Anna's. I'll take care of Louisa until you get back."

"When did Arthur leave?" he asked, trying to put sequence to things.

"This morning when the fog lifted a bit. Go on. Louisa's resting right now. The pains have let up again. She'll be needing you when the time comes."

He stumbled to his feet.

"You light a good fire, then take your bath cold. It'll clear your head," she said, pushing him toward the door. "But don't stay in too long or you'll catch your death." Impulsively she hugged him, and he clung to her a minute. "Go on now," she urged. "Louisa'll be fine."

He wasn't so sure. Pains driving hard, then stopping. He didn't know how much more she could take. Why wouldn't that baby come? Would it die in the struggle? Would Liza die?

Would she die? Sitting in the tub, in the misty, foggy darkness of his brother's cabin, the question came at him like a sharp sword teasing vulnerable flesh. He leaned forward and stuck his face into the icy water. One, two, three...he counted to 60. He surfaced, spewing and spitting, gasping for air. Would Louisa die?

Would Louisa die?

The question fired, not a jabbing sword, but a ball from a cannon now. There was no dodging, no ducking. It was no new question. It was an old one, one that had haunted him from the beginning, ever since they had married, in one way or another.

Knees drawn, arms wrapped, he looked squarely at the open cannon of his fear. He forced himself to say it out loud, to put name to his fear. "Maybe Louisa will die. Maybe I will lose her."

He remembered the first time he had felt the poke of that jabbing sword: last winter, when John had raised his hatchet against Old Alki. *What if John hadn't come to his senses? Dave, what if you hadn't been there? Louisa, there's no sense in asking those questions.*

But it was all he asked anymore—all those "what ifs"! What if another cougar comes out of the hills? What if more renegades cross the mountains? What if, what if, what if... What if Louisa died in childbirth like Pamelia?

He had tried everything—looking ahead and guessing, making adjustments. He had moved her into town and given up their claim. He had worked himself into a state of frenzy, badgering the Indians, begging for information. He had gone out of his head whenever the name of James came up.

Feeble firelight gave off a small breath of heat, and he groaned, staring into the orange-blue flames. They twisted and curled, and he saw the twist between him and Louisa. She had found her faith, but he had succumbed. He was living in a world of his own brutal imagination.

A violent shudder rippled through his body. He leaped to his feet, sluicing the icy water from his body with quick, sharp strokes of his hands. He toweled down. Feeling in the gloom for his clothes, he started to dress, trembling not only from the cold but from the truth he had stumbled upon. No wonder he hadn't found any peace! Fear had consumed his faith!

Arthur found him trimming his beard, leaning over the mantel and squinting into Mary's mirror. "Saw Williamson the other day. He said to tell you he had that mirror glass for you. Want me to help you cut it?"

Christmas. So far removed from his thoughts. "You get Henry?" he asked, unwilling to think about Christmas or Louisa's new mirror. He had forgotten all about it.

"He's over at the house right now."

"Thanks, Arthur." He brought the razor down, taking one final stroke. He wiped the remaining soap lather from his face, then slipped into his shirt. "What's he got to say about her?"

"I don't know. Didn't stick around—hurried over because I thought you'd want to know he was here."

"Thanks again, Arthur."

They stood quietly in the open door, looking out, listening to Christmas carols drift up the road. "That Mrs. Butler sure can play the piano. Nice to have one around this year," said Arthur.

She was playing his favorite song. He knew the words by heart. *Watchman, tell us of the night, what its signs of promise are...* It reminded him of Louisa's promise, her sweetbriar. "You going down to hear the Governor now?" he asked.

"Think maybe I will."

"Tell me what he has to say."

"All right, Dave."

He plunged up the road.

Henry Smith was a tall, slender man, and David liked him a great deal. They shared many of the same opinions and were about the same age, although Henry was probably a year or so older. It was a shame he lived so far out, thought David. They had probably seen each other only three or four times in all the months Henry had been back. It seemed odd to him right now to need to be so dependent upon someone he saw so rarely. "How is she?" he asked as soon as he entered the cabin. She looked worse, if that were possible—even weaker, even whiter.

"That baby just doesn't want to take a peek. Sometimes they do that. Don't know why." Henry tried to smile. "What they need is a good prod in the seat. Kind of like my mother used to do with the fire poker when it was time for bed and I didn't think so."

"What are you going to do? What *can* you do?"

"Oh, we have ways of giving them a poke."

David's heart plugged in his throat, and he glanced quickly at Louisa. She moaned and tossed in the bed, their bed, and a sickness rushed against his eyes. He stood helpless, the sickness pounding, magnifying the tightened muscles along Henry's cheeks and Mary's worried face.

"We're going to have to get this baby born," said Henry.

"What are you going to do?" David repeated, sinking weakly into the chair by the bed. He groped for Liza's hand, and she clamped hard, hurting him, caught as she was in the throes of yet another contraction. She didn't seem to know he was there, though.

"I'm going to have to force this baby out—one way or another."

"How are you going to do that?" David felt nausea bubble. He got to his feet. Maybe if he walked around...

"I'll be real frank," said Henry. "She may not make it. The baby probably won't. All this starting and stopping business is just never any good."

He couldn't believe what he was hearing—Henry talking on and on and on, explaining it all, showing him his instruments so he wouldn't be frightened. But he *was* frightened. "When?" he asked. "When will you do all this?"

"On her next contraction, coming up. Talk to her, sing to her, keep her thinking of something else beside the pain."

"But she can't hear him," whispered Mary Ann, skin white and tight beneath her eyes. Her mouth twitched like Louisa's, and David turned away, unable to bear it.

"Of course she can hear! David! Soon as I yell, you're to hold her. And I mean *hold* her."

"Hold her? What do I do?"

"This may sound crazy to you," said Henry. "But I've been reading some books. There's some that believe a part of the brain can hear and smell and feel even though the main part can't. Lots of people are brought back from the very brink of death because they hear the voice of someone they love."

"Louisa's not dying!"

"David, she is. She's lost a lot of blood and she's terribly weak."
He rubbed his cheeks.

"Listen, Dave. She knows your touch, your voice. Your love for
her is what's going to pull her out of the shock. She's going to
want to leave us. It's up to you to not let her."

It was too fast. It made no sense. He stood dazed, unsure, arguing, then Louisa began to whimper, spittle dripping from the corner of her lips as she arched her back. "Do something!" he cried.

"Mary!" said Henry. "Come down here! There's a chance the
baby..."

David spun, but Louisa's teeth were still clenched. She rocked
on the mattress. Sweat poured from her temples. She panted.
Suddenly her eyes glassed over and blood drained from her
cheeks.

"It's tightening, I can feel it..." Henry's bottom lip was
scissored between his white, even teeth. "NOW!" he screamed,
plunging down with one hand on Louisa's stomach, moving
quickly to the end of the bed. Louisa's scream shattered above
his, and she came off the bed, eyes unseeing, a thing gone
mindless with pain. But David caught her as she came down, and
she fell silently into his outstretched arms.

"Talk to her!" Henry yelled, working fast. She was so cold, so
still. *"Talk to her!"*

The words came from a back shelf of his mind, where he had
shut them away—useless, fancy words that meant nothing to him,
but that meant all the world to her: *"I will lift up mine eyes unto
the hills, from whence cometh my help. My help cometh from the
Lord, which made heaven and earth. He will not suffer thy foot
to be moved; he that keepeth thee will not slumber. Behold, he that
keepeth Israel shall neither slumber nor sleep. The Lord is thy
keeper; the Lord is thy shade upon thy right hand. The sun shall
not smite thee by day, nor the moon by night. The Lord shall preserve thee from all evil; he shall preserve thy soul. The Lord shall
preserve thy going out and thy coming in from this time forth and
even for evermore."* The truth exploded in his mind at the same
time he heard the far whimper of a baby's cry. Fear and confusion emptied from his mind, and the ache held for months let
go. Oh, Liza...

She lay quiet upon the sheets, eyes sunk deep and dark. It seemed he saw Betsy's eyes. "Oh, Liza," he wept, drawing her still body to himself, bending over the bed and burying his face in her wet, stringy hair.

"David?" It was Henry, speaking to him from the end of the bed. "I've got her cleaned up. Can you climb in with her? She needs to know you're there."

"What if I held her in the rocking chair?"

"I'd rather she lie flat."

"I've always rocked her when she's been frightened and sick."

"Then maybe you better."

"Liza," he whispered, lifting her from the sheets. Mary handed him a blanket and he wrapped her carefully, tucking her head to his shoulder. She lay limp in his arms, the dead weight reminding him painfully of Betsy. But she was breathing, so he stroked her and held her and rocked her, smelling her sweat and pain and blood, feeling her frailness against his strength, willing and praying that she might grow warm under his touch.

She heard his voice in the foggy darkness. "Liza..." She stirred, too weary, too sore, too fragile to even open her eyes. She knew he held her, rocking her, and she was comforted. "A little girl, Liza. You had a little girl." She felt him pick up her hand and then there was the tiny, moist clasp of a baby's fingers tight around her own. Oh, David, she thought.

Her head was against his chest. She could hear his heartbeat steady against her cheek, and it seemed to give her strength. "Emily Inez," she whispered, resting her head heavily against him. He pressed his head to hers and she fell quietly asleep.

Epilogue
December 31, 1853

"It would require hundreds of pages to set forth a moving picture of the stirring frontier life in which she participated. Louisa Boren Denny is a pioneer woman of the best type. 'PEACE HATH HER VICTORIES NO LESS RENOWNED THAN WAR.' "
—Emily Inez Denny

"You're a fool!" Doc Maynard stuck a foot out to stop David. "You're a fool if you think you can take her back out there like this!"

David stepped over the boot in his path and proceeded to Tommy Mercer's wagon, dropping in a pile of comforters and pillows. He climbed over the backboard to arrange them into a bed. When he was finished, Maynard was waiting.

"Whatever's gotten into your head? Taking Louisa out there like this! It's not hardly a week gone by! Anything could happen! You know that!"

"She wants to go, Maynard."

"Dave, my boy!" Maynard blustered, shocked and grieved, lost in the face of foolish reasoning. They had already had apologies and explanations regarding Louisa's childbirth. Like men caught in circumstance and genuine affection for each other, they had looked past the errors to Louisa's better health. "You can't be doing this! What if something happens while you're gone? What if—"

David cut him short with a sympathetic smile. "I've quit asking those questions, Doc."

Maynard took a step backward. He wore a heavy Hudson Bay coat and his raccoon-tailed hat. "You're taking her out to get back at me. I know what you're doing. You don't fool me!"

"I'm not doing anything to you. I'm doing it for Louisa. It's something I should have done a long time ago."

"You're still angry. You think Smith is a better doctor than me."

David laughed out loud and pressed his hand onto Maynard's shoulder, feeling the thickness of the wool coat. "You know that's got nothing to do with it, Maynard. *I'm* a better doctor than you when you're drunk."

Maynard didn't think it was funny. "Now you're starting to sound like Arthur," he bristled.

"Arthur? Me? I'll never sound like Arthur, Maynard."

"Dave, take her out in the spring, when the weather is decent." He flapped his left arm, interrupting the soft fall of snow, and bounced his toes into the earth. But David pushed past, anxious to be on his way. The last load had been taken out; there was only Liza and the baby.

"Come out and have a cup of tea with us someday," he said, and waved. If he hurried, they would be home before nightfall.

"Where are we going, David?" Louisa wrapped her arms tighter about his neck, feeling the strong gait of his stride as he carried her outside.

"For a ride."

He looked down at her, smiled quickly, then looked back up to check his way. They came to the wagon and he lifted her into it, settling quilts and blankets about her warmly. "You all right?" he asked.

"David! Where are we going? And what are you laughing about?"

"Just a minute. I'll be right back."

He returned with Emily Inez, wrapped double in a buckskin from Jim and George and the soft pink lambs'-wool baby hood and bunting that Louisa had ordered with her egg money. The baby's translucent eyes were shut in sleep, webbed with tiny blue veins spreading out to her temples. With her pink cheeks and small, soft-pink mouth she sucked contentedly on her bottom lip as David tucked her in next to Louisa.

Louisa felt the bounce as David climbed round and up onto the wagon seat. Lying still, heart pounding, she could see trees passing, tall and dark green, getting lost in the snow and approaching night. *They were headed north on Tom Mercer's road!*

Her heart quickened. Could it be? Did she dare hope? David had been gone for hours each day since Christmas, and today he had made her go over to Mary's. *Was it true?* Twisting, she could see his back. He sang softly, elbows balanced on his knees, bent over the reins—like so many times coming across the prairie. She could see the swinging neck of Tib and Charley, white and black, pulling them onward. "Oh, Emily Inez," she whispered, kissing the infant's cheek. "We're going home."

The wagon stopped. David took the baby, and, after what seemed like eternity, returned for her, plucking her from the warm nest and carrying her easily in his arms toward the cabin. The woodpile had an inch of snow over one end. David stepped over a fallen log, taking a wide step around a stump. She smiled, staring into his face, admiring his jaw from this angle, the white fog of his breath passing through his nose. He sensed her stare, looked down quickly, and smiled. They rounded the corner.

"It's grown even since I saw it, I think," she said, when he set her down on the stoop to lift the latch. She touched the sweetbriar's thorny stem.

"It's too cold to grow, Liza." He swung the door open and stood aside, waiting. "Go on," he urged, his eyes dancing with his secret, and when she stepped inside, she gasped in wonder. David had decorated the cabin just like when they had been married! Cedar boughs were strung and hung from rafters. They draped the mantel and looped the door. The scent of outdoors was poignant, and candle flame softened the gloom and put old shadows upon yellowed newsprint, newsprint repasted and mended. Her brass candlestick sat on the table. Her blue-down dishes sat in the crate. Her comforter, patched and squared, was spread over the fir bed. And at the foot of the bed was her open trunk, carted across the prairies and used for storage—only now it was filled with hay and sheeting, and on it little Emily Inez lay asleep.

"Oh, David," she whispered, seeing it all, hearing the crackle of fire, the hiss of the stove and bubbling coffee. "Oh, David."

"Look." He caught her chin and brought her face to meet the wall where her empty mirror nail was imbedded—only there wasn't an empty nail anymore. Her mirror, all shiny and bright and whole again, reflected their faces, and she flung her arms around his neck, burying her face in his shoulder. "Oh, David," she whispered, overwhelmed by his display and measure of love.

He gathered her in his arms. The door closed with his kick. Darkness fell as he blew out the candles.

"Louisa?" he asked, lowering her into the warm bed.

"Yes, David?"

"Do you love me?"

She laughed. "You know that I do."

"Even though I've been a fool?"

"Even though you've been a fool." He thought he heard her laugh again. "David?"

"Yes?"

"What about the horses? You've left them out in the cold."

"The horses! I've gone and left them out in the cold, standing in the road!" He reached for his boots and jacket. "Just a minute, Liza, I'll be right back!"

Cold air swept in twice—once when he left, and once when he returned. The blanket was warm on top of them, the colored squares and patches hidden in the night. And on the door, still swinging from the jolt of David's boot, hung three hats: a baby hood, a sunbonnet, and a cap.

BIBLIOGRAPHY

1. Bagley, C.B., *Scrapbook,* Vols. 1, 12, 15, 5. University of Washington, Northwest Collection Room.
2. *The Bible* (King James Version).
3. *Blazing the Way.* Seattle: Rainier Printing Company. © 1909. By Emily Inez Denny.
4. *The Buffalo Are Coming.* New York: Alfred A. Knopf. © 1960. By Gus Tavo.
5. *Chief Seattle.* Caldwell, Idaho: The Caxton Printers, Ltd. © 1943. By Eva Greenslit Anderson.
6. *Chief Seattle—Great Statesman.* Illinois: Garrard Publishing Company. © 1966. By Elizabeth Montgomery.
7. *Chronological History of Seattle.* By Thomas Prosch.
8. *David S. Maynard and Catherine T. Maynard.* Seattle: Lowman and Hanford Stationery and Printing Company. © 1906 by Thomas W. Prosch.
9. *David's Diaries.* Seattle: Museum of History and Industry.
10. *Denny and Boren Family Files.* Seattle: Museum of History and Industry.
11. *Denny Family Pamphlet File.* University of Washington, Northwest Collection Room.
12. *Doc Maynard.* Seattle: Nettle Creek Publishing Company. © 1978. By Bill Speidel.
13. *Dubuar Scrapbook,* Vols. 77, 82, 86. University of Washington, Northwest Collection Room.
14. *Duwamish Diary.* Seattle: Cleveland High School. © 1949.
15. *Empire of the Columbia.* New York: Harper and Row. © 1967. By Dorothy O. Johansen and Charles M. Gates.
16. Fonda, W.C., *Scrapbook,* Vols. 5, 6. University of Washington, Northwest Collection Room.
17. *Four Wagons West.* Portland, Oregon: Binford and Mort, Publishers. © 1931. By Roberta Frye Watt. (Used by permission.)
18. *Frisbie Scrapbook,* Vol. 1. University of Washington, Northwest Collection Room.
19. *Genealogical Notes—Denny Family.* Seattle Public Library, Main Office. By Margaret Thompson.
20. *Huboo.* Seattle: University of Washington Press. © 1980. By Vi (taqwseblu) Hilbert. (Quotes used by permission.)

21. *History of Seattle*, Vol II. Chicago: The S.T. Clarke Publishing Company. © 1916. By C.B. Bagley.
22. *History of Seattle, Washington*. New York: American Publishers and English Co. Pub. © 1981. By James Grant.
23. *History of Washington*, Vol III. New York: The Century History Company. © 1901. By Clinton A. Snowden.
24. *Oregon Trail*. Rand McNally and Co. © 1972. By Ingvard Henry Eide.
25. *The Oregon Trail Revisited*. St. Louis: Patrice Press, Inc. © 1972. By Gregory Franzwa.
26. *Picturesque Pioneers*. Seattle: Dogwood Press. © 1967. By Henry Broderick.
27. *Pioneer Days on Puget Sound*. Seattle: C.B. Bagley. © 1888. By Arthur Armstrong Denny.
28. *Pioneer Reminisces*. Seattle: Museum of History and Industry. By C.T. Conover.
29. *Pioneer Reminiscences of Puget Sound*. Seattle: Lowman & Hanford. © 1905. By Ezra Meeker.
30. *Pioneer Seattle and Its Pioneers*. Seattle. © 1928. By Clarence B. Bagley.
31. *Post-Intelligencer*. Seattle, Washington.
32. Private manuscripts: Henry Smith, Henry Yesler, John Denny, Mrs. Carkeek, Sarah Latimer Denny, Louisa Denny, Emily Inez Denny.
33. *Sealth—The Story of an American Indian*. Minneapolis: Dillon Press, Inc. © 1978. By Mel Boring.
34. *Seattle*. New York: Alfred A. Knopf. © 1977. By Gerald B. Nelson.
35. *Seattle*. New York: Doubleday & Co, Inc. © 1972. By Nard Jones.
36. *Seattle Daily Times*. Seattle, Washington.
37. *Seattle Heritage*. Seattle: Superior Publishers. © 1955. By Ralph Bushnell Potts.
38. *Seattle Memoirs*. Boston: Lothrop, Lee and Shepard Co. © 1930. By Edith Sanderson Redfield.
39. *Seattle's First Physician*. Clinics of the Virginia Mason Hospital. Dec. 1932, Vol. 12.
40. *Skid Road*. New York: Viking Press. © 1952. By Murray Morgan.
41. *Sons of the Profits*. Seattle: Nettle Creek Publishing Company. © 1967. By William C. Speidel.
42. *Souvenir of Chief Seattle and Princess Angeline*. © 1909. By Laura D. Buchanan.
43. *Washington's Yesterdays*. Portland, Oregon: Binford and Mort, Publishers. © 1953. By Lucille McDonald.
44. *Westward to Alki*. Seattle: Superior Publishing Company. © 1977. By Gordon Newell.
45. *When Seattle Was A Village*. Seattle: Lowman & Hanford. © 1947. By Sophie Frye Bass.